MOVING
THE
TASSELS

MOVING THE TASSELS

PAUL JAMES HATKE

ReadersMagnet, LLC

Moving the Tassels
Copyright © 2021 by Paul James Hatke

Published in the United States of America
ISBN Paperback: 978-1-954371-15-6
ISBN eBook: 978-1-954371-16-3

All rights reserved. No part of this publication may be reproduced, stored in a retrieval system or transmitted in any way by any means, electronic, mechanical, photocopy, recording or otherwise without the prior permission of the author except as provided by USA copyright law.

ReadersMagnet, LLC
10620 Treena Street, Suite 230 | San Diego, California, 92131 USA
1.619. 354. 2643 | www.readersmagnet.com

Book design copyright © 2021 by ReadersMagnet, LLC. All rights reserved.
Cover design by Ericka Obando
Interior design by Renalie Malinao

DEDICATION

To Rose ... so very patient and understanding

CHAPTER I

It's been a strange year, and it's been a strange time. "Possibly recognized as the most tumultuous decade of the 20th century," so said Mr. Greyson. He is the principal at school. He also teaches history. His lecture was only a couple of weeks old when the aassassination of Robert Kennedy occurred. The time moved on and the tumult continued. There was the break from school and some evaluation of this year that has held so much violence; so much turmoil. My escape was the lake, my summer refuge. I have always enjoyed being near the water. We would make trips to the lake whenever possible. It was something that took away the problems of the world. The lake seemed to wash away the war in Vietnam and demonstrations on college campuses. It seemed far away from TV news that was airing current events of the day. There were other things making news such as equal rights and civil rights protests, and of course assassinations. Things needed and some not needed.

A calmness was at the lake. Trees stood high with many shades of green, and the dark water held a mysteriousness to it. Sometimes it glistened from the sun catching the uplifts and occasional whitecaps that were a welcome sight on the warm days, and all of this is an appreciative time away from school.

I was seventeen and a little naive, but there was so many things that would draw questions. Why was so much happening at this time? It wasn't like this in the 1950's. Well, I didn't think it was. There were many incidents that would challenge Mr. Greyson's claim of this time. The period of WWII was often discussed by the people who lived through it. For now, there were different news-making events taking something away from the break from school. It was like summers have always been a fun time of excitement. Now, our country has been on some shaky ground and many of us in our teens are uneasy. A lot of kids wonder what's next.

June had a few things different from last year. It seemed notable, maybe because of my age. The days moved way too fast. The good times could not be taken for granted. Picnics and girl watching, swimming and cooking out. Girls in bikinis. Oh yes! Bikinis are being worn more and more. Very eye popping.

One of the things that made these months especially memorable and fun was learning to water ski the last part of June. That was pretty cool. This was the first summer for the chance to ski and it was a thrill cutting across the water, feeling the power of the boat that was pulling me. Greg, the father of one of my friends, taught me, and it helped that he was so patient. He encouraged me to slightly lift the tip of my skis to cross the wake when moving back and forth on each side of the boat. That was advice that worked out well. I must have wiped out thirty times earlier. You'd think I would have caught on quicker.

July went by in a hurry. Only one chance to go to the lake and ski. There was a little more feel with the water ski, and some fishing was done on that outing too. Fiberglass boats were lifting their bow above the water and making wide sweeps. This was fun to watch as the passengers enjoyed the movement and during some of this a kind of a trance was put upon me as wind would blow a girl's hair into a disorderly fashion, maybe my subconscious presented this being a work of art. A note of confidence was at this time at the lake I had my first sexual experience with a girl. Her name was Edna, and she was fairly good looking, and really built. She was wearing and showing off her swimsuit. It was somewhere between a two-piece outfit and a bikini. White in color with black stripes that would narrow and widen like waves. She was at the lake at the same time some of my friends and I were, and the two of us had some private time together. Unbelievable.

Back at home there was our yard to take care of, and a number of others. There was some money saved. There was some money to spend, too. At night, some of us guys would roam about. We met a lot of girls. Even some that were from other parts of the state, and some from out of state. That was great. This irresponsible part of my life was better than could have been hoped for. The world continued too. It wasn't fun and games every day. The number of jobs lined up in our area had started to increase. Sometimes I found myself too tired to go out after working all day. Additional work was on the upswing.

There were a number of requests for hedges to be shaped up, and there was even the asking to sculpt some small evergreen trees that were very near the house of one client. The skill to do this had not been achieved by me at this time, anal the people were understanding about it. A few attempts brought out with chagrin this so called monster-piece. It had to be explained that the shaping would be better in a standard way. Overall summer had been a lot of fun, and making some money was a plus. And again it removed the thoughts of the newspaper headlines.

August was a very hot and humid month. Just walking outside would bring on a sweat. It felt like the plastic wrap that is used in storing foods was covering my arms and about every part of me. It is very uncomfortable. Yard work is very hard on the hot humid days. Any opportunity to make it to a lake or any body of water was appealing. The chance of going during August did not come around as much as had been wanted.

If someone's home had air conditioning, there was the chance of being asked inside, and that was some relief. August can be stifling. My parents have talked about getting air conditioning, but usually the decision ends up with the excuse of too expensive at this time. For now, we'll get by without it. It would be nice if my parents would find a way to budget for it. A color TV would be all right too. The family needed to modernize.

School will soon be starting, and it doesn't have air conditioning either. That doesn't really matter so much at school. We have the oscillating pole fans, but that only helps some. The comical part happens when papers get blown off the desks. At least there is an excuse for getting up out of the desk seat. It was funny seeing the frustrated look on the face of a teacher. If there is any consolation it is everyone has to suffer through the heat, and if everyone has to go through with this it seems all right. Even when those accustomed to a cooled off room have to stick it out, it makes people that work outside and sweat feel better prepared to deal with the discomfort. Kind of bringing others to our level. This doesn't feel so bad when thinking about it. And the number of days for putting up with heat and humidity will soon pass.

Most of us kids at this time have other things on our mind. The warm nights and days would be giving way to the cooler days as fall nears. The colorful season. Even when all those reds and golds and yellows turn to that rust color, and on to the brown. Very pretty colors adding a lift of the spirit. My English teacher last year told us that when mentioning this season, it should be referred to as Autumn. "There is more description with the word

Autumn he emphasized to us. One might think he were acting aloof, or something like that. Anyway it's a nice time with leaves changing, dropping everywhere and giving ground cover that a lot of people do not want. It provides leaf raking jobs which give me additional work and some additional money. Raking leaves is not so difficult a job. Usually piling the leaves will allow for at least one good dive into the heap of the colorful mix. When you're seventeen there is still a lot of kid in you.

A few weeks had passed and my mother had me going to school to fill out enrollment information. "Make sure you apply for something that can be useful, you understand? I have a check that I've signed for the cost of your books." She handed it to me. "Take some classes that are taxing" she continued as her voice rang out like a bell.

Mom and Dad have hopes for me to go to college. I wasn't sure about college. That is the same with a lot of things. Things keep popping into the mind. Those assassinations of Bobby Kennedy and Martin Luther King a few months earlier deeply bother me. Then there seems to always be the threat of "THE BOMB." It doesn't make much sense. Another thing to question is the attitude of some of our neighbors. They want to bomb everyone! Kill anyone that imposes a threat or is different from them!

There was a man telling my father: "As far as I'm concerned they could wipe out all of Southeast Asia and then finish off those Goddam Kennedys!" The guy that made these remarks does this all the time. He had remarks about Martin Luther King that were along the same lines as the Kennedys. Maybe the language was even worse. He also wanted to drop an atomic bomb on North Korea for capturing the USS Pueblo and holding the members of the Ship prisoner. To hear him tell it, he was right up there with Admiral Nimitz. He speaks to everyone on the street as if he were some type of authority, but he sometimes acts like a whacko.

This is a man that is fairly well-respected in our neighborhood. He goes to church every Sunday too. He keeps a nice yard. He will say these things, and it seems many adults share the same ideas. This finds its way down to the kids. We are taught things in church and school about justice equality, love thy neighbor, and then... well as earlier pointed out, there sure are a lot of confusing things. There are a lot of kids in my age group that feel the same. A lot of them are taking action with protests. The war in 'Nam, and the draft. Some of the protests and demonstrations seem to be getting out of hand. Some kids are going to extremes. The walk toward school can stir up a bunch of world problems everybody has to face. Maybe the problems have been around forever.

While continuing to walk and mulling over this and other things, my name was called out, "Hey, Wes! Wes Patterson, wait up, I'll walk with you." Looking around, there was Dickey Brink. He was a friend from school. He was going to register for school also. He was built kind of odd. Sort of an oval shaped person, you would think he was very uncoordinated, but he wasn't. He was quite agile; more so than probably anyone expected, although there was a clumsiness in some of his manners. Something that was interesting was how well he took a joke. Guys would make fun of how he appeared and it could bother most kids, even hurt probably. He might make a remark on his own appearance, or just laugh along with what had been said. A disarming tactic. This was not in my own makeup. Few others could take such kidding. Dickey did. Deep down there was some sort of respect for someone that handled this.

"It's pretty neat isn't it? Us going to be seniors he commented with some enthusiasm.

"Yeah. Yeah, it sure is." Considering what he had said, it took some of the sting out of the thought of going back to school. One more year. Then it came to me again. What would be going on in a years' time? I will be eligible for the draft and with Viet Nam being a hot spot... and when not actually prepared for college. College is tough it's been said. It's easy to flunk out. The armed services are tough too. It's a challenging world. As for college, my older sister will be a senior in college. She applies herself. That line about applying oneself has been mentioned from both of my parent's numerous times.

We walked on as a breeze brushed around, cooling my forehead. It is always refreshing to experience these little wind gusts. Even if summer is closing out, the feel of the autumn season is nice. The breezes take kind of clear unpleasant thoughts for a few seconds. As we neared the school, this three-story structure kind of loomed unlike it had in earlier years. That was odd to me. When reaching a different maturity, the school shouldn't be so daunting a structure. That's kind of weird. The winds were dying down or were being blocked by the school, and soon we came upon a line of kids that was growing. The lines gathered, and we joined in. Dickey stood just in front of me as we took our place.

"Are you doing anything later, I mean after we get this signing up stuff out of the way?" Dickey asked.

"I don't know. What are you doing?"

"I was going to stop by the drugstore. My mom has a prescription she wants me to pick up. I'm having my meal there too. You how, at the luncheon counter," Dickey related. "If you go there with me, I'll buy you a soda."

"That sounds good to me."

"What's going on with you guys?" A voice called out as Wayne Borden made his way toward the group that was registering. His appearance shocked or at least surprised most everyone that had assembled. He had let his straight, dark hair grow for the last three months and it probably needed trimming when we completed our junior year those months ago. He was wearing these eyeglasses that were popular with hippies and some rock and roll musicians. His clothing looked bright, with reds and yellows on his shirt standing out in contrast to the almost prosaic garments of everyone else. His clothes did not fit in at all. Everything about him was a bit too showy. With all this flashy appearance the strangest thing about Wayne was his being a member of the National Honor Society.

"We're here like everybody else. Trying to get the classes arranged. Letting the school and teachers know we are coming back here," Dickey calmly explained to Wayne.

"Oh, yes, we pay homage at this time to our parents and the school moguls in order to carry on as a part of the 'great society' that we are now a part of," Wayne said in an oratory way, but left no doubt of the sarcasm he had in mind. He started talking about something else, and I had no idea what he was saying. He liked to go on with bombastic talk. A bunch of big words.

The details on signing up were not at all bad, and well organized. This was good. People of my age have little patience. Sometimes some clowning around would be in the mix. Wayne stretched his neck looking back and forth to take in any activity.

"I meant to ask you, where have you been this summer?" Dickey asked Wayne.

"California, young man" the answer came. "I have thoughts of staying there. They have mountains to the east. Ocean view to the west. The movie industry. Hinterlands, and San Francisco has very radical people trying to remedy the situation at hand. There is a lot happening that may interest the proletariat.

"Did your parents say anything to you about the length of your hair?" I asked, and looked again at Wayne's hair and then found myself distracted by the unusual shirt he was wearing.

Moving the Tassels

"They told me I had to have it cut prior to the first day of school. I knew my parents would give a warning, and I had better listen or find another place to live."

The line moved fairly well, as the people working at the enrollment and designing of the classes went according to the number of students, and the year. They had their act together, as Wayne put it. There were these large cardboard signs that varied in color. Red for freshmen. Yellow for sophomores. Black for juniors. Then green for seniors. Someone had talked about a colored-coded student body. It was one of those things that wasn't completely understandable, but I laughed at it as if it was a sophisticated joke.

At the bookstore you would hand course information to one of the attendants. Then you walked around collecting books for each class. There were some good used books bought when possible, and my intention of trying to be thrifty. The cashier looked the check over carefully that Mom gave me and the lady filled out the amount and handed me a receipt. Dickey made a quick jaunt up the stairways with me following as we had the job of taking our books to the lockers. The locker assigned was on the third floor. How much fun is this? Climb these stairs every day for the entire year. Seniors are supposed to receive some kind of consideration. It was a slight struggle to get all the books in the locker and put them in a not-too-haphazard arrangement. Dickey was about a hundred feet down the hallway making an effort to do what I was working on.

We left the school and began talking about the location of the lockers. "We should have demanded a locker on the first floor," my complaint barked out.

"My feeling too. If we just go along what they decide to give you, you're going to be walked over from time to time," he muttered. We made our way toward the drugstore. Wayne spotted us and caught up before we left the school property. He decided he would join us. The three of us walked to the drugstore having a discussion of how school should give upperclassmen greater respect.

At the drugstore all the stools at the lunch counter were vacant, so we took the three nearest the door. Wayne began talking again and then spotted something that caught his attention. "I would stay in California if I were through with high school. It was the best damn time. I bet I laid a different girl every night," he boasted in a voice that was too loud. There was some doubt in his bragging on such things. He craned his neck continuing to observe someone or something. It became apparent that his eyes were on the parents of a girl he used to go steady with. They walked in different aisles of the drugstore. They recognized him, even through his glasses and wild attire. The thoughts could almost be read by the mother of his former girlfriend. She was probably thinking how relieved that her daughter and Wayne were no longer dating, or going with each other. The lady and her husband walked out the door without saying a word to Wayne. He watched them leave and showed a funny look on his face.

The waitress at the counter gave the three of us a certain look, and it was clear that she would put up with little nonsense. She took Dickey's order, along with the soda I asked for and began fixing a hamburger. Dickey said he would be right back and walked over toward the pharmacy area. She looked at Wayne, asking if he wanted anything and he didn't.

"So what subjects are you taking this year?" Wayne asked me, but there was a little doubt he could care less.

"English of course, and Economics. I signed up for a Sociology class..." Before finishing the subject rundown, Wayne has spotted someone else.

Moving the Tassels

"Wait a minute!" he interrupted. He darted outside to speak to some guy and girl that have walked past the drugstore window. Dickey had then walked back and said the prescription had been taken to his mother's by a driver for the pharmacy. He looked around one way and then the other.

It didn't bother me having Wayne leave, but it triggered the thought about Edna and our time at the lake when he mentioned laying different girls.

"Where did Wayne go?"

"He saw some people and acted as if he were coming back," I said. "With Wayne, who knows?" and there was a feeling in my shoulders that drew a shrug of confusion.

The food order came through and placed in front of my friend. He was eating his hamburger when mustard plopped on his shirt. It kind of stood out against his light striped shirt. He was unaware until it was brought to his attention by me. A few brushes with his hand only smeared it further. After we finished at the lunch counter, we left, and headed in different directions.

There is a pool hall near and with idle time available, it seemed ok to step in for a minute? There always was smoke lifting over the lighting that would suspend over the tables. This smoke was like a part of a fixture. In the corner was a guy that looked to be glued to a pinball machine. There was the sound of flipping action and bells, and he shook it in an attempt to register a higher total of points. There wasn't anyone recognizable or known in there so I walked out.

The idea came to me. Maybe stop by Arlene Wilson's home. She was a nice girl, pretty and very attractive, and always found time to talk whenever I came by.

A few steps could be saved by cutting across the groomed lawn that approached the door of her home. Looking around it was obvious that this was the best-kept property on the street.

Plants and shrubbery looked very professional. There was a great deal of work involved in this, it came to me that it was never noticed before. A funny looking doorbell was beside the doors. When activated the tones rang out loud, and it reminded me of the TV show about the family that was confused by the sound of the doorbell. They didn't know the reasons for it. It brought on a laugh thinking about it.

"Well, how are you Wes?" Arlene asked as she opened a door.

"Doing good, I just came from school. You know, signing up for classes. There is so much fun in doing that."

"Would you care to come in the house?" she opened the door wider as she invited me. This was the first time ever to have been invited in her house. It's usually a talk on her front porch. A house such as this would probably refer to the porch as veranda. The entrance was double doors, and how many houses has double doors?

"Thanks. There really wasn't anywhere to go," I said.

"Nowhere to go, and nothing to do so you decide to come by here," she commented, laughed and threw her head back slightly as her long brown hair bounced with this carefree motion. It caused me to laugh, realizing what a stupid thing it was to say. Her parent's home was decorated with an expensive flair. Her father had a catering business and restaurant, and it was often advertised on the radio. Her family was probably set financially. To look around in this home, there would be no argument about it. The floors were a dark hardwood with a high gloss, and placed about were carpets that had colorful mixtures and fringe on the sides. These may have been Persian rugs; it was hard to be sure. There were a couple of white marble figures set about. Expensive looking portraits and artwork. Everything was so orderly. Bouquets of flowers sat on a table in the 1iving room and another table near a stairwell. A scent of roses was in the air, and I was familiar with roses. The furniture was new or looked new. We sat on a sofa twice the size of the one in our home. It was cool in the house also. Wow! They have air conditioning! The house was bigger than many in the area, but not all that big. Continuing to look around, it occurred to me that my mouth was open as my eyes wandered. This is kind of embarrassing. But this home, inside and outside, was just very nice. This was that almost mystical home I would see from the street. The place where Arlene lived and breathed. It was something.

It had nearly skipped my thinking that she had two older brothers. A framed family picture showed all of them at a table. Her brothers used to be seen around a few years ago. They never had much to do with me, but one of them went out with my sister a couple of times. One attended an Ivy League school, Dartmouth or Princeton, something like that. The other, the one that dated my sister, was in the Air Force. Arlene told me he was temporarily stationed at the Pentagon. Everything involving her family worked out in an impressive way. Her family had great character.

Arlene, would you run up to the food mart for me?" her Mother' asked as she walked into the living room. "I beg your pardon, I didn't realize you had a visitor."

"Mom, you know Wes Patterson, don't you?" she questioned. "Why, yes, I do. I didn't recognize you at first, Wes. How are you?"

"Doing just fine," I answered, and felt like hiding my head in shame. Mrs. Wilson was a very pretty woman, and it was disconcerting talking to an adult that was as old as my mother, and yet Mrs. Wilson could turn heads of most of the guys the same age as me.

"I'll go to the store for you," Arlene told her mother. "Do you want to go along with me, Wes?" she asked.

"Sure.

"Here is a short list of the items I need, and a twenty," Mrs. Wilson said as she handed the list and money to Arlene.

"Got it Mom," she responded. "I'll take your car if it's okay?"

"All right. I expect change.

"I'll bring back your change, Mom. Come on, Wes, time's a wasting," Arlene said to me in a spirited mood. The car we were going in was a Camaro. It was not a teen's car but it looked sporty. I thought about Mrs. Wilson cruising through some of the drive-through restaurants in this car. How dumb can a guy be, thinking of this to myself?

Arlene drove like an instructor. One might have thought her enthusiasm when we were getting ready to leave her house would carry over on the streets and we would be barreling down the road. This was not bad though.

"Have you met the new family in the Cranston neighborhood?" she asked.

"No. It's the first I've heard of anyone new."

"They're from California. Two boys and a girl."

"Why would they come here? California has so much. We were just talking to Wayne Borden, and he had recently returned from there. He was impressed with California. Moving from there to here is like going backward,"

"Don't you like it here? I can't thinly of any place I would rather live. I've been to California, and they do have a great deal there. So much going on. But, well, this is where my true friends are. The school. My family, cousins, well many of them. I plan to marry and have children and live here for the rest of my life!" She stated this like a pep talk for our city.

Her attention to the road while driving could be considered admirable. Her profile was something. Her face, from any angle, was picturesque. She did things right. Her clothes were neat, pressed, and clean. Always tasteful. I don't think I ever saw her wear a tie dyed t-shirt or sweater. Her attention displayed something some guys like me look for in many girls. It is a quality of intelligence above normal. She handled the car like an adult and made smooth turns. Nothing was jerky about her driving. She had good road concentration. It made me wonder why someone like her would even speak to me. On my part there was a lot of work to do; a lot of growing up to do.

"Sometimes things just hind of fall apart around here. You how it goes. Like expecting a big Christmas and ending up with a gift you can neither use nor give to someone else this being said with some sarcasm. It was sometimes done to hint at dissatisfaction with everything in general.

"Oh, I don't think I've ever had anything like that happen," Arlene said in that typical upbeat way. My thoughts ran on that she has lived a charmed life. It seems that some people do. Arlene pulled into a parking spot, positioned the car between the lines and began talking to some guy she knew and she and I stepped out of the car. He didn't know me and made no effort to meet me. Arlene gave some introductions, but we both kind of grunted at each other. It was better when she said goodbye to him. We then walked into the store. Most of the employees in the grocery knew her. One might have thought royalty entered through the door. The store owner even said hi and started asking her about her parents. It's little wonder she ever would leave. Everyone seemed to adore her, myself included.

I helped her with a couple of items and we were soon going back to her home. It was nothing that surprised me when another car pulled up from the opposite direction and the driver started talking to her. This was something that other drivers on the road often found annoying. We were blocking the road, although no traffic was coming, and she and some other girl were gabbing about facial make-up and then about the song by the Rolling Stones playing on the radio. They said their goodbyes, and we continued toward her home once again.

"You don't know Flora, do you, Wes?" she asked.

"No, don't think so. I thought I knew a lot of people, but compared to you I'm a hermit"

"Oh, you know many people. I have just been seeing some that I know from here and there. You understand how that is?"

"I guess so." There was an uncomfortable few moments after this comment. It seemed time to go home, or anywhere. It did occur to me that Arlene would talk to these people but never be critical about anyone. She never made any remarks of how someone looked or how they dressed. She was a very decent human being. Maybe that's the secret to living a charmed life. We soon arrived back at her home.

"Did you want to come inside?" she kindly asked.

"No, I had better be going home. I have to go over what I will be taking as far as classes. My Mom will be asking about them. See yah around I told her, and soon felt like a real jerk. I could have stayed at her house and talked to her, but it was a feeling of being out of place. Why? Who knows? Perhaps a kind of intimidation. It was that home, maybe. The place where she lived. Sometimes one feels like a fish out of water and afraid of how or what words might be used. This is not because of being stupid. It is hard to explain.

If telling Arlene about this, being Arlene, she would certainly understand. Then again maybe she wouldn't. Damn! It's confusing, and how do you understand what her house was or how it was decorated that made me feel so small? Arlene was always a nice person. She never tried to put me on the spot. Sometimes it was hard to be around a girl and talk to her just as a friend. Someone like Arlene was a girl like that. My thoughts were jumping all over the place at this time. Oh, Arlene. If only the talk with her were on my terms. It would be great if she would go out on a date with me. It's a strange thought. I can talk to her as a friend, but if we were on a date, my words would really be fumbling all over the place and the self-conscious bit would make it that much worse. Sometimes a guy trips over his tongue and his own feet. It probably didn't matter. Her going out with me is not likely. At least not yet.

The sun beat down on the back of my neck while I was walking along the road, heading for home. It was puzzling to me that the better part of the day could have been spending a couple of hours at Arlene's and watching her talk about music or the new family that moved nearby. It would have been something to enjoy, being around her. God, am I ever stupid!

Our house was in sight and here I was not really wanting to be here. What was there to do? Mom would be checking out the schedule for my classes. She would most likely ask why this or that subject was not part of the plan. This was not a thing to be bothered with right now. Why didn't I stay at Arlene's for a while? She asked me. She was nice enough. God! That house! It was really some house. "Am I ever stupid!" the words came out aloud. If walking and avoiding Mom was possible...

"Wes, what are you doing? Did you get signed up for everything?" she asked with a kind of hope in her voice.

"Here's what I'll be taking," answering, as I handled her the slip of paper with the subjects written out in a very legible handwriting. "And here is the receipt for the books. It's about the best I could do," I continued and felt guilty while saying this. Mom looked over both pieces of paper.

"Well, there could have been a subject or two that you might have taken that would be better in preparation for college," she said. The disappointment in her saying this was noticed, and Mom wanted me to notice this, for sure. My face probably gave her one of those goofy looks that had been developing and showing the stupid side of me since puberty. The world was easier to accept before that came along.

We continued to talk about subjects. It was obvious that my schoolwork was not on par with what my parents had hoped it would be. My sister's approach and success with the school didn't help either. She was a model student. The television was on and a check of the stations showed nothing of interest. Still my eyes focused on something regarding Nixon for a few minutes. "Mom I'm going to go to my room for a little while."

Lying on the bed and looking up at the ceiling, the thought of college came out. One has to really buckle down for that. There would be studying all the time. What subjects does a person take in college? My sister knew what she wanted. The school had everything laid out, and what subjects she would need to take. With me it was much different. What major? What anything? And here's my Mom telling me to take high school classes that are going to benefit me in college.

Then the thought of Viet Nam came to mind. This was on the news nearly every night. Major magazines did big stories on this too. Some of the pictures would get to you on the front page of a magazine with war torn places, and guys stretched out on gurneys. It was one of those things of the day. It caused a lot of young people to consider our involvement in the war. After thinking about the magazine pictures, the studying didn't seem as bad as before.

There came another thought of Arlene. She had an unusual name in a way. I didn't really know any other Arlene's. Arlene would go to college for sure. She would apply herself like my sister does. She didn't need to concern herself with Viet Nam, but she more than likely had concerns. She was thinking about getting married when she was through with school. Why would a girl go through all of that studying just to get married and raise a family? That's a thought, to marry Arlene and raise kids. Man, I'm going too far with this. Just Lying in bed, and then the thought of the flowers in her house came to me. The roses came through. Over the summer there was work in people's yards with particular flowers, and especially roses. That distinct aroma. Arlene's home has flowers in vases when nobody is expected to visit. Arlene's parents weren't putting flowers out for me. Absolutely not! Flowers and school, and accomplished people. Where was I going? My dream state went from one thing to another. Time to turn over and press my face in the pillow and catch forty winks. What is forty winks? There came a weird notion of driving a tractor on an uncle's farm.

Upon awakening, it felt sort of weird. My head had an unusual feeling. It was like the brain was this mess of molasses and it was lying all to one side. The balance on my feet was difficult as I placed a hand on a wall to keep from falling to the floor. Wow, what happened? Sitting on the bed for about a minute helped to clear this experience. A check of the alarm clock displayed twenty minutes after eight. It took a minute, then was the understanding that it was evening and not the morning. In the front room Mom and Dad were at their usual places watching the television.

"Well Rip V., you decided to join us! I called out when we had supper, but you slept through that," Mom said, smiling. "Can I warm something up for you? We have much left over."

"No, I might fix a sandwich, just not all that hungry," my response came as the earlier dizziness came over me again, but left my being just as quickly.

Dad sat in his favorite chair, hardly moving. That was the old man. It wouldn't be a respectable thing to call him that to his face. He would not want that from me, or it might make him feel bad. He worked hard to provide for us, and it might be that he was just too tired to make much conversation. With Mom it was different. She worked in the house keeping it clean, vacuuming, preparing all are meals. She had little time to relax during most of the day but she always had something to say. Mom was a talker for sure. When Dad talked, the words demanded more attention. His utterances usually meant business. It frequently meant some sort of trouble. Usually the one in trouble was me.

The door opened at that moment and my sister Kate walked in. "I'm home!" she blurted out. She worked at a dairy stand part time, and attended college. She seldom disappointed our parents. With just the two of us kids it must be that one did the right thing and then there was the other. She toted in some books as she came through the door. She always had books. It seemed like this was year around.

I fixed a bologna sandwich and told mom and dad I was going out for a short while. So, here it is, walking down the street taking a bite of the sandwich, now and then, and trying to find someone to hang around with for a while. Everyone was gone. It was hard to figure where they all went to. These were my regular friends and not a one to be found. There was Wayne and Dickey earlier, Arlene too. Wayne was difficult to be around, and Dickey was not really one to hang out tonight. At least not right now, although our friendship was becoming a bit stronger. There was no doubt Arlene was the one to see. So often the case, my thoughts went to Arlene. To go over to her house right now might come across as an imposition. No need to do that. If nothing else we were on good speaking terms, and God forbid messing that up. It was best to go back home. The darkness had completely set in, and there was this moping along kind of sorry for myself feeling.

The sandwich was finished, and the decision to go a slightly different route came to mind. There soon appeared a familiar pond some of us used to fish in. The sound of frogs croaking and other things making a noise for mating or something such as that was all around. The water looked peaceful. It had a dark color, and it seemed to have always looked like that. If you took a drinking glass and dipped it in the water then held it up in daylight, the water looked kind of clear. Just a couple of years ago some of us guys were trying to build boats and float them across this pond. None of them did very well. And whatever happened to the boats? If Arlene were here with me, it would be great. She would make things perfect right now. We could be on a boat. Oh boy, ---is that ever wishful thinking.

Nothing much happening. Where is everyone? Friday nights like this are usually full of activity. Maybe everyone is out on a date. I would be if I had a car. What's the use of having a driver's license if you never get to drive a car? If the old man would let me use his car, some dates would be coming around, and maybe even a date tonight. Damn! There's not even a girl that would go out with me at this time. It is as well to go home.

CHAPTER II

A family from California did move nearby and acquainted themselves with many of my friends. Two boys and a girl. One of the boys was only twelve. The other two were teenagers. Arlene had told me about them moving here, but I hadn't met them. There also was some local guy, Mickey, that had been dating my friend Jimmy's sister, and his family had just moved a street over from Jimmy. "The people one meets in high school could possibly, and probably, shape a person's life more than the classroom subjects, even when studied with serious intent" said our sociology teacher. Maybe so. All of us guys said she was a really good-looking girl. It's always exciting meeting a new girl.

Jimmy's house was a popular place to gather, and it was there that Mickey was introduced to many of us. He was soon to be Kathleen's boyfriend. He had been seeing Kathleen for a few weeks, and they had gone out on several occasions. Since recently moving nearby and being one of the new kids to start associating with my group, it was not surprising that he took to Jimmy's sister. Kathleen drew the attention of a lot of guys, it was not surprising that he took to Jimmy's sister. Kathleen drew the attention of a lot of guys. She was very pretty. She had long black hair, and dark eyes, accented with noticeable eyebrows that showed a hidden intelligence. Very alluring and there was her temper that was so explosive that some of the guys began calling her K. D. Nitro, or Katenitro. It fit, too. She would go off for no reason and was known to start throwing the first thing she could pick up in her hand.

Mickey was an all right sort. About six feet tall, dark complexion, brown hair, and readily noticed by the girls. He had a motorcycle and sometimes took Kathleen out on this whenever they went on a date. "I'll see ya around, Mick,' I told him. "And best of luck,' without elaboration. My meaning was good luck with Kathleen. One could easily pick up on her body language and from what could be read she was just about done with the time she had spent on Mickey. No doubt he would soon find out. My puzzling about his taking her out on a motorcycle brought a question. What does he do for dating in winter? Maybe it's an easy answer: Probably uses the old man's car.

There was a party on the last Saturday night in September at the home of a girl named Teresa that many of us knew. She lived about five miles south of most of us, and we had met her through some others; she took to our group in a good way. She lived in a moderate house, nothing too fancy, but nice and well kept. Teresa's mother allowed us to use the basement for the party, and she stayed upstairs while we listened to 45's and danced some. The basement was finished and had red carpeting that was too thick. Nearly everyone was tripping while crossing the floor. This was sometimes used as a tactic to land in the arms of some girl. Sometimes a girl would reverse the action.

The furniture was nice stuff. There were two leather chairs, a sofa and a loveseat. Then as a temporary measure there were some folding chairs available. Often the real furniture was taken by a guy and girl that were involved with one another. It was just a typical thing.

It was not uncommon to turn up the music a little louder than necessary so the adults could not hear what we might be talking about, and with music being up louder than needed it sometimes kept older people from coming around. Teresa's mother was more understanding than some parents. She came downstairs about every fifteen minutes to bring pretzels and potato chips, and a potato chip dip she made that tasted rancid. Most everybody would throw it out, or flush it down the toilet in the basement restroom. She made of trips filling this bowl or than one. She was always smiling, and it was easy to see that she was really checking on us. It reminded me of security guards that punch a clock at a location. They made their rounds at nearly the same time. She did the same thing. If some guy and girl were into a serious kiss, they knew it might be interrupted with periodic visits would drown out the footsteps of one walking down the stairs. This was a party without a chaperone, and yet it actually was being observed often, but she was too nice a lady for anyone to say anything.

The two oldest of the kids that had moved from California were at the party. The boy was named Alan, and like me he was a senior in high school. He was quite different from most guys that we ran with. He wore bellbottom blue jeans and that covered his shoes and scraped the ground. He often had a pea jacket, like those worn in the Navy, and although the climate here was colder than Los Angeles it seemed wearing this jacket was too much on many days. This particular night was balmy and a windbreaker would be more than what was needed. His hair was longer and stringier than most other guys, and he had a degree of arrogance that was probably going to cause him trouble before long. He made it known that he didn't like living here. His hair, although different, was not such an issue. There were a lot of guys that were wearing their hair a little longer than they had before. The clothes were not making an impact so much and styles were beginning to change. Alan just had a chip on his shoulder, or something. He just didn't try to meet people halfway. It was so obvious. He talked about how boring the party was too. A couple of the guys told him to shut op or leave. He finally sat in a folding metal chair and pouted the remainder of the night.

His sister Sally was about to turn sixteen. She was much different than her brother. It was my first time meeting her. And the guys that told me she was good looking were selling her short. She was a knockout. She might have had the prettiest eyes I had ever seen. Unlike her brother, she was much friendlier, and she quickly discovered that all the guys around here were so interested in her. She would draw interest no matter where she lived. Sally had dark hair that fell to her shoulders, and such attractive facial features that were highlighted by those exquisite catlike eyes. At the party she wore a tight fitting red sweater and a dark blue mini-skirt that was above her knees, and there was not a guy at the party that would criticize the way she was dressed. Some of the girls at the party were commenting to each other as she passed them by. Mickey was at the party with Kathleen, and they were occupying a good part of a sofa. When Kathleen moved her eyes away from Mickey, he would be checking out Sally. He was cool about it. He would have to be. Kathleen could catch him doing this and erupt like a volcano.

One of the guys, Randy, had an immediate impact on Sally. He liked her, and she liked him. They were an item for the next three weeks. Randy had recently split up with his girlfriend, and he had been torn up over this. The timing was right for Sally. At least it seemed to relieve him of what he had been going through. When thinking about Randy, there would be a bitterness that would surface. He dated some fine looking girls including his last girlfriend, and even after this recent breakup, he had a number of girls that wanted to go out with him. His father gave him a car, and he worked part time at a department store, so he always had money to take girls out. It had me drawing a comparison on who had this and that, causing me to feel sorry for myself. Money was not easily acquired, and having less than what was hoped for made my attracting girls difficult. Randy had a lot going for him. He was used to reining in the girls. After the party ended, I rode home with my best friend at the time who was Greg, and this was brought up.

"What do you think about a guy like Randy? He has all this good fortune, and thinks he has it so bad. By comparison if I had what he has, well, I'd have it made. No wheels, and asking my dad for the car is always no. I'm the one that has it bad, not Randy." My complaint had a quick response.

"Wes, when you start moping around feeling like this and crying over how bad things are, and how bad you got it, and so forth, you're whipped!" he explained. "It's best to put that stuff behind you and start laying out some plans on what you can do immediately, and what your long term goals are."

This was so different. Greg never talked like this before. It caught me off guard; kind of dumbfounded me. How about this? It was like having a big brother talk to me. Greg had really grown up over the last year or so, and maybe part of it was because he had enlisted in the Army and had a few weeks before his military duties took effect. Maybe it's time to listen to him. He was older. He might have some sound advice. No one around listens to my gripes. Nobody wants to really talk sincerely like this. Talking to my dad about girl problems...well, who knows what he would say? Dad just wasn't the type to bring these problems up to. Greg dropped me off from the party and upon entering the house were my parents watching the news.

"Home so soon?" asked Mom, as I stood with my hands grasping the high back of a chair not being sat in.

"Teresa's mother shut things down at eleven; Greg gave me the ride home. There wasn't much else to do." This is the weekend and high school kids want to be out on weekends. There was a desire to be out. On a Saturday night during the school year, all teenage kids want to be out. The budget didn't allow for spending too much.

Besides, Greg had to get up early in the morning for some family matter so he wasn't staying out. This weekend thing, not making the best of it has happened too many times. Arriving home earlier than expected and it being too late to go back out. This kind of makes for a bad weekend. A person my age sort of feels as if he is missing out on everything being home this early.

"We weren't quite expecting you home so soon, Wes. The late show will be on soon. Do you want to watch it with us?" Mom asked. This always seemed tough. My parents were good people but not part of my social life. Not while I'm seventeen! But my Mom was at least trying. She was almost always kind. It wouldn't be right telling her that nobody my age would want to stay up and watch TV with their parents on a Saturday during the school year. No need to say this. Just the mentioning of goodnight and off to my room. There was the thought of going back out and meeting up with some people at the drive-in restaurant, but that might not be a very good idea. Going there would take some time. No wheels. For now, just lie back on the bed and figure out where to go with my life. Yeah. That's what need to be done.

The face of Sally entered my mind. God, she had it all. Pretty face, and nice smile. A very nice figure. Why say figure? She had a body! She was looking right through me at this very moment. My thoughts cleared of her as this dreamlike state had me so taken by her for a minute. Then thoughts of Randy probably kissing her at this very moment were beginning to torment. Greg had good advice, and one thing he talked about was to think on other things. Capable things. It is not always so easy.

It would have been nice if Arlene would have been at the party. Arlene and Sally would have gotten along just fine. Arlene could have told Sally about how goofy Randy is. No. Arlene would never talk about Randy even if they got together, decided to marry and he jilted her at the altar. It still would have been great if Arlene would have been there and danced with me. It would have been nice to dance with Sally. Feel her up close. Good God! Sally and Arlene. Maybe there's a girl for me that lives miles away. A girl that doesn't know our crowd. That would work out good. That's a dumb thought. Someone like that living miles away. How would I get to see her? No car! Thinking about this, it came to me that the bus lines run near here; not far from where our home is. Well it is some sort of solution. What a way to handle a situation! Well, Greg said to work on what could be done and make plans for the future. Sally and Arlene. Oh, my!

It was Sunday morning and Mom woke me to go to church. "Wes, are you going to church at the usual time?" she asked.

"No, I'm not going this morning; not in the mood to go."

"Mood or no mood, you're going sometime today!" Mom countered with an unusual intensity in her voice. There was no doubt she meant it.

"All right, all right, I'll go." It would be better to go now, rather than with Mom and Dad. Dad doesn't go half the time anyway.

What the hell? Then other thoughts moved in. Does God get upset if you start talking about hell, especially on Sunday? Or just thinking the words before going to church? Is it OK to think about girls in church? This guy will wink at that girl. She might flirt slightly after he winks at her. Then they both might get focused once again on what is being said. In a few minutes, they're back to doing the same thing. Damn, what stupid thoughts!

Moving the Tassels

After returning from church, it seemed a good idea to give Greg a call and talk to him about what he said to me on getting my life in order. He couldn't be reached so I went out walking and decided to be a little businesslike while out. Several stops can be made at some of my neighbors' houses. Not a bad idea setting up leaf raking jobs that would not be too long off. Most of the places were okay. The people that were spoken to were friendly, cordial people. My yard work had some quality, and most people were decent to do business with.

One guy was different. While waiting for him to answer the door, there were loud sounds and all sorts of rumbling in the house. An anxiety came around and so did a decision to walk off, but he had then come to the door.

"What the hell do you want?" he asked, as he rubbed his face hard with both hands and looked like a dog that was about to attack. His hair was kind of all a mess, and his clothes looked as if he slept in them.

"Didn't mean to wake you up, but I was wondering if you would be interested in having the leaves of your yard raked and gathered in a few weeks?" The question to him brought out a stammering in my voice.

"You didn't wake me up. Does my yard look like such a mess that the few leaves that are on it are a big eyesore to your old man, or some other complaining son of a bitch around here?"

"No, sir, not at all, sir!" my answer back was as if at attention in the armed services.

"How nice to know. No I don't want you laboring on my property to gratify this bunch of nosey bastards that live around here!

"Yes, sir" After answering him, I backed away on the walk that led to his house and stumbled but caught my balance.

"If I change my mind, I'll say something to you," he said in a milder tone. Maybe he felt bad about how he talked to me, but stopping by here again is very unlikely. There was cause to be curious why he started letting his yard look as it did. Just a year ago it was trimmed neatly, and he and his wife were often working outside. There was talk that she had packed up and left. Stories varied as to why, and possibly with who.

After making about a half dozen contacts and anticipating a time to do this, it was time to walk over to Greg's. He might be home by now. He wasn't, so going by Arlene's house was a good choice. At her house, four cars were in the driveway, and there are often family times on Sunday. Turning around, an immediate force of wind was pushing at me. There were leaves falling from this and the odd whirl of leaves that sometimes comes about as it moves in unusual paths. It reminded me of about five years ago when finding myself in the middle of one of these, and it seemed to hold me centered and at peace for a long time. There was a protection of sorts that is not easily put into words. With this turning of air it could have given a comfort around the surly neighbor that was spoken to earlier. Some of the things that pop up in nature are weird, but interesting.

Returning home was much the same. Mom and Dad were watching TV, and my sister was studying at the dining room table. "Have you completed your homework for tomorrow?" my Mother inquired.

"Everything that had to be done was done yesterday."

"It sounds as if you could do some extra work on your English, son," Mom hinted, and I sort of ignored what she said. "Do you have any upcoming tests that you could prepare for? Studying in advance can usually make tests and the pop quizzes much easier, and your grades would most likely reflect this."

"That sounds like the pits, to be doing extra studying on a weekend," I said.

"With your report cards over the last few years, any extra time with your nose in the books would be a big benefit," my father chimed in. With that, perhaps pretending to study for a while would do. He didn't say much very often, but with Mom going on about this, and my remarks, there was little doubt he would say something regarding schoolwork before too long.

The dining room table was what seemed best suited for study. Across from me was my sister Kate, and she was reading over something in a textbook. Her concentration was amazing. She would study for sometimes two hours at a time and hardly move. It was like being near a statue that processed information. How does she do that? I could read and pronounce certain words that even some of the better students couldn't do, and yet struggle to relate any of the text that was just read unless it was completely interesting.

"What are you studying now?" I asked, just to break the silence at the table.

"It is psychology. We're going over a section that deals with treatment of psychoanalysis. We are covering some of the discoveries of Sigmund Freud as he worked in this field. Dream interpretation and sometimes how early sexual behavior affects people long after an incident of some sort."

Psychology sounded like a tough subject and probably much to learn about this but whenever someone says something that refers to sex, it is only natural for a guy my age to be more attentive. It was surprising my parents were not alerted, or didn't have something to say on this. They continued to watch whatever there was on TV at that time. What the hell, this is taught in college. It's not like she was taking a course on how to kill someone and dispose of the body without being caught. The name was familiar.

Sigmund Freud's name is frequently mentioned. Most of the time, his work in this field made him seem an overeducated bore.

My books were barely used. These were seldom opened outside of the classroom. Kate's books would be dog-eared on the soft covers after the end of the semester, and the hardback books would show signs of use on the opening of pages, and wear on the spine and corners.

"Do you want something to drink?" I asked, maybe giving her a break. This was after a tiresome ten minutes and feeling already burnt out on studying.

"Not yet. There are notes I need to write down and go over, so I want to finish up on this before taking a break."

How she does it, I haven't the foggiest. Maybe studying only appeals to some family members. It's fascinating, that someone can bury their nose in a book and continue reading and grasp what the writer is trying to convey. If I go to college and have to do what she's doing, it's doubtful I'll be able to get through.

There was a book from a class that was to be read before the end of October, so that would occupy my time for a while. It had a lot of information on Adolph Hitler, but oddly it was for my English class. The cover had a building that looked something like the facade of a castle. Centered on top of the building was a circle with a swastika located inside the circle. Bold lettering was on the book, and typically, the author's name was not looked at. There was mention of a book Hitler wrote called "Mein Kampf" and this was discussed in a history class of my junior year, but it was hard to remember what the purpose was for this book. The translation meant "My Struggle," and it had me curious about what Hitler struggled with. For what it was worth I thought about struggling being age 17. If multiplied by 2 and then subtracting the multiplied number from this year, it would be 1934. In 1934 Hitler was seeming to be moving the Nazi regime where he wanted it. In another 11 years, 1945, it would all come tumbling down for him. In another 11 years from now it would be nearing 1980! Wow, numbers are a wild thing when you think about them like that. Maybe math should be given more attention.

Earlier, paging through the book began to be disconcerting when all the German names and words slowed my progress. I "kampfed" through a few pages, then put it down. There was a curiosity if Kate had ever read this, but once again her eyes were intent on the subject of psychology, and there was no reason to interrupt. Time for a drink of water or something. So into the kitchen and filling a glass with water, stretching and a need to rub the back of my neck. Ah. The telephone rang and Mom answered it.

"Wes, Greg is on the phone for you," she said, holding the receiver and looking kindly while I came take the call.

"Hey, what are you up to?" asking eagerly. He told me he was returning my call and was out with one of his uncles for a short time, and was trying to get in touch with all his family members before Uncle Sam shipped him away.

"Where do you think you'll end up at?" I kind of prodded, and asked if he had given thought about orders to go to Viet Nam.

"I've been trying to prepare for anything. It's like a baseball player when he is at bat. He prepares for a fastball coming across the plate. But his eyes have to watch for a curveball, or a sinker. Whatever is being thrown to you, you have been ready and aware. Preparation can have you in a position to react sensibly,' he related, and again this had impressed me. Who did he talk to about this? Maybe his uncle. It was so strange that this crazy-acting guy I had been hanging out with the last couple of years had become so mature of late. Before he took on this new side of his personality, we would talk about girls most of the time. He would make comments and put on gestures that were downright indecent.

Anyway we kept trying our best to figure girls out. No doubt he was going to be missed when he did leave.

"Say, I have an idea. Why don't we go get something somewhere, you know…get something out to eat tonight? If you're not doing anything, we could hang out some and grab a hamburger tonight, somewhere," I suggested.

"You know, that's a good idea," he told me, without getting into his new philosophical mode. He said he would stop by around five, and it sounded good. Now it had to be cleared with the parents.

"Mom, Dad. I'm going to eat supper out tonight, that is if you say it's okay," trying to look meek, for some reason.

"You know we like to have our Sunday dinner with all of us at the tables Mom answered back."

"But Greg's getting ready to leave in a few weeks to go wherever the Army decides to send him to!" I cried out, and searched the look on both Mom's and Dad's face for some reproving remark.

"Maybe we can let them run to their restaurant this once, since Greg is going to be in uniform soon," my Dad interjected, and it almost caused me to forget the house I was in. This is not my old man that just said this! My dad did have this patriotic part of himself though that must have weighed on him some, so he gave an okay. This patriotism was admirable.

"Okay, I'm willing to go along with it this time, but we don't want our Sundays to be taken lightly. We are still a family, and there are expectations to keep the Sunday meal together,' Mom added, but she gave her approval too.

This was not such a big deal, going out for a hamburger with one of my friends. A couple of things were involved though. This bit about Greg going to be gone for military duties soon, and not knowing when he would be back. The other thing was to finish up the weekend. The thought of the weekend about to end, and there was nothing to tell about. Going back to school tomorrow and someone asks, well there was the party Saturday night, and on Sunday time was spent with a buddy of mine that was going to be away in the Army very soon. It sounds better than saying my studies were tended to and then there was supper with my family. That just wouldn't cut it to some of the kids at school.

There were some things to ask Greg. He actually sounded like someone that knew what could be done to get better organized. When a senior in high school doesn't know where he is going in his life, at least talking about it with someone is a start. If he goes too far out, it is my thinking it was Okay. Greg would be gone and probably wouldn't be talking to anyone about what was said anyway.

It would be good though to talk about stuff and get suggestions on what to do. Greg seems to understand. And, well, being a senior in high school, one should be laying down some kind of base for the life ahead.

There are not a great number of restaurants around to choose from. Greg had decided to go to a place that was located on the other side of town. While driving there he listened to the radio station that older people would listen to. It played music that most kids thought was square. The deejays were stiff too. Everything was so serious. Oh well, it was his car, actually his father's. I was a passenger, and this was one of the nights out for him that were dwindling down, so if he wanted to listen to that, who is to complain?

"Are there any girls that you're going to write to?" I'd ask.

"Sure there are. Shirley, Candice, Edna. Oh! I'm going out with Edna Wednesday," he added.

"On a school night?" I exclaimed, but not too loud.

"We're going out for a short while. Nothing serious," he said calmly. Thoughts came in about Greg and Edna. It was an unusual pairing. I wondered about Edna. she was never encouraging me, but was one of the girls that just has a fellow mixed up on where he stands with her. She wasn't as pretty as a lot of the girls that were around, but she was shapely. Stacked might be a better description, and there was often the thought that Edna and me might get together again some time. Then again Greg, my friend, is going away for a while, so he should get the chance to be with her for a last time.

"Is this where you're taking Edna, Wednesday?"

"No, we are going to see a movie and eat at the seafood place across from the theater," Greg said in a thoughtful way. Greg was reflecting on how things were. He was thinking on this, and it appeared so. He might have been tearing up, but he shook that off. He then pulled into the place we would eat. We walked in and took seats at the counter.

"What will you guys have?" the waitress asked.

"I'll have a piece of coconut cream pie and a cup of coffee," Greg ordered.

"Anything else?" the waitress asked him.

"That'll do?'

"Is that all you're getting? I thought you wanted to get a big dinner," I spoke excitedly, and tried to keep my voice controlled. It occurred to me that too many times my voice came out whiney when trying to emphasize something. Controlling my voice from this pitch was always needing work.

"It's enough for now. Wasn't it you that was telling me how little money you have?"

My expression might have had some effects. He was cracking a smile.

"If you decide on something else, let me know? This one's on me," I offered, in a feel good way.

"Wes, you never buy. I wasn't expecting anything, and besides I ate a late lunch," Greg commented almost as if he were turning down my generosity.

"Hey, old man! It might be a long time before you're around here again. Besides, I figure there's a payback to you for a couple of burgers or a pizza or something," saying this somewhat sheepishly.

"Hey! Okay, how about a bowl of chili to go along with it?"

"Yeah, good deal,' my voice tapered off, wondering about the cost of a bowl of chili. Never in my life had I bought a bowl of chili out before and hadn't seen it on the menu. Nonchalantly my eyes roamed over the menu again, slowly, without making much about it. The chili was on the other side of the menu and it was about the same price as double patty burger. My breath eased after seeing this, and casually the menu was placed aside.

Our dinner went well, and we talked over a number of things. He mentioned that he had given thought to getting married. This was very surprising, and this confusing side of his personality was something he had been doing a lot lately. His outlook on things, his attitude, and just so many different things. There was a maturity that continued showing through. He even had better posture than he used to. He had his hair combed neatly, but he always did that. He also always wore his clothes well. Maybe I was thinking too much about this. It was impressive though in the way he had begun acting and carrying himself.

"Are you thinking about marrying Edna?" the thought had overcome me. Edna was such a curiosity, and she was so different. Greg mentioning marriage and this relationship with Edna was a thing to ponder. Was he planning to marry her?

"I like Edna," he said, "but there might be, and probably is, some other girl I'll meet while serving in the Army. There's a lot outside of our little part of the world here, and I think somewhere, no matter where I go, I'm likely to find the one. It's kind of a kismet thing. As far as Edna, we're just friends. It doesn't go too much beyond that."

This left the door open for me to go out with Edna. If Greg really liked her I would in no way have any thoughts of asking her out. Greg is just having a friendly goodbye when lie goes out with her. Once again the thoughts moved toward a girl that doesn't give much indication that she wanted to go out.

Greg dropped me off at my house. It wasn't late, and Mom was right in me needing to study. Procrastination had been mastered; had it down! There was some review of questions for an upcoming test at school. Our class knew we were having a test this week, but unsure of the day. It could be tomorrow. Sitting down and mulling a few things over, it dawned on me that some maturity could be nearby after all, In the past there was never any care about studying a little extra in the way of review for a test. When placing my book down, Mom saw what was happening and gave a look of surprise. No doubt she was wanting to ask me about this new studious behavior, but smiled, turned around and continued putting a few things in order in the kitchen.

School is funny. We have things drilled into our heads, and after we get out, how often do we use them! A long time ago I asked an English teacher about diagramming sentences, "Is anyone going to ask me to do this when working at a job?"

"It is important to understand how to communicate in the working world. If you understand the parts of speech, and how to convey your message to another, it will improve relations," I remarked and walked away after saying okay. It was a polite way of leaving. There was some despair because it was lost to me what he was saying after the first couple of words. Sometimes a teacher confuses a point my explaining too much. There is probably a better way to get the point across.

**//

CHAPTER III

The middle of October brought on a rain and strong winds that had some of the people complaining about leaves blowing in the yards I had recently raked. You might have thought it had been my fault, and the wind was in league with me to drum up more business. This was not only a silly reaction by some, but I was no longer in need of cleaning up leaves thanks to the new employment that came my way a couple of weeks ago at a neighborhood grocery. The store had been operational for about 15 years. A medium-sized building that sat in a small shopping complex. It did good business with the nearby neighborhoods. My dad might have had something to do with my getting hired. He had some dealings with the store owner, and his comment after finding out that I was hired was, "You might as well do something that draws a few dollars. It's apparent to me you're not going to be playing sports for your school."

The sarcasm was nothing new. My dad thought sports were one of the few things that made life worthwhile. He felt he might have made the big leagues in baseball at one time. His son should be of the same mind, and play everything the school offered. He also expected me to excel in all of these. He has been watching the Olympics and possibly thinks his son should have the talent to participate. It would be a challenge for me to even hold up a fist in silent protest. The Olympics and sports are very entertaining, but desire has to be there. The participation every day is too much a sacrifice. It would be too difficult in bringing myself to this. I enjoyed baseball, football, and basketball. There was even an attempt at track my freshman year.

Dad urged this last season and said hurdles would help with agility. Agility maybe, but lack of speed was a big drawback for running hurdles. It might be on record that the slowest time ever was when I competed against a team in state. Let me say the laughs were as painful as if not more so than embedded cinders on my knees when a trip over the last hurdle finished my track pursuits. Basketball tryouts had just started a few weeks ago. My passing the ball was fair. My quickness was less than it should have been, and my jump shot was not good. As for jumping and rebounding, maybe about average. There was a tap on my shoulder about 25 minutes into the practice. Cut again on the first day. It seems that competing in high school sports were not suited for me.

This could work out though. Attending the games is enjoyable. Playing in games is a lot of fun but not the sacrifices of long hours of practice. It seems the fun of playing sports under a coach's authority had become a job. What quickly happened was being cut from the team and landing a job that pays a little money. It occurred in the span of a few days. It could have been worked out, but at least now there was reason for not participating.

The new job paid minimum wage. It wasn't difficult. Hired in as a bag boy, but the job had a number of things that went with it.

Saturday mornings usually meant having to be up and out of bed instead of sleeping off the Friday night outing. There was also work one or two hours after school on the weekdays. This aside, there was a girl of interest that was working there too. This was great for me. There is usually a desire for female company. I had not even held a girl's hand in a long while. She was a cashier, and we started going out occasionally. Our boss, Mr. Tromvek, didn't like the idea of people dating coworkers, so we kept quiet about this and tried to be nonchalant toward each other when in close contact. Her name was Rebecca, and she had a kind of reddish brown hair and trusting brown eyes. Her hair actually looked dark brown. But if you looked at it and thought of red there seemed to be a hint of red. She moved almost dreamlike. If she had worn a dress down to the ground, you might think she was skating across the ground rather than walking. She had a fine figure and was smart. She most likely was too smart. With me there is always a draw to intelligent girls.

It was nice to be out with Rebecca, but the only way to go on a date was to double date. This had to be arranged, and there was not given much time to be alone with her. It would really be enjoyable being somewhere that didn't have me so self-conscious, and one may sense Rebecca felt much the same.

There was a day the two of us were back by the freezer and were caught up in the moment. We must have steamed up the window in the door of the nearby freezer. She pressed her body against me, and my thoughts were beginning to lose my sense of what was happening in this grocery. Everything other than her was secondary. Our actions were going far when we heard the stockroom door being thumped. Rebecca released her arms from around me, and we both stepped back quickly. Rebecca looked composed.

Looking toward the door was Yance. He slowly walked in. He was one of the older guys that stocked groceries, did a bit of everything, and also held a position that was almost assistant manager. Yance was built strong. As a stock boy he fit the description. He was thick and stocky. His hair was light and thinning, and he kind of resembled a character on a popular western television series. He had the easy going personality that the guy on TV had. And he was forever wearing khaki pants and a white collared shirt. He saw us and smiled. There was this feeling of blood blushing my face. Rebecca looked at me for just an instant. "Becky, lane one needs a cashier," he said very calmly.

"Yes, of course, I'11 be there in a second."

There was a box of canned green beans close to me so it might look good to pick these up and put them in a cart. When moving out the stockroom door and down the aisle, an intentional noise got the attention of Yance and he noticed me taking this where it was to be placed. Surprisingly the shelf was in need of the product, so it felt kind of good doing this. This feeling of being spotted with Rebecca, not knowing if Yance might say something about Rebecca and me preyed on my mind. He entered the door slowly, so maybe he didn't see us embracing but it was something that can bug a person. Later, talking to Rebecca that night on the phone about this, she suggested it best that we should break off our relationship, at least for a short while.

Nothing was said to either of us in the following days so it figured we had escaped being seen. The feelings between Rebecca and me had cooled considerably. A powerful interest remained in her, but it was a one-sided thing. We continued only to have a relationship as friends. She was fearful that something could happen at work and cause us to lose our jobs and carry this stigma with us in the future. In a week's time, she had the interest of some other guy.

One Saturday the store was doing slow business about an hour and a half before work was over. There was only a younger girl and guy in the store. They were in some ragged looking clothes. They had me concerned when spotting them putting cookies and other food items in a large purse she was carrying and inside the shirt he was wearing. There was an excitement at the idea of confronting them. It felt like a police operation. Quickly moving around, I put myself in a spot between the exit and this couple. My position at the end of an aisle was strategic and from behind it my voice called out, "Halt and turn over the goods you're taking!"

"Go to hell, you clown!" the girl screamed back at me. The guy began to run so I tackled him before he reached the end of the aisle. He forced his knee into my chest, and his girlfriend swatted me with her purse. It was a challenge being knocked around, my arms and hands moved to cover my face. There were stacked items that crashed to the floor causing a lot of noise. About that time, there was a scream resounding from somewhere in the store. I had fallen to the floor but grabbed at the ankle of this guy and held on while taking swats from the girl's purse, and he started pounding at my head. We began wrestling on the floor, and I grabbed hold of this guy to pin him down like the wrestlers often do on TV. Suddenly there came a sharp pain on my side, and my hold had to be released. The girl had kicked so hard it was a reason to lose strength from the pain. He pushed me off and got to his feet immediately, and the two of them glanced back for a second and scampered out the door.

"Wes! Are you okay?" the familiar voice of Rebecca had called out. She rushed to me and reached around to hold me. Damn, did it ever hurt! A reflexive jerk tensed my body. Her release was quick, and tears nearly came about from the feeling in my side. These were fought back turning into a display of pain. There were no real tears to show, and no actual crying. Looking into her eyes there was that familiar feeling of love that had come over me. The pain had been sharp. A cringe to avert what might look like crying was a struggle too. Even though our relationship had changed, there was a tough guy appearance that showed itself. She helped me to my feet and then called the store owner on the phone. He must have told her he would call the police, and she also checked again to see if there was need in going to the emergency room at the hospital. I assured her there was no need to go and to let the owner, Mr. Tromvek, know my condition was not serious.

There were two police cars that pulled up near the entrance of the grocery just minutes after Rebecca made her call to Mr. Tromvek, and both officers walked in with aplomb. "How are you kids doing today?" the older of the two asked.

"We're fine, but as I said on the phone to our manager, we had an attempt of stolen goods, and an assault on Wes," She had gestured with her hand toward me to the police. She then continued, "There was a young man and woman pilfering items when he tried to stop them," Rebecca told them. Did she ever sound professional in her account of what happened? Not a bit of hesitation. She then finished setting the groceries back in order that had been knocked over.

"Are you okay, son?" he asked after hearing Rebecca's report.

"Yes, sir" the words came out like a modest hero. "Just a little roughed up, but I..." at that moment I let out a cry of pain once again, turning my shoulders while feeling under my arm with my fingers. The sting of the kick was lingering.

"Let's see what we got here, young fellow," the policeman said as he lifted my arm and examined around the shoulder blade area. Yance had just walked into the store and had a very surprised look on his face.

"Hey! What's all this?" he called out with a rare show of emotion.

"We had some boy and girl attempting to walk off with a few things and Wes approached them," Rebecca related to Yance. "A snuffling came about and they ran off. Wes was..."

"I'm okay!" I interrupted in a raised voice.

"We can take you to a doctor, or hospital," Yance said. It was the first time ever being around Yance where he showed so much concern. He might have worried about his job with this happening. It was kind of interesting that he acted as he did. It was also interesting to see that Rebecca had qualities of a reporter the way she handled herself and described what occurred.

"It might be a good idea to have a doctor check you out, son," the older policeman said. He had me breathe deeply to check on my discomfort, and looked in my eyes directly when he had me answer his question.

"It's just tender in this kicked spot, but I'll be fine sir," my explanation convincing the officer.

The worst of the pain on my side had let up in a short span of time, and movement came about okay as a turn here and there was uncomfortable but bearable. Donna, one of the older employees, had come to work and clocked in. She looked around, picking up on the confusion. Rebecca began explaining what had happened.

Yance asked me again of my status. I reassured him, and he told Rebecca and me that we could punch out and call it a day. Rebecca was scheduled to be off soon anyway. My time called for another hour on the schedule, but as things had turned about it seemed unnecessary to continue working the last hour as it was offered. Yance then picked up the receiver of the phone and continued the conversation he was having with Mr. Tromvek.

Rebecca walked up to me and asked, "How are you feeling?" My thinking was that she was coming around after seeing my performance in dealing with the girl and guy that had been confronted. Ah, that image really does get them!

"It's not as bad as before." Reaching my hand under my arm and touching around gently. It would have been the same words to her if the pain had been intolerable. Job or no job, we are getting back together after my display of courage and leadership.

"I'm so glad. I was worried there at first, but I see how you're moving well. You did good, Wes," she let me know. For a second or so, it seemed a timely situation and beneficial that the incident occurred. Then she says, "My boyfriend is picking me up shortly. Can we give you a ride home, or somewhere...anywhere?"

"No." It almost came as a shock. "A little walk might be what is needed," then a forced bit of a smile. All the stupid thoughts about getting back together with her had come crashing down.

"Well I am happy that you're all right. I'm going to go now and probably see you here at work next time...Hero," she said, as if adding that hero bit could help in building up my morale. When she talked about her boyfriend, she could have just as easily struck me in the side with a knife where I had earlier been kicked. The hurt was probably worse. She turned and walked out the door. This was very hard. The worse part of the day.

"God almighty," I said in a whisper.

"Did you say something?" Yance asked.

"Nah. Just deciding to head home. Going home a bit early," came my reply.

The walk home was so lonely. It was like the world had turned on me. For a few minutes Rebecca and me were back together. We were thrown together in a circumstance that one sees in the movies. There was me in the heroic scene. There was the movement toward the enemy and taking them on bravely. Getting knocked down but not giving up, at least not easily. Then there was assistance by my "Florence Nightingale". This was looking good. It was feeling good. Even after my injury. Continuing to walk along and seeing this over and again in my mind. Then Rebecca's boyfriend. That son of a bitch! Why did he have to come by? Where were they going? With this continuing to play over with scene after scene, there was almost a feeling of tears welling up in my eyes. Without realizing it, my home was very close. Getting there just now was not desired so a deliberate walk past our home with an add on of the next couple of streets would tack on about a mile's distance before walking into a house that would most likely have questions I was in no mood for.

The layout of the nearby streets was dull to my thinking. A group of rectangles grouped together, with straight views toward the ends of each street. Trees had been planted by most of those that bought these homes, but there still was a lack of charm that a road might have with a bend here and there. Something about that stirs the imagination. Girls have curves and so should streets. My, was this thinking ever profound!

An older couple lived on the west side street, a block over from our home. They used to have me mow their lawn and do yard work for them. There was even an unusual friendship with them. They were Mrs. Carla Cray and her husband Fred. It was almost as if they were my grandparents. My grandparents on both sides of the family were dead. Barely knowing my true grandparents, this was sort of a substitute of grandparents. We had lived hundreds of miles from both and only visited on what was termed special occasions when they were living. It was so weird. All four grandparents died within a two-year span.

Mrs. Cray spotted me walking down the street and motioned for me to come to her front door. I walked up the driveway and then onto the walkway.

"Hello, Wes, how are you?" she asked in a quiet tone.

"Fine, ma'am, and you?" This was about as polite as I could be. There was a desire to try and be nice to them. Something caused me to be this way. If substituting them for a pair of my actual grandparents, then a show of respect should be present.

"Mr. Cray has had a setback. He has been diagnosed with lung cancer.

"I don't know what to say," came out of my mouth. Cancer scared me, because the mere mention of it seemed to mean the end. My parents talked about it at times. They said a cure would be found one day, and something else would arise and be as bad. I surely didn't want to see Mr. Cray die. How would Mrs. Cray would get along without him? They were always together. They remind me of a picture once seen of an elderly couple sitting on a porch swing going over memorabilia. Some people that got together were just meant to be. This dumbfounded sensitivity lingered as my thoughts moved along.

"I thought you would be interested in knowing about this. Freddie has always thought well of you."

"Yes, ma'am. I mean I... I'm sorry. I'm just... I don't know what I am. Just sorry." Typical of me to botch a response with this disconnected sentence. She must have understood, as she nodded her head and the corners of her lips turned up letting me know that she did.

"I'll stop by to see him sometime," I said, while feeling sort of numb and trying to get over the shock.

"I'll tell him you were by. He is resting at this time and it is what he needs, and I thank you for your concern," she said. A motion from me indicated okay, and a silly wave of my hand then showing one of those partial smiles you can feel yourself do under conditions like this.

Back to the walk toward home there was a number of things again going through my mind. Why does this happen now? I really like these people. Sometimes they listen and talk to me when I can't even talk to my own parents. They do listen. There was this mature understanding that was hard for me to find. They offered advice. What was disturbing was not having been by to see them since the last part of July. One of the other kids took care of their lawn and it didn't seem right to be stopping by.

Then it came to me that my side was of little consequence. It was sore, but Mr. Cray having cancer was something of greater concern. Mr. Cray was a smart man. He would often talk to me. Sometimes he said things that were way over my head. He would continue on and explain what he meant in simpler terms if he picked up on my lack of understanding. He said something at one time that gave me cause to reflect on, "Our place in the world probably differs greatly from what our Sunday morning lecturers would have us believe." This sentence was deep. It would upset some people for sure. This thought and the walk home continued.

My parents' house was in sight as I started to turn the corner. In what seemed but a minute I was facing the front door. Without reason I walked around to the back door, opened it, and Mom and Dad were talking about something. The discomfort was here once again. It always felt like an interfering with what they were discussing.

Wes, I didn't think you'd be home quite this soon," Mom spoke to me with more sincerity than expected.

"We had things covered at work today, and Yance let me off a little early," and shifted my eyes toward Dad. He didn't say anything but acknowledged this. There was no mentioning of the confrontation at the grocery. There were some minor cuts and a bruise or two on my face, but standing with the light behind me caused a shadow on my face somewhat. Dad would more than likely hear about the incident, but at this time there was no need to discuss it. The decision was to say something about Mr. Cray.

"I happened to go by the Cray's residence on the way home."

"Oh my! It's been some time since you have been there. How are they doing?" Mom inquired.

"Well, I was passing by for no reason and Mrs. Cray signaled to come up to the door, and she told me Mr. Cray was pretty sick." After saying this a chuckle had to be repressed. It just came to me at this more serious moment that Mrs. Cray called Mr. Cray Freddie. The unexpectedness of hearing of his condition was disturbing. What was just odd was her calling him Freddie. That was a boy's name. Fred was a man's name. But then thinking on this, Mrs. Cray had been with him for so many years that she must have thought of him as Freddie when they were dating and first married. It might have been a special name like sugarplum, or darling. A name that kind of endears one to the other. During these thoughts my mother had been saying something.

"Wes! I've been speaking to you!" Mom cried out.

"Sorry Mom, I was lost in thought. This thing about Mr. Cray.

What were you saying?"

"I asked if Mrs. Cray needed any help from us, or any of the neighbors?"

"I'm not sure. She seemed to be doing well. I might stop by again soon and checks I said, and still kind of turned these things over in my mind. Then came the thought of my face having some marks on it. It didn't need to be examined. The store scuffle. Rebecca, and that goofball she was dating. Yance's reaction to what had happened. The police coming into the store and getting information. It was sort of a dragnet situation, but not like the murder cases or anything. No detective questioning or asking for the facts, or whatever detectives actually say. Mr. Cray being laid up. There he was just deteriorating away. God Almighty! Then another thought of Rebecca's boyfriend. He was a real bum, and I didn't even know him. Why do these silly thoughts run through my head? There was a need to lie down for a while.

"Mom, Dad, I'm going to go to my room for a few minutes and rest."

"Sure, Wes," Mom acknowledged. "There'll be some dinner on the stove that I'll warm up for you when you want. Have a nap." Dad just nodded his head and smiled as he often did.

I pulled the shades to block the light. It was a cloudy day and the sun had not really shone through, but in order to nap for a spell it was best if the room was dark. My refuge, my room. How often the case, finding myself flopping down on the bed and staring at the pictures on the wall. There was a picture of a horse grazing in a field. There used to be a picture of a trio of girl singers in skin-tight pants and sexy blouses, but it disappeared one day while I was in school. My pictures were not always approved and my Mother had that Victorian upbringing, trying to make believe sexy girls and such didn't exist.

Another thought popped into my head. Why did Mom say nap? Little kids take naps. Is she always going to think of me as a little kid? The old man doesn't want that. That's for sure. He thought I was getting too grown to play with toys when I was about to turn nine.

While lying on the bed everything thought about earlier returned. Things were spinning through my mind like a school of fish moving through an area of water. There was this jumpy feeling. It was impossible to relax. The cancer Mr. Cray was suffering from. The two people in the store, stealing and fighting. That girl told me to go to hell. That was kind of comical. If I had said anything back, we might have stood there exchanging insults. She should have been busted in the mouth. She was a smart ass. Yeah, busted in the mouth and then really work over her boyfriend. If substituting Rebecca's boyfriend for that guy he could have been knocked out cold. They weren't all that bad. Just trying to swipe a few things. Maybe they were hungry or something.

A dream wandered through, following my half asleep rest. Raking leaves and picking up dead tree limbs, then packing them down to carry them to the front yard later so the garbage collectors could pick it up. Then the rumbling noise of the garbage truck started coming down the street sounding in my ears and the sound wouldn't go away. There was now the idea of getting the leaves and limbs out to the front. The house where this was cleaned up was different from all the others. Did Mom and Dad move? It might have been Yance's house. No matter. A fast run to the street to ask the driver of the garbage truck to wait, but he said Rebecca was waiting for him. He laughed and the thought was Rebecca's boyfriend is driving the truck. But he had gray hair near his temples and lines in his face. He looked way older than Rebecca's boyfriend should look.

It was almost midnight when I awoke. That silly dream almost seemed real. It was dismissed while walking into the kitchen. There were some cold pieces of chicken in the fridge. It would sandwich up good on some toast.

"Wes, let me fix something for you to eat Mom spoke out as she walked toward the kitchen.

"This will be enough. Seriously. I'll fix it and watch TV with you and Dad in a couple of minutes." I ate some of the chicken and potato chips and drank some tea that was sitting in the refrigerator. The toast popped up darker than what was wanted but still okay. I went on into the living room where Mom and Dad were watching the late show. It was an old movie with one of those old actors that was popular during World War II.

"Feeling okay, Wes?" Mom asked calmly.

"Yeah, uh, fine," my answer came with a twitch and the soreness was still with me after some movement. Then I plopped myself down on the sofa and watched the show with them. Mom was looking my way, trying not to be too obvious. A discreet move of the hand over the side of my face that took the most punches caused a striking pose of reflection. There was also some cover up with my elbow on the armrest.

"No date or nothing going on tonight?" My Dad spoke up. That was a rarity. Maybe he knew something happened. Maybe Mr. Tromvek called and told him what went on at the store today.

"Not much of a weekend," came my reply. It was upsetting to waste a weekend. This is a night to be with some girl, getting consoled for what happened and the pain endured. Maybe Arlene will hear about the fight at the store and contact me tomorrow. The musing continued.

Mom looked at me suspiciously, and Dad did too but then looked away. She then had to ask, "Did you have enough to eat?"

"Plenty enough."

"Did everything go okay at work today?" They knew about it. A five-dollar bet would say they knew. Mr. Tromvek must have called during the napping and told Dad.

"There was a skirmish with some shoplifters," I told them in some sort of mumbled voice.

"You're okay, Wes, aren't you?" Mom asked as she showed some emotion in her voice.

"Of course he's okay; he's fine. Aren't you, Son?" Dad butted in. It was one of the few times he seemed to have concern for me. He actually cared deeply for me no doubt, but it was seldom evinced. At this time, he didn't want Mom to go into the mood of trying to baby me. My Dad wanted me to meet the tough times without backing down. He understood how a man is supposed to handle things out of the ordinary, and when a young man is getting near the draft age, he had better stand up for himself. Mom wasn't always going to be there. She wanted to baby me. It was easy to see, and it was nearly felt. And deep down there was this want for someone to comfort me. Mom was just being Mom and supposedly at this moment she was fighting off the maternal nature she had. That was because of my Dad. He was overruling this time. Mom and I both wanting to hold each other because it got a little rough today.

Thoughts wondered about. The idea of squeezing Rebecca would be fine. That damn boyfriend of hers! And it would be something if Arlene made over me. Either one of these wonderful girls. There remained this mixed up thinking, but it could be either one of them close by and everything would be better'

Then it began to add up. It was when Rebecca was with that guy she was seeing after the commotion at the store. Arlene or no Arlene. Being moved aside by some guy that got the girl, Rebecca... rather had the girl and didn't do anything to merit her affections.

"Wes! Are you sure you're okay?" Mom had called out in a louder voice.

"Yeah, Mom. Of course," my answer came and trying to soften the last part of my response.

"Son, your mother was talking to you," Dad said, as he emphasized me paying attention.

"Sorry. Just thinking over the day's happenings. Kind of lost in thought."

"That's okay, Darrell," Mom said to the both of us as she glanced at me and looked over at Dad. She almost never calls him by his first name. If he was called by his first name five times in my life, it would be astonishing. Then there was Mrs. Cray and her calling Mr. Cray, Freddie. My God, do older adults ever surprise me with what they sometimes say. Thoughts continued to move all around and then attention was back to Mom and Dad. It was funny for a couple of seconds, so I walked up to the nearest window to look outside. This thing of calling my dad Darrell. He might finish the job that the two kids in the store started if anything but Dad was said in reference to him. It's hard to imagine addressing him in any other way.

"Hey Mom, Dad. Sorry about how I am acting."

"Now we understand today has been very..."

With an intentional interruption to Mom, I continued my apology. "No, Mom, let me finish! Today...it was just kind of a lousy day and now it's just a day gone by. It should have been mentioned when I came home, but Mr. Cray and all, well everything just went kind of crazy, or goofy, or whatever it did and it was a tough time talking about the store thing. And, well... you know sorry."

"We thought you were injured worse than you let on. The both of us are thankful that you weren't hurt any worse than what you were. It must have been a scary thing," my mother said in what seemed to bring about some relief for her. Dad had just moved his head in approval. The decision was to let it go at that. What the hell? There was no real hurt physically. Sometimes in the past being beat up had felt much worse. The real hurt was concerning Rebecca and her boyfriend. The real problem was the fact that there wasn't a girl to comfort me. Here was unjustified blame on some guy I didn't even know. Why put him at fault for liking Rebecca? She was pretty and had a nice body. She was smart. She had a lot that a bunch of guys might like. The two of us might have continued our relationship if not for working at the same place.

"Do we have any soft drinks?" my question came as a dry mouth brought on quite a thirst, and a deliberate walk toward the refrigerator.

"There should be several on the top shelf," Mom replied.

"Do either of you want something to drink?" I asked, and it was probably the first time to show some courtesy tonight in having asked them.

"We are fine her response came, then she added, "Your Father and I are going to turn in shortly"

"Okay. There might be something on TV worth staying up for a little while yet," my words came out with a bit more authority The television was left on, and the sofa was a feel of comfort for a period. Just then car lights showed through the folds of the draped windows. The lights were brought down to the parking lights. and then the sound of a car door shut. My sister Kate's voice was distinguishable as she said good night to her date. It sounded as if she kissed him good night, and the fumbling of keys scratched at the door lock. Before getting to the door she had it opened.

"My! Wes, I wasn't expecting you," she said, smiling broadly. "Sorry for not getting the door," came my apology, but it made little difference on the effort to go to the door. It was awkward and there had been enough things going wrong recently.

"Well, it's time to use the bathroom and get some sleep. There was no intention to be out too late tonight. I'll say goodnight, brother."

"Get your rest Kate," I responded, and liked the idea of having the late part of the evening to myself. The Late Show was on but the interest in watching it had subsided. The earlier rest had me restored my energy and held off sleep.

Television has really changed things. Right now there is a black and white TV airing many broadcasts that are now in color. The Hennesseys down the road have had a color TV for several years. The first time I saw it about ten or eleven years ago, it was very snowy looking with bright bands of color that ran horizontal. If that is color TV, you might as well do without. That was then. The last time seeing a color TV that had on a good program was a few weeks ago, and the color was so much better. We're moving from a black and white era to a color era. The news stations are doing a great amount too. The Viet Nam war is on the news

Moving the Tassels

with film of true killings and maiming. Some of the well-known magazines have even harsher pictures. It is definitely getting a response from kids in college. And the Haight-Ashbury thing on the west coast last year has spawned something for sure. This bit of imagining kind of a conversation with Rebecca was a new sort of stupid. It continued though. "There are many things that concern me in this world of today. The war in Southeast Asia, and cancer that attacks so many, young and old.

Rebecca might be, or could be, a reporter. She certainly handles herself well. She should be spoken to with some intelligence and maybe some authority. The voice of someone that was well educated. She would chime in if I did this. She was that kind of person. My thoughts on this stopped for a couple of seconds. How do you speak intelligently on current events if only going through the motions in school? Then came the thoughts of Rebecca's boyfriend. Is this guy up on the latest news? Can he talk to Rebecca about Viet Nam, and cancer, and civil rights, and all the other things the decade of the sixties seems to have brought into light? He probably doesn't talk to her about such things. He probably whispers those sweet nothings in her ear and rubs against her body.

Oh, God, what am I doing? Just driving myself crazy thinking about things like this. The Late Show was signing off at this time, and just as well. I turned the television off and watched as the picture on the screen collapsed to a white dot. It was time to go onto bed. Get some extra sleep. It had been some day.

CHAPTER IV

It was the usual Friday night high school game. I was waiting for a friend, George, to drive over and give me a ride to the game. George was an acquaintance and recalling how we struck up a friendship is not clear, but it wasn't anything to regret in befriending him. My parents liked George. At least my mother did. She must have seen George as a positive influence on me. George was studious. He was a year older and attended a local college, although preparing to transfer soon. It came as no surprise that he was also doing well in college. Most of my other friends were doing their schoolwork with below-average grades. My grades were right there with them.

Back to George, he was very friendly to my parents. My father never objected to George coming around, and my Mom would usually speak to him, sometimes talking for quite a while. She used to get tickled at how he would argue nearly any point. Sometimes when George was making his point, and my Mom would counter, I would have to interfere in order to speed things up and get them to finish their discussion, or better put, their conversation.

"George is pulling in the driveway Mom, I'll be back sometime after the game," yelling this out while exiting the door. My Mom ran to the door calling as if I were going away and possibly never be seen again.

"Hello, Mrs. Patterson, how are you?" George called out to my mother in a louder than normal voice.

"Hi George. You boys enjoy the football game," Mom said, as the strength in her voice seemed to drop off some. My hope was to get us out of the driveway quickly. My mother and George could get started on their long-winded gabfest and what then? We'd miss half of the ballgame if this chat between them didn't move along.

"Come on, let's go!" I eagerly said.

"We've got plenty of time," George assured me, then he asked, "How did you get the night off from work?"

"The schedule has me going in tomorrow morning. They have to give some time off once in a while, you know?"

"By the way, we're picking up someone that is going to the game with us," George said, in a direct way.

"A girl!" my eyes opened wider in excitement. "Roger Blackwell. You know Roger, don't you?"

"Yeah, I know Roger." It was some effort trying not to sound too disappointed. He was one of those people you didn't care to hang out with. A pretty girl would have made it nice to sit beside in the car. George dated some really good-looking girls. Most of the girls he went out with wouldn't give me the time of day if George wasn't present. It is a letdown when you picture momentarily a Miss America and then realize you're kicking around with some guy like Roger. Maybe he was an all right sort. He's just difficult to hang around with. He always seemed a bit odd. In a way you could feel sorry for him. Maybe George did too.

"Didn't Roger join the Marines?" I asked, just partially interested.

"He did. He's home on leave," George replied. The drive to his house was short. He lived the next street over. We pulled up to where he lived and George honked the horn.

"Hey Georg-o!" Roger yelled out. He shut the house door and took a few long lanky strides to the car. His movements were similar when he walked. He had that military look all right. His hair had been cut off to just a burr, and he was wearing a plaid shirt that didn't fit quite right. That was just Roger.

I had opened the door, and Roger jumped in the back seat. He stretched his arms wide gripping the back seat on both sides of himself as he centered his position in the car. "You know Wes, don't you, Rodger? Wes Patterson," George asked him.

"Oh, yeah, I know Wes. How's it going Wes?" he asked as he slapped the back of my shoulder, and a sharp sting was felt.

"Damn!" I cried out.

"What's wrong, Wes?" Roger asked in a bit of a smartass tone. "Ah, nothing," I said and felt the sting from the slap on my shoulder, yet not wanting to make too much of this. We were heading toward the ball field as Roger and George started up a conversation, and my thinking this was going to be one of those nights that a person just wants to be done with. There were a number of things about how much might go wrong tonight, and then another thought came to me. He is a Marine now and has been through boot camp. That can toughen up a guy. Those old stories from my dad about his brother, my uncle, and how the Marine Corps had made him "tougher than rope" as Dad put it. My mother's brother, an uncle on the maternal side of the family, was a lifer in the Marines, and he was also a drunk. My mom said he held the Marines in the highest regard, above everyone and everything. He was ready to fight for them, drunk or sober.

Both uncles had seen action in World War II. Now there is this other marine in the car with me, and it's like he is wanting to start a fight with me to show his prowess.

"Hey, you're not saying much, Wes!" Roger said, "Cat got your tongue?" he continued. "Loosen up it's Friday night." Just then another slap on my back came from him.

"Son of a bitch! Would you cut the crap?" I called out angrily. He's probably going to do that again. If he knows he's getting to me, a guy like that might keep up the harassing. He's wanting to show how bad he is. He's in the Marines now and wants to kick my ass. There was always the feeling that I could handle myself, but it wasn't in my best interest to get into fights. Roger was not all that tough before, but now, well he probably learned a lot. He might have learned some hand-to-hand combat maneuvers, or judo or something and was planning to use it on me. He might have been taught some tactics on killing a guy. This was a miserable feeling, and uncomfortable.

My face was feeling hot. I rolled the window down. The air coming through the car window helped and felt good.

"Roll up that window...the damn pneumonia hole," Roger yelled out to me.

If he would only get pneumonia… Well maybe it's not the thing to be wishing, but if he wasn't here it would be better. It's not that cold, was the thought that came to me. No need to push it, and maybe it would help in rolling up the window anyway.

"How long did you say you were home for, Roger?" asked George.

"I fly back a week from tomorrow," he answered. "Woo-hoo! Look at that carload of girls!" He called out. "Let's live it up!"

"Is the training tough on everyone?" George inquired, directing Roger's attention back inside the car, and it was as if George might consider joining up.

"I like it. Everything was good except the pool work," Roger answered and seemed respectable for a change. "Georg-o, you ought to chase down that car. There's a girl in there for each of us, and one left over," he added, and started back to his old Roger ways.

"What's the pool work?" George inquired, as his interest continued as genuine.

"Swimming!" was his direct answer. "I had to learn to swim. I never learned and I was given some so-called lessons that practically drowned me. The instructors kept calling me darling and sweetheart as they prodded me with this pole that had a hook on it. They would say anything to try and get to you. You have to have a determination, and that's what those guys are looking for. The Marine Corps wants you to better yourself. I thought of you often, Georg-o, while going through my swimming lessons. To this day I can't breathe through my nose correctly. You remember my nose, don't you, George?" Roger said, reminding George of something.

"You mean when I broke your nose?" George said, and kind of chuckled.

"You broke it when we got in that fight a couple of years back. Still can't breathe right," he went on and then made some stupid-sounding snort that had the three of us laughing.

This eased some tension. It helped with the way that I felt. It wasn't quite as bad for now. It was a well-remembered fight when, George and Roger had gotten into it. There must have been fifty kids watching. George put it to him too. George was fit. He handled himself well. He told me his father used to box and drilled him in this skill. If things got bad between Roger and me, George would probably step in and keep things from getting out of control. Roger would not be quick to test George ever again, Marines or no Marines.

We were going down the highway and Roger was carrying on, yelling at every girl he saw. It didn't matter if these girls were with their boyfriend or not. We'd probably end up getting into a fight tonight anyway with someone. If he would shut up, it would be better.

George pulled the car into the high school parking lot and parked. The three of us got out and went toward the ticket booth, and once again Roger was saying something to just about every girl he saw.

"You need to calm down some, Roger," George told him almost like a parent would.

"I guess. You know it feels so good out tonight, and I would sure enjoy some pretty little dish having hold of my arm," he responded. After that, a goofy look crossed his face.

Inside the gate we looked to find some seats. It was crowding up, and as we walked along the cheerleaders were calling out one of their rhyming cheers and going through twists and turns, stepping up and back, side to side. It was an enjoyable bit they were doing.

The pompoms were like an extension of their arms and accented the movements. Three girls moved in step toward one goal as three others moved toward the other goal. They then joined with two girls along each side performing cartwheels, and then one of the cheerleaders came to the group doing backward handsprings until the entire group circled up and shouted something which was muffled and not quite heard. The movements were good nonetheless.

"Hey there! Hey, how about joining me after the game? We can bounce around all you want," Roger yelled out to the cheerleaders. George with his face holding a serious look, grabbed him by the arm saying something that quieted him. What he said to Roger was unknown to me, my being a few feet away. He did calm himself momentarily.

There were some bleachers with the top row empty, and we decided to occupy these seats. Most of the time we stood to get a better view. The continuous sound of the crowd seemed to rise to the top of the bleachers. Glancing toward George, it was perceptible of his locked in attention to the action on the field.

"You never played high school football, did you, George?" I asked, and wondered why he didn't play.

"No, my father didn't believe in organized high school football," he answered matter-of-factly. George would have been very good at this. He reasoned out everything he attempted, being practical, and it usually granted him success. He had patience and applied himself. He would make a good coach if he desired.

Roger had his interest in some girl. The way it seemed, he had his interest in every girl. At first I only saw this girl he was eyeing as she walked behind a small group of kids. Roger could care less about football. He was out to have fun, and who could blame him for that, but his pursuit in the girls at this game would surely be a problem. Then there was spotted a long-haired brunette that drew his attention. It wouldn't be the thing to say to him, but he didn't stand a chance with that girl. George might though. He could have his pick of girls. The pretty brunette moved on.

The thought of Arlene showing up was something that tugged at me. Both good and bad. She came to football games frequently; many times with a date, and even if she was here with some guy, it was best not think about. It was always nice to be around her though. If we happened to see her here, Roger would surely make a play for her. This would be embarrassing. Arlene would have nothing to do with him. She was very nice but would surely let him know where he stood with her. Then again girls so often confuse guys like me. When you think you are just starting to understand a girl's thinking, she'll do something that completely puts you off balance. A classy girl such as Arlene might just go for a fellow like Roger. God Almighty! This could drive me nuts!

Fortunately, we did not see her at the game. In a way I had hoped we might run into Arlene. It would be a change for me to introduce a pretty girl to George. She was so pretty and had a lot of class. He was often introducing me to girls like her. Just once it would be nice to do the same in having him meet a girl like Arlene. For some reason he didn't know her. This was kind of surprising.

"Hey Georg-o! Are you dating any special girl now?" Roger asked all of a sudden, almost along with my same thoughts.

"I've been out with a couple of girls from school. There's one particular girl in my history class that I've been meaning to ask out," he remarked as he looked over to Roger for a second. He then looked over the football field and scanned the kids moving about.

The lights coming down on the field had a bright clean look it gave to the field. The colors that the teams wore and the cheerleader's outfits sometimes sparkled. That girl he likes in his history class would have to be something. Maybe she sparkled like some of these girls. A sparkling goddess.

The game had gone back and forth and it was coming upon halftime with a tie score of 14 to 14. Most of the game went on and was it barely noticed that both teams scored twice. Maybe the three of us had been scouting too much to see who was in attendance. There was another girl I wanted George to meet; then again, maybe not. She might be attracted to him. Worse than that an introduction to Roger was something to consider. He no doubt would make this uncomfortable.

"Let's walk around the tracks George suggested. We went along with this and weaved through others going here and there. In a short time, we were on the opponent's side of the field. It was my school's opponent. Neither George nor Roger had attended the same school as me. Glancing up every so often, it seemed someone might appear in this group that would be known. Strange that all my friends were no shows tonight. Eventually we did see someone but not who was ever expected. It was my sister Kate and her friend Carol. It couldn't help but be noticed that Carol was wearing bell bottom blue jeans. Like so many other things, the clothes were taking on a different look too.

"Wes!" Kate called out. There was a desire to continue moving on in a way but it was better to stop and talk.

"Kate! I didn't know you were going to be at this game. You didn't say anything about it," and then felt kind of funny at this time. Now would be an appropriate time to introduce everyone.

"Kate, Carol, this is George and Roger. My sister Kate and her friend Carol." Introductions always seem awkward to me. Teachers used to go over the etiquette of this. It always seemed silly, but it's better than no introduction at all. George acted with some character about himself. He said something, and noticing Roger was like watching a hungry dog that had raw hamburger tossed his way.

"Kate and Carol," Roger said aloud. "Well, you two girls are something to see." He continued with Kate... "Kate, yeah...KP. Do people call you KP?" he asked and began laughing some.

"Usually they don't," she answered.

"Well you can be on KP anytime wherever I'm stationed," Roger said. Where he was going with this one I couldn't be quite sure, but who would want their sister getting involved with him? Or Carol. I didn't know Carol too well, but who would wish this guy on any girl?

"Listen, it was nice meeting you, George and Roger. Wes, see you at home," my sister said as Carol nodded and thankfully the two of them walked off.

"Say, that's some woman your sister has grown into," Roger remarked.

"I didn't know that you knew her."

"She was seen around the neighborhood over the years. Her friend isn't bad either." After he said this, I could have thrown up. Then, regrouping, it dawned on me they didn't want to be around this goof, and why should they?

"My sister is a senior in college," I blurted out. My reason doing this was not really known. Maybe the age difference would deter him.

"Kind of surprising they came to a high school game," I added and then thought again, knowing nothing could discourage Roger. He would probably figure a slap in the face was endearing touch.

The teams were coming back on the field, doing warm up stretches before the second half started. The three of us walked back to our seats and took a position that was little closer to mid field. The second half was a blur to me. Concentrating on the second half was less than that of the first. My high school team lost 31 to 24., but details about the game were puzzling. The game was over and the three of us walked back to the car. George recommended getting something to eat. It was a good idea. We walked through the crowd of mostly high school kids that were leaving and going to their cars or rides. The car was parked in a spot that let us exit without dealing with too many cars. It was a quick trip, and we were soon at a drive up restaurant.

"Do you want to order from the car or go inside?" questioned George.

"Let's go inside!" Roger suddenly said. "Besides I have to piss like a racehorse." George laughed at his remark. It was fine by me to go inside. The chances of getting in trouble didn't seem as likely. The park and order spots were where most of the fights started. Our young marine would no doubt provoke someone into one thing or other. There were a few guys out the door as we were going in. He stood in the way of two of them. These guys moved around him. It was apparent they weren't looking for any trouble. There was a musing, maybe a wish that one of them would have decked him. As brazen as he was, it could have happened. We entered through the glass door and checked out where to sit.

Roger continually bothered me. His presence was disturbing. Marines reminded me of strong, silent types. The type of person that one looked up to. Instead, here is this big mouth that happens to be a marine. He shows little respect to anyone, or anything. This wasn't a guy that just wanted to have a good time. He was like this before joining the Marines. He sort of reminded me of another guy by the name of Norb that used to hang around last year. He got into this joyriding thing where he would steal a car and drive around like he was real cool. He harassed me a couple of times to cruise around with him.

"Hey, chicken shit. Let's go around and maybe pick up some girls. Here are the keys to a Pontiac Lemans. What d'ya say? Or are you gutless?"

"Let me set you straight. I'm not riding in a hot car with you or anybody else. If the cops caught us, my old man would kill me. So find somebody else to ride with!" He looked disappointed when I said that. He never bothered me again. If he was ever caught was not known, the word never got around. He was one of those kind of people that always got away with things. If I would have gone riding around, there would be no doubt that would be the time he would get caught, and it would be deep trouble for sure. Roger was kind of this type. He made me think of Norb.

We sat at the counter and sure enough the waitress had to fend off some of Roger's comments and advances. She moved well. Graceful kind of and swung her hips just so. Not too much. Waitresses are approached by jerks like him all the time, no doubt.

This was probably not new to her at all. It was even a surprise when she flirted with me. She wrote down what we wanted off the menu and placed the paper slip under a spring on a wheel that was taken by the cook in the kitchen area.

"The waitress kind of goes for you, Wes," Roger remarked, and I crouched at my seat a little, expecting another slap on my back, but soon lifted up, throwing my shoulders back some, and after a few seconds gradually correcting my posture. It might have been for my appearance to be taller in my seat. Maybe older too. George then asked about the Marine Corps. Whenever George talked to Roger it was noticeable that he, Roger, showed a respect that he seldom put forth to others. That was okay. If he wasn't bothering me, it was that much better. Maybe talking about the Marines was a good thing for him. He did show a better side of himself when talking about them.

"We are stationed in San Diego," he seemed to boast. "It's quite a city he added.

"I've heard that it is nearly perfect weather," George commented.

"Yeah," Roger answered back without putting any interest in the mention of the weather. "Let me tell you what happened not too long ago. One of my friends and I went in town and we were looking at the girls, whistling, making remarks, checking all the girls out, when we saw these three greasers and decided to start a fight with them," and he must have been thinking about telling this to us, because he began laughing over his story.

"Three of them?" I asked, surprised why two of them would start up against the odds.

"What's a greaser?" George asked, as we both wondered what a greaser was.

"It's a guy that combs his hair back and puts a lot of hair oil on it to keep it in place," Roger explained. "You know. Oil; grease!"

"Why three?" asking in a louder voice so he would be sure to hear me.

"Oh, yeah. Well we had finished boot camp, and our Drill Sergeant told all of us that he had been tough on us, but now each one of us could probably whip up on any three guys on the street. We figured that we could not only handle these three guys, but three more of their friends. Let me tell you those greasers were tough. They were getting the best of us when some other Marines saw what was happening and broke up the fight. A good thing, too, or those guys might have put us in the hospital.

It was a helluva time," he said and chuckled after saying this.

"What are the girls like in San Diego?" George asked with a different enthusiasm.

"Let me tell you, you'd enjoy seeing them. A lot of good lookers, many of them are tanned and stacked. Many of them have that senorita look, dark hair and eyes. They walk differently from girls around here," he finished saying. He described them with his hands moving side to side as if his hands were on a girl's hips, and he continued, "Oh yeah, moving in a sexy way and not trying to be too sexy. It doesn't make sense, but some of these girls, by not trying to be too sexy seemed to be even more so."

"Ah, here's our foods my interruption broke through. The waitress served me first, and it felt a little special. She then put the other orders in place. It was different trying to understand what had just been told us about those San Diego girls. This wandering mind goes in all directions, especially when pretty girls are the topic.

"Is there anything else I can get for you?" this was asked of all three of us, but she was looking more at me. Roger nudged me. I shook my head no and kind of smiled.

There was a second nudge on my arm from him, "There you go." He was trying to encourage me in a low voice after our waitress walked to some others that were seated. There was just something about this guy that would piss you off. Even at that, the name on the tag was picked up on. It was Charlotte. That was a very likable name.

We finished our food, paid our bill and took off for a midtown shopping center. There was a club we were going to, and it was so crowded that they wouldn't let us in. The fire marshal strictly enforced the numbers, and there were two guys at the door keeping count of those entering and leaving. A few weeks earlier another club that was located a few miles from here had burnt to the ground. No one was injured, but it triggered a high alert to those watching the door.

"What's the name of the place that is out in the country?" Roger asked. "It's about forty miles from here, but they let everyone in, and serve beer to anyone that has the money." He then squinted in a concentrated effort to come up with the name.

"That's The Cooper's Barrel House. It's further than I want to go tonight," George made it clear to us. That was good news to me. If we go somewhere like that, it would be preferable not to be around Roger. There would be Roger, getting us into a brawl with a bunch of country boys. Adding booze and some country boy seeing his girl being flirted with by Roger would be a disaster in the making.

George suggested we call it a night. He told us he had developed a headache and didn't feel like doing much other than getting home and going to bed. The thoughts of someone punching Roger were to break up like an awakening dream.

"You've probably been studying too hard," Roger said with the laugh that was beginning to be customary tonight.

"Maybe so," agreed George. "It's a lot different than high school."

"What are you planning to do with your education?" Roger asked, with a note of sarcasm.

"It's not definite but possibly get in med school," came a thoughtful, sincere answer. He then rubbed his eyes and winced as his headache continued troubling him. We had sat at a traffic light for a few seconds, and the glare coming through the car windows allowed a look on his face showing he was going through what might have been a migraine. I didn't even know if he got migraines, and wasn't really sure what they were other than a bad headache.

"Dr. George! No. Dr. Georg-o! Sounds even better, doesn't it? I would think you could make a living breaking guys' noses and then fixing them after," Roger kidded, and easily patted him on the shoulder. The rest or the drive home was just so-so. We listened to the radio. I thought about the breaking of Roger's nose and started to laugh; trying to suppress it only to feel it cause a tingling in my nose. It must have brought on some thoughts from the other two. Maybe they figured it was silly on my part but nothing was said.

We pulled into Roger's driveway. He said he'd be seeing us, then stepped out of the car. George then drove to my house and dropped me off. "See ya," I said. George acted as if he had been hit in the head by a hammer. Maybe something more should have been said. Something about getting better, but it wasn't and the big Chrysler backed out of the driveway and moved down the street. I was hesitant to move. The lights were on in the living room, and Mom and Dad no doubt were watching the news. It would have been nice to have gone somewhere else. It was too late to go anywhere, and too early to be at home. Though being home, might as well go inside.

"We expected you home a little later," Mom said. Dad looked at his watch and then back at me.

"How did the game go, son?" he asked.

"Our team lost by a touchdown," I answered, then mentioned seeing Kate at the game with her friend Carol. "It's unusual they go to high school games still."

"Did they sit with you?" Mom asked, and this seemed a ridiculous thing to ask.

"No, they just talked a little and then went on. I think I'm going to wash up and go to bed,"

"Good night, Mom said.

"Good night, young man," my Dad said. Now here was my Dad saying things like that just to make me aware that being an adult was only a short time off.

After using the toilet, washing up, and brushing my teeth there was a little grimy feeling. A shower would have been appropriate. Maybe a shower in the morning will do. I went toward my room. It was on the other side of the house, away from the other rooms, and there was the walk past the living room again. This was a time to kind of sneak by and not to disturb Mom and Dad. The idea of answering more questions was not an engaging thing, and with Kate still being out, they might stay up chatting until she got home.

There was this comfort of crawling into bed, but the downside tonight was being wide awake. These sheets on the bed were something. They were purchased when I was in the sixth grade. They had cowboys with horses on them. If my friends saw these it would be humiliating. By the age of twelve a guy doesn't want these bed sheets. My mom! She doesn't understand the struggle of being a boy, and a teenage boy, soon to be a man. There are some things a guy would not be able to live down. Why does my mother keep everything until it's threadbare? Cowboys! Well there are a lot of programs on television that are westerns. How would it be in the Old West? Now if George, Roger, and I were in the Old West going from saloon to saloon, some gunslinger would more than likely shoot Roger. The tombstone might read:

Here lies Old Roger, a lady's man? No! Just an old codger. He met up with a lady near the squeaky saloon door; He was shot twice by her, and Rodger the codger is no more.

The evening was replayed in my mind. There was some relief that the night was over. Now a picture popped into my thoughts. Roger wearing boots and spurs, a black vest and a black hat. He would prop his leg up on a chair and maybe have a toothpick sticking out of his mouth. His chin would be jutted out and that bothersome grin on his face would be obvious. Making a come on remark to some woman. In a flash the picture of him sprawled out on a floor was playing out. Then the woman that shot him was blowing smoke from the barrel.

The saloon chick had cleared the smoke from her pistol, And everyone was beginning to wet their whistle.

Then everybody in the place would start to cheer, Adios, Roger, sip some whiskey, chug a beer.

That's a rotten way to think of the guy, but he just brought things on with the way he would act.

Roger! What a weirdo. Why does George hang out with someone like him? Why does he hang around someone like me? Maybe all three of us are weird. Then the thought of the waitress at the restaurant was present. Was she playing up to me? She was pretty. Dark eyes and hair. That wouldn't be bad. Damn! She must be five or six years older than me. She could care less about me. She was acting like she did to avoid that goofy Roger. She's too old for me. Those pretty eyes though. Dark and mysterious. Then the thought of the girls from San Diego came to mind. Those girls were probably something else. They probably wore tight blue jeans and tops that showed their midriff. My eyes were

Moving the Tassels

beginning to feel very tired. Sleep was upon me as my eyes closed with a last thought of the football game.

Morning came, Mom and Dad were talking about something. It was probably political, something one of them read in the newspaper. They did that a lot. The smell of coffee was in the air. A cup could taste good this morning. Mom and Dad put cream and sugar in their coffee. It turned the coffee a blonde color. It didn't even look at all like coffee after doing that. Oh well.

It was a good time to shower and dress, eat, and get ready for work, before taking on anything else. Then came some thoughts of last night. That waitress, Charlotte. She was the reason for a dream... wasn't she? Her face, it was pretty...pretty attractive. Her face kept showing itself even during sleep. Most guys would go up there again tonight to see her. It's something to think on.

Ah morning. Rise and shine. Yep, time to get up out of bed, clean up, and see what Mom has fixed for breakfast.

The following Friday we decided to go to another football game. George called Thursday saying he would go on Friday, and mentioned he had a date on Saturday. So this was okay. We asked my friend Greg if he was interested in going to the game. He wanted to go too. His free time was moving by rapidly, and he was enjoying his friends' company before he served his country.

Dinner was over, and it was time to clean up before George came by. This was an away game and located in the next county. It was a good drive from my home. It would be a decent thing to offer a couple of dollars for gas money. Calculating the costs and what this budget allowed was always haunting me. It's one of those things that the not so wealthy deal with. There's not a bankroll to throw around. Things would be okay.

"Your friend George is here!" Mom called out. Again, the tone in her voice made it obvious that she liked George. She liked that he was a good example, an approved friend. After mentioning that he was wanting to get into med school, his stock had risen. She showed even a higher opinion of him. A diversion had to be done. Mom and George would start talking on and on. Some movement toward the door hurriedly with intention of interfering with their conversation was needed. They would get started talking, and we would be running late. Dad was in his usual chair, and he acted like he had wanted to talk to George too. You'd think a celebrity was stopping by.

"I'll be right there, George!" I called out, and was shutting the door, nearly catching Mom between the door and the doorjamb. She gave me a not-too-happy kind of look. She just opened the door again and waved. George was doing something in his car and didn't see my Mom. Humph! That worked out well. I opened the door and hopped in the car.

"Hey! What's Dr. Georg-o up to?" A smirk grew on his face. Then he laughed about it. He kind of got a kick out of this and answered, "Not a doctor yet. After I am, I'll let you be the first to know. I'll bill you. Big time! Roger too."

"No doubt you will. By the way, here's a couple of dollars for gas," "No, thanks. My pop filled the car up this afternoon. No need for it." He backed out of the driveway and headed toward Greg's. It got me thinking. Anyone else would have taken the two dollars without hesitation. He's surely different. It might be another reason so many girls like him. There is a decency about George.

Greg lived nearby. We were at his home in minutes. Greg jumped in the back seat and, unlike last week with Roger Blackwell, there was a much more at ease feeling having Greg along. Greg could get kind of crazy at times, but it was different, and he had really shown a difference in behavior lately.

"Greg, what are you doing these days?" George asked.

Moving the Tassels

"Uncle Sam is going to be my next boss. I enlisted in the service and will be leaving this gracious place before long. Looking forward to the challenges too, but have to admit, I'm already getting a bluesy type feeling. You know how you want to go but know how much you'll miss things and people?"

"We all have to spread our wings at some time, don't we?" came the response.

"Greg's going to be one of the guys that have a lot of tales about him. He'll be a legendary type, kind of like Alvin York, or Audie Murphy," I jokingly threw into the conversation.

"As earlier said, there are many challenges, but there's no need to be so foolish trying to be an all-out war hero."

"You never know with a big galoot like you!" Just after saying this I felt a wrestling hold—part headlock, part nelson—applied by Greg. It was not a hard pressure, and we both laughed about it the next few seconds as he released the maneuver.

George had his input with "Okay, you two guys ease up on this or the both of you will be dropped off at the recruiting office and have the Army take you two off my hands immediately."

"That's all right with me! Greg told George. "The bus halls me off from here Sunday afternoon. My liberty as it is called is limited, so what's the matter of another day and a half?"

"Man! Sunday afternoon. We should have thrown you a party," the words came from me in a reflective way. There was a concern for him. But then, he was older and strong, and surely he'd be fine.

We continued to talk as we traveled the distance to the school that was hosting my school tonight. It didn't seem to take too long. We drove passed farmland and silos and fenced property. All of the land was so spread out. This school was out in the sticks. There came into view some lights and a modern-looking building. George turned in the lot that held many cars and found a parking place in a reasonable location. Then the three of us made our way to the ticket line. The football field was behind the school that was twice the size of my school. We were soon inside the fence and approaching the asphalt track. There were drums and brass instruments sounding out, providing a tempo for those now marching through an open gate as they exited the play area.

The ballgame was just about to start as we found our place in the bleachers. We were at the highest seat, and like many people we opted to stand rather than sit, just as we did last week. A chill in the air came on as the darkness covered grounds that were unlit from the football field's lights. A smell of popcorn was drifting near, and cheerleaders were calling aloud to get the crowd into the game. There were a few people I knew from school, and it seemed only right to call out to them. Strange as it was, there must have been more classmates at this far away school than the nearby school last week. Some chatter with some of them was taken in.

Greg didn't seem to know anyone here, and George didn't either which was unusual. A continual amount of scrutiny went on, taking in those my age that were in attendance. Attention was not completely on the game, but spotting who was there. Sometimes there was a check of the players going through their tasks. The time moved from one quarter to the next as the defenses played good for both teams. The half time score was a seven to seven tie. Many of the high school kids began moving from the stands to the track as they joined an already large group that circled the track a couple of times during the first half of the game. Then Arlene appeared. She was walking on the track with some guy, probably her date for the evening. I called out as loud as my voice would carry.

"Arlene!" She looked my way and waved. She then grabbed the arm of the guy she was with and moved toward us. Her date looked in the general direction as she wove through others in the stands and held the hand of this guy she was with. Who was he? Naturally there was an immediate dislike of seeing him with her.

"Wes, my gosh! So good to see you," Her eyes went to Greg and George. "And who are your friends?"

This is Greg, and this is George," I said and moved my hands their way to finish my introduction.

"I'd like you to meet Ralph Durant. He was nice enough to bring me here tonight."

"Hi," the word came from my mouth, trying to make it more than a grunt. "Nice to meet you," I continued with a touch more of respect in regards to Arlene. Glancing at her, she had that pleasing look on her face that she so often displayed. She wore a light coat covering a pullover sweater, and blue jeans. She looked like a million bucks!

"It's some game, isn't it?" Greg added.

"It sure is. Both teams are giving it their all."

She might ask something that happened during the game and an answer wouldn't be available. Not a truthful answer. There was discomfort that might have been noticed. What I had wanted was to talk to Arlene the rest of the time while we were here, but she and Ralph had decided to move on. My heart sank. Here was another guy interfering with a great girl that should be with me. Arlene was special, and in my deepest thoughts the obvious was she happened to be a very nice person that had no interest in me. She probably never would consider me beyond just a friend. It hurt to know it was this way. It really did hurt.

The second half started and reactions on my part were much the same as the first half. Seeing who was there. Once in a while taking in the game. Watching the girls that most likely went to school here. There were three girls walking together and looking up toward us guys. Then George stared directly at this one girl. She was a blond that moved in a spirited way. She wore her hair flipped on the ends and it bounced off her shoulders as she moved along with her friends. She focused in on him, as he did the same in her direction. He then stuck his hand up and signaled to her with his hand cupped except for his index finger. She came to a halt with her friends and spoke to them, then walked up the steps and through the bleachers to join us. She was wearing some burgundy colored jeans that might have been part of the school colors. A knitted sweater covered her upper body and looked really good on her.

"Do you know that gal?" my curiosity had me asking.

"No, but I guess I might soon."

"I thought it might be your date for tomorrow," George didn't comment. He kept watching the blond-haired girl moving toward him. Greg started with a comical announcing: "George is at the 20, he's at the 30, he's at the 40, he's midfield."

"That's enough," suggested George as he watched this girl move under his spell. He and this girl were about to meet when he finally took a couple of steps toward her. It was interesting to see. George was kind of a Svengali. He had her under control. They talked for a few seconds and walked to Greg and me. The girl's friends went back toward the track and began to make their circuit again. That did nothing for my morale. Greg probably didn't care.

"This is Sissy," George offered. "Greg and Wes, he gestured with his hands. The controlling hands that had just lured this girl up the stadium steps. We both said hi in that kind of shy schoolboy way. It was unexpected for Greg to be that way. He was anything but the timid type. My balance was off and a quick action with the foot stabilized me. After doing this the scanning about was the next thing, just seeing if my off balance step was observed. There remained an uncomfortable feeling for whatever reason. The game went on and Sissy and George stood away from Greg and me. Greg said something of the way George treated

Moving the Tassels

girls. He had a way, but very unusual. After a few minutes Sissy walk back to the track to rejoin her friends. George regrouped with us.

"Do you have a date with her?" Greg asked of him, and the devilish grin returned to his face from when he was calling George's progress like a sports broadcaster.

"She gave me her phone number. I'll probably call her some time before long."

"Sissy. Certainly a pretty Sissy with a classy chassis," Greg said, again grinning wide.

"The way she walked up here, you'd think you knew each other," I added.

"No, but she was easy to talk to. We should talk with a little more privacy." That sort of ended the matter about this girl he had just met. George had his own way of meeting girls and getting to know them. If he wanted to drop the talk about her, that would be fine. Greg remained quiet, picking up on this too.

The sound of a pistol shot was the indication that the football game was over. My school came away with the victory, 20 to 14. Hey! Glad they won, but details of the game were not picked up very well by me. This is what many kids do. Come to the games to socialize and look at the girls and guys from other schools.

The three of us were walking out of the stands and toward the car. One more thorough look around, wishing to see Arlene for a last time tonight. The lights continued to shine brightly on the field and everyone that was near. The crowd moved along as we did. Here was the thought. What if I did see her? She's with that son of a bitch Ralph, and that last view of them together... and thinking about it would only upset me. In a short amount of time, we were in the car and leaving toward our turf.

George drove to the restaurant we had stopped at last week. We entered the restaurant the same as last week, and my scouting the place was for the waitress that had served us last week. A different waitress came to where we were seated at the counter. The lady that brought us menus and water was wearing slacks and a puffy white blouse with a dark vest. She looked a lot older than most girls that do this work. She might be close to 40. It had me thinking why she chose this kind of work. In another three or four minutes, Charlotte, the waitress from last week, came to where we were and took our order. She acted as nice as she did last week, but was much busier. We gave our food order then waited longer than last week to have it brought to us. Charlotte brought the food orders and sat each order in front of us. She again showed that nice smile.

While we were eating we talked to Greg about his leaving Sunday. It had me wondering why he was spending time with us this last weekend, and he mentioned without me asking that he was going out with Edna tomorrow night. Some other things were talked about that meant little to me, and we finished our food. The older waitress handed our checks to us, and we paid at the cash register. I was looking around for Charlotte just to make eye contact but could not find her.

We got in the car and headed for home. It wasn't much of an exciting night, but sometimes you enjoy what you can get out of it. Greg was let out at the driveway of where he lived. We shook hands firmly and my words were, "My friend, it looks like this Army business will work good for you. The same situation may be in my future."

"I have a recruiting officer's name if you want it?" he teased, and again showed that look on his face.

"Not at this time."

George wished him luck and we drove off, soon coming to the front of where I lived. While opening the car door, it was necessary to give some appreciation. "Thanks for driving to the game."

"Glad to do it. There could be interest in a new girl." He raised his eyebrows some, and gave a look as if he had the world at his command. He might have a good grip on it. He then drove off. I turned toward the house and opened the front door. Mom and Dad were at their usual places in the living room with the TV on.

"How was the game?" Dad asked.

"We won! It was close, but we won!"

"Have you had anything to eat?" Mom asked. One could almost bet that she was going to ask that.

"Yeah, we stopped and ate at a drive-in restaurant. Time to clean up and go to bed." After using the bathroom, the walk to my room was a stealthy undertaking. For sure my parents wanted to question me more. It was sometimes like being on a television program where the detectives keep grilling suspect and waiting for him to own up to a crime. They would often make me feel guilty for just being out with some friends. There is trouble understanding this.

Some strange thoughts entered my thinking. Arlene and Ralph guy, Then, there was Greg leaving for the Army Sunday. He has a date with Edna tomorrow. He'll probably try and lay her before he leaves. She'll most likely go along with it. One of those good-bye things. Old Ralphy boy won't be laying Arlene. He might want to, and who doesn't? But she isn't one that does that. She doesn't bed down with just any old guy.

It was then one of those things to think on. What she did with the guys she went out with was anybody's guess. It was bothersome thinking about it, but that was just how it was. If she was sleeping around with a bunch of guys; it would be mentioned no doubt. A sparkling girl like her sleeping around? Something like that would practically make the newspaper headlines.

Edna came to mind again. We were together back in the summer shortly. The lake and all. Still something to think on. It was electrifying. She could really excite a guy. The following week she was dating somebody new. The idea of saying something to Greg would not be smart. Let it rest.

Then the hand motion of George toward that girl Sissy. God! That was like hypnosis or something. He had control of her. He knew he did when he made eye contact with her. Just wave her in to where you are. He didn't even move until the last few steps. If only to have that power. To move my hands that way to Arlene. Have a confidence and power. Damn! Then that hopeless feeling began to set in.

Now Greg's voice seemed to echo. He's at the 10. He's at the 20. He's at the 30...Greg was right. George sure handled it differently. Greg was funny too. He carried on in the past and then he acted so different when we were coming home from a party not long ago. It was hard to tell what mood or what side of Greg was showing up. He is a Comical person and then dead serious. He might have the Army bit on his mind and this acting out works for him.

It was kind of a crazy weekend. These thoughts twisted around in my head for a few minutes. There was still a feel of the football field and a smell of popcorn. It could be visualized, the school that dwarfed mine. The thought of Greg, my friend, going into the Army. The thought of Roger in the Marine Corps and not being there tonight. That was a good thing. There's a homework assignment that needs to be done. It was something to work on in the morning. My God! These thoughts about all sorts of things. Rebecca might have to work tomorrow. That would be great. We would work in the store tomorrow afternoon? I pulled the covers over my shoulder, exhaled and dozed off to sleep.

CHAPTER V

The holidays this time of year are often bleak when looking out of doors. The colors of autumn have passed, and the gray that carries through most of the day can sometimes be depressing. Today is different, of course. It's Thanksgiving. I slept longer than usual because there isn't school, and there isn't work. Those redolent seasonal smells of good foods being prepared had my nose sniffing in the direction of the kitchen. Mom arises early on this day every year and puts in most of her time fixing different things that she takes pride in doing. There is something about this day that one has to enjoy. Our family becomes better on this day.

My sister Kate is having some guy over tonight when we have our dinner. His name is Len Cunningham. It struck me that his family was wealthy. This thought that they always had money continued to come to me for some reason. There was never evidence that they had a lot of money. It was just a feeling. His last name gives me the impression of an old family with inheritances that go back to feudal times. More than likely I'm completely wrong. Len is a private first class in the Army and has liberty, as he referred to it according to Kate, until Wednesday of next week.

He mentioned some military time that was not grasped, but that was no big deal. We will talk with him maybe at our dinner table, and he might explain the way time is kept in the Army. Now if anyone occupies his time tonight, it will be Kate. The old man might grill him on the military too.

There was some interest on the television as Mom was preparing our dinner, and my Dad was kind of sprawled out in his favorite chair as he watched TV. The morning moved pleasantly to the afternoon, and before long it was just about dinnertime. Dad would sometimes go into the kitchen and try to help out, but Mom had things going the way she wanted and excused him from being there. She liked to have her kitchen, her special room in the house, to herself. She had an apron on decorated with flowers placed in something like a tea kettle. It looked to be new and gave Mom that homey look.

Dad went along with this, leaving the kitchen. He also gave a hint that he was building up his appetite. His stomach started making noises, and he said that the growling of his stomach went from left to right and back again to the left. Dad so seldom shows a comical side of himself that it was a moment that should be remembered for the remainder of my life.

The television was on and there were some parades from New York that were broadcast. A couple of celebrities were being interviewed and floats were moving gracefully down the street. This day has a way of making people join together, unlike any other holiday. It seems to be better than Christmas. Dad and I continued to watch whatever was aired, and it began to move the day along.

The time passed along into late afternoon, and Kate started putting on her makeup, taking the bathroom as her own about 3:00 p.m. and fixing up for over an hour. Mom was trying to coordinate the different foods, and Dad was still watching the television when the doorbell sounded. Some rumbling was heard as Kate was moving quicker toward her room and Len was at the door most likely. No need to keep him waiting, so I called out, "I'll get the door!"

When opening the door, it was by habit to study over our guest. He, Len, was wearing a medium weight jacket and a hat. The hat he wore had a silly look to it. This continued to amuse me. What was there about this hat? Why would he wear this thing? Nobody wears a hat! If a hat is worn, it's not the type that he had on. This was something out of the 1940's. Of course it was very practical in regards to my Dad and some of his generation. It kind of went out with the Eisenhower era. Len did remove it when entering our home.

"Wes, tell Len I'll be right there," Kate cried.

"He can already hear you, Kate!" I called out, and with some courtesy drew the door back to let him enter.

There was this desire to laugh as my eyes attached to his hat. It was camel colored brown with a shade darker band that circled above the brim. How square. "Hi! I'm Wes, Kate's brother."

"Len Cunningham, Pri...sorry. The military, you understand?"

"Len, how are you? I'm Kate's father," Dad said to him as he had come to his feet and approached the door.

"Very fine, sir, and you, sir?" Len asked as he shifted that bizarre hat around and clasped it under his left arm so he could shake hands with Dad.

"Doing fine. Let me take those," Dad told him and took the hat and coat Len had worn. Dad had never met Len before, but there was little doubt in my mind that Dad liked this hat-wearing Army goof. "This GI haircut doesn't give much in the way of warmth on a day like today, so my hat seems to help cover where there was once hair," Len commented in reference to the burr haircut and his hat. For some reason, there were expectations for him to wear his uniform. He wore instead a dark pair of slacks and a white long-sleeved shirt and tie with three colors of striped blue. The stripes were in a diagonal direction, like half a chevron. His shoes were black and shined like dark mirrors.

"You look like a civilized human being," Dad told him. It was obvious that my dad thought this group of young people, excluding Len, were growing up with odd ideas, including one's appearance.

"Hello, Len. So happy you could join us. I'm Kate's mother," and with her introduction she brushed her hands lightly on the front of her apron then grasped both his hands with hers and smiled broadly. She truly looked very happy to meet him.

"An honor to meet you, ma'am," he responded, and bowed slightly. He resumed his resolute stance in a very polite way. He was making points with my parents for sure.

Kate then positioned herself at the doorway between the dining room and the front room that Len was standing in. Kate had on a light brown v-neck sweater with red trim and white blouse underneath that had an attractive collar that was worn outside the v-neck. She was wearing a skirt of nearly the same shade of brown, and red knee socks with a penny loafer shoes. She looked to be something other than a college senior.

It was as if she were a sophomore in high school. It was very modest, and no doubt Mom and Dad approved. She should have had a more appealing outfit on for all the time she spent getting ready. It probably made little difference. Len enjoyed seeing Kate, and Mom and Dad were pleased to meet him. They had a look about them. One could read the thoughts that they already had Len in mind to walk down the aisle with Kate. He showed a manner that others didn't. Kate had dated some goofs. Maybe a few guys were all right, but most registered as duds.

"Len, I'm so glad you could make it," she said to him as she neared him and grabbed his arm, leading him toward the dining room. He said something back to her, but it couldn't be understood. It didn't really matter anyway. Kate was delighted that Len was here. She walked with him from the dining room and directed him to the kitchen. Mom and Len continued with the customary pleasantries.

Mom then stepped where everyone could see and hear her. She was still making her dinner preparations, but solely for our guest's benefit said, "Dinner will be about six o'clock."

"That would be fine, ma'am!" our soldier boy offered.

Kate and Len took a seat on our sofa. Dad had turned the channel to a football game that was on, and they watched along with him. The game had my interest too. It was a good one to watch. There was little else to do for now other than watch and wait on the dinner.

Mom had the table set and was placing the different dishes in a particular order. The table had a clean white cloth, and the silverware was wrapped up in cloth napkins like you'd see in a classy restaurant. Mom was trying to impress Len as much as Kate, and it showed on Kate's face that she enjoyed how Mom had set the table. Dad walked to the oven range where the turkey was placed and sliced about a dozen pieces from the bird and also worked on the drumsticks, laying them side by side next to the slices that were on the largest plate we had in the house. He also put two gravy boats on the plate. One was a dark brown color, and the other much lighter.

The dining area had windows located opposite the front door, and these were building up a frosty look from the warmth of the food and our gathering at the table. It was a comfortable feel with the five of us taking our seats as we started passing the different dishes around until everyone had what each wanted on our plates. If Arlene or Rebecca had been there, it would have been perfect.

Dad said some sort of blessing, and we began eating. We said prayers over our food only once in a while. This might have been done to impress Len, but we did act different on this day. About two bites of his turkey had been taken and Dad started asking Len about the Army. Len's answers came after chewing the food quick and swallowing. He answered as though he were speaking to a commanding officer. Most of what was said was barely heard as I was moving my fork to my mouth like it was my last meal. It would have been respectful to have listened. Often too much is missed out on. The possibility of me in some branch of the service was not too many months away.

After a few minutes, Mom looked over at my plate and rose to bring in a pumpkin pie. There remained much of my regular dinner, but who is going to turn away pumpkin pie? Then a thought entered my curious mind. If Len's family had money, you would expect him to be something other than a private.

Our doorbell rang, interrupting the meal and my first thought was that perhaps it was one of the girls…Arlene or Rebecca—even Edna would be fine.

"I'll get it!" I called out, putting down my fork and napkin and moving quickly up from the table, trying to bring my voice into a more mature composure. With some effort was also a discipline to my walk. There was a desire to run to the door, anticipating the appearance of a young lady being outside.

"Dickey! What are you doing?" I questioned with some disappointment.

"Wes! I have to talk to you," he answered in his excited voice. With a need for privacy it seemed best to step outside.

"Mom, Dad, I'll be right back in," pulling the door shut behind me and giving a look to my friend, letting him know this was a piss poor time to interrupt one's meal.

Wes, I... I...think I killed my father," he said looking up to me as if there was a magic powers that could erase the terrible moment and make everything okay again.

"Killed your father?!" I cried out. Why? How, wh, wh, why?" a stuttering came out. It was so weird. Then came this shaking, and a thousand thoughts began to race through my mind. The cold of the night air was intensifying being and then a trembling that couldn't be controlled. This uncomfortable spasm overtook the movements of my body.

"Can you come with me? 1 have to go back home! I have to see if my mother is okay. And see if Dad is...oh, God! I have to check," he rambled on without giving me an answer.

"Yeah, sure, just let me tell the folks and grab a coat," I quickly said, trying to get a sentence out of my mouth through the continued trembling. Walking back in the house, there came this look that was expected.

"Dickey said something about checking on his mother. She's probably okay, but he is worried; it's not real bad. He just needs a friend in this situation for now; sometimes someone in our own age group can help on something that may not be too bad. OK?" I related this, trying again to smooth over what they may have initially thought. It rattled the dinner, and all of us. "Be back before long, really," I added, and gave the most sincere and pleading look that could be put on my face.

"You can go, but get back soon, or call as soon as you can. Make sure. I don't know if I like this. Company being here and upsetting this and all," Dad continued. His grumbling went on and he wore it on his face.

"Yes, sir, fine, sir."

"If I can do something." Len stood up as the words left his mouth.

"Maybe your father should drive the two of you over there, or let you use his care Mom again suggested, and Dad changed the look on his face as if to say he would but he surely didn't want to.

"No, we'll be fine. I'll know more as we walk to his house. Let me talk to Dickey," came my response and hoped they wouldn't ask too much more.

"Wes. I'd like to know more about this. There should be more information. Him just coming to the door at our Thanksgiving dinner. It's not the thing to do, Son," Dad said in frustration, as if he wasn't getting the message across to me he had hoped to.

"Dickey said something about checking on his mother. She's probably okay, but he is worried; it's not really bad. He just needs a friend in this situation for now; sometimes someone in our own age group can help on something that may not be too bad. OK?" I related this, trying again to smooth over what they may have initially thought. It rattled the dinner, and all of us. "Be back before long, really," I added, and gave the sincerest and pleading look that could be put on my face.

"You can go, but get back soon, or call as soon as you can. Make sure! I don't know if I like this. Company being here and upsetting this and all," Dad continued. His grumbling went on.

"Yes, sir, fine, sir."

"If I can do something," Len stood up as the words left his mouth.

"No, no, Len. Everything will be fine. You stay seated and have your dinner; finish your food," Mom told him as she forced a smile. Kate was showing a disappointment, maybe bewilderment on her face. What started out perfectly well had become a disquieted event.

"Be back shortly," I let them know and threw on my coat placing my arms in the sleeves and covering my shoulders, then pulled the door closed behind me.

"I'm glad to have you going over to my house, Wes. I didn't know who to talk to. I didn't know what to do."

"What happened?" my voice now questioning in full unbroken tone.

"Mom and Dad were fighting over what my Dad told her he found out. They were right there in the kitchen. They didn't hide it or nothing, right in front of my little brother and me! My Dad called my Mom a whore! He said he found out she worked as a prostitute before they were married. She tried to quiet him but he kept on yelling!" Dickey franticly told me. "I can't believe it! It can't be true! I just can't believe it!"

His talk and movements were beginning to surface, and it made me nervous trying to figure out what to do. We could call the police. What would they do? Would they think I was an accomplice? They could run the two of us in! Boy, would that ruin the rest of Thanksgiving. If things aren't bad enough! As strange as this felt, and with all the confusion, there was something exciting about it. If something with the police happens, my Dad would probably really give it to me. Mom would be in tears, and then there was Kate, poor Kate, saying goodbye to Len. Len walking off wearing that goofy hat. He wouldn't want to be involved with a family that had a convict doing hard time. That hat means nothing.

God! What am I thinking? I don't even know what Dickey did. He never gave me all the information. He stopped at my house just to have someone to help him get through this ordeal, whatever it happened to be. Dickey isn't like this!

"Dickey, what the hell did you do for sure?" I now demanded to know.

"I really don't know! When my dad was throwing mom around, I yelled at him to stop. He wouldn't do it, so I picked up a skillet and swung it into his side. He kept hurting mom as she cried out, and I bumped him to have him face me, then I smashed the skillet in his face. He went down on the floor and blood was pouring on the floor. Mom screamed at me and I was so scared I ran out of the house and down the street with no idea where I was going. Just scared. I saw that I was over by where you live. I didn't even know I was near. I didn't remember. I just walked up to your door. I thought you could help."

The information helped. Now there was something to work with. What to do was another matter. At this point, a picture came to mind of what happened. We kept walking fast, sometimes running as the night showed a little fog. We walked faster as we went through the fog. It seemed odd that the fog lifted as we neared Dickey's house. There were no police cars around. There could have been sirens or an ambulance or something. There was nothing like that. We walked up to the door, and Dickey walked in with me following.

"Dickey! Where have you been?" his mother cried out and ran to him. She hugged him, and he was much surprised.

"Mom, I'm sorry. I didn't want to hurt anybody. Not you. Not dad! Nobody. I'm a skunk. I didn't want to... hurt dad. Is he hurt... bleeding...?" His words blubbered out between sobs. About this time there was the feeling of discomfort. The "I wish I wasn't here" kind of discomfort. Then my eyes located Mr. Brink lying flat on the sofa in the living room, his face partially covered with a compress on his nose.

"Dickey, I called everywhere trying to find you! I was about to call the police! I was so upset in trying to find you," Mrs. Brink told him as she seemed to then first notice me. "Your father is okay. His nose might be broken. It bled! God, it bled so. He said his ribs hurt too.

"Mom, I'm sorry, but I didn't know what to do."

"It's okay, dear boy. My son," she went on as she continued to hold him.

Now is a good time to leave. Now's the time to call Mom and Dad. "Oh, boy!" "Mrs. Brink, excuse me, can I use your telephone?" I asked as composure set in, and everyone seemed to be all right. Just then a tug was on my pants leg, and I almost peed in my pants. Looking down, it was Dickey's little brother pulling at my pants leg.

"Sure, in the kitchen, on the wall," she instructed.

While stepping through the kitchen, it could not go unnoticed that things were strewn about, and a large bloodstain on the floor. There were a few smaller drops of blood making a trail. With a little effort of moving left and right and avoiding the stains, the phone was spotted on the wall and in reach. It was partially pulled from the wall, but still capable of being used. I dialed our home and Mom answered. After her inquiring of what was going on, things settled down slightly.

"I'm taking off," I told Dickey's mother. "Is everything going to be okay, do you think?" Dickey was wiping away tears and dragged a handkerchief across his face, cleaning up the show of his emotions.

"Wes, I didn't mean to mess things up for you today," Dickey said apologetically.

"It's all right, everything is fine," Thinking about this for a second, my posture grew with shoulders pulled back and kind of a heroic feeling came over me. It was for no reason. Arrival, phone call, and going back home. What was heroic about that?

Mrs. Brink came nearer and also had a little to say. "I am sorry we troubled you...I don't think anything like this has ever happened.

"Mr. Brink will be OK?"

"Well, yes. He'll be up and about, thank you for coming by and helping us:" she said, as she had calmed down some.. "Can we drive you to your house?"

"No, thanks. It's probably good for me to walk."

"Thanks, Dickey told me as I was walking out the door.

"Yeah. See you at school." After saying this my glance went to the sofa where Mr. Brink was stretched out. He was too banged up to pay any attention to me. Dickey had really decked him with the skillet. It was strange why they were not going to the emergency room or doing something about him. From just the look of things, it seemed obvious that his nose was most likely broken. It was swollen almost the size of a fist, and it looked to be resting on his face. His ribs might have damage too, but that didn't show like the nose.

The walk home was about a mile, and it was good to think things over while making my way home. I couldn't help but think how Dickey's family would handle this. He and his dad would definitely have some things to talk over. His dad might retaliate. Hellfire, Dickey might bust him in the nose again with the skillet. That would certainly finish the old guy off.

Dickey surprised me. And Mrs. Brink. How is she going to explain things to Dickey? Was she really a prostitute when she was younger? For all she had been through tonight, she remains a pretty woman. She's a nice lady. We almost never discussed anything such as prostitution at my house. Any mention of sex was sort of hushed up. Even when Dad explained the facts of life some years ago, it was almost comical. The closest thing recently talked over pertaining to sex was my sister's discussing Sigmund

Freud's psychoanalytic work and the influence of sex in regards to human beings. Freud must have been onto something. It's all us guys talk about.

Most of the fog had disappeared. It was still dropping a dampness all around, but it was better. The trees that lined some of the roads were showing a pretty winter scene, though it wasn't winter yet. Streetlights made their gleam through the branches, and while walking home, there sometimes was the scuffing of my shoes on the blacktop. Then there was this loneliness and the sounds of my footsteps were so clear. This part of the world was mine now. There was some sort of peace. There were cars parked in many driveways and on the side of the road. No doubt many were celebrating the holiday. Here, just passing through unnoticed, there was the haunting quiet on the streets. Now, looking at the light and exhaling in an upward direction, there came the formation of small clouds. It was like being a very young boy just discovering that this sort of night air makes these billowy figures.

Without giving too much thought to it, I started walking by the Cray home. The lights were on, and there were two cars in the driveway. Maybe Mr. Cray is better. It wouldn't hurt to stop by and see. A second thought on this kept me from going there. It was Thanksgiving, and this was a family night for sure. Sometimes they treated me like family. Dickey Brink had stirred enough up in this regard. It was best to walk on past and turn toward my home. The family is expecting me back.

There was this heroic feeling that fell over me. That was a laugh. I was so scared when Dickey first stopped by that the trembling of my hands and voice was uncontrollable. A chill with the chattering of teeth was so bad that it couldn't be stopped. My anticipation was so broad one could only guess what was to happen. If Mr. Brink had been capable; he might have come after me. A laugh came to me as Mr. Brink's smashed up nose and a probable stumbling in his step would make his movements take on that of a drunk. He might not be doing anything to anybody for a long time.

"Why didn't Mom or Dad insist on driving us to the house where Dickey lived? Don't they care?" The questions came in a quiet voice to myself, trying not to disturb the night too much. "Well, sure they care. Mom said something about Dad driving, and even me driving, but it was obvious he didn't want this. But maybe he should have been more forceful. I didn't want him to drive, and maybe he understood that Dickey did need to talk it out and explain the craziness of the night. There was someone that walked out of the door of a house just up the way. This conversation with myself should now be silent.

Thoughts continued while the walk continued. I was on our street. There will have to be the question-and-answer session with Mom and Dad. The layout of what happened and why. They will want the details. This will have to come across tactfully so Mom, especially, wouldn't be embarrassed.

Then there was Len.. Boy, did he ever run into a Thanksgiving Day. He'll have some stories for some of his Army buddies. Here he'll be with some of his pals out at a bar somewhere, drinking a few beers and talking about their girlfriends back home. One of the guys will have a story about the pretty blonde with green eyes and damn good looks that make all the others around as envious as can be, just wanting to be with her. Then one of the other guys will talk about the girl that was real sexy and bedded down with him just before he returned to duty. He'll probably exaggerate enough to make it more interesting. Then they'll start on the weird things that happened. That's when Len will have his say. He'll be wearing that hat, and the guys will probably think he deserves what he got for wearing that stupid hat. But he'll continue on with his tale of the goofy Thanksgiving that one of my friends messed up for everyone.

Arriving home, I opened the front door and was quickly bombarded with questions. The puzzled look on everyone's face. No need to lie out of it. Just be honest, yet not disclose too much. I related that Mr. and Mrs. Brink had an argument that went too far, and then Mr. Brink got out of hand. Dickey thought Mrs. Brink was about to be hurt so he tried to help her and in doing so knocked Mr. Brink off his feet and unconscious. My father had a tough time buying into this.

"That little guy knocked his father out? He doesn't look like he could do that."

"He used a skillet, and that knocked out Mr. Brink," and this explanation quieted things momentarily. My father understood. He chuckled at the thought of it also.

With all of this out of the way, for the time being, we sat at the dinner table. Mom asked if I wanted anything else to eat since my meal had been less than complete. There was so much left over, and my appetite had increased. Mom put some of the food on a plate. Even cold turkey would be pretty good. Len was still here. That was surprising. He looked comfortable as he sat on the sofa, and Kate sat beside him, but not too close.

"How about playing cards, or a game of some type? Mom suggested. Dad's eyes rolled at the thought of it. He would give in no doubt, but anyone that knew my Dad understood this kind of socializing was not what he cared to do. We began playing Scrabble. Dad would just as soon be hog-tied and fed arsenic. There were few things my Dad seemed to enjoy. Sure there were some things, but he would seldom let on. For the rest of us, it was an enjoyable time. It took our minds off the interrupted dinner, especially for me, and the games seemed to calm things. Dad wasn't any good at this, and he showed his dislike by declining to play more than once. When we finished, Mom was the winner. She knew words that fit in the spaces that most people couldn't begin to know.

My appetite began to come around. "I'm going to check again on the leftovers?"

"Let me fix you a plate," Mom offered.

"If it's no trouble, and maybe a piece of the pie. Kind of have a craving for this, and it might hold me over. Mom said something else about warming up some leftovers, so a grunt was given and a repeat about the pie. The knife in my hand was going at the pumpkin pie but changed course and cut into the pecan pie. There is a certain texture felt through the blade. No need to be conservative with this. Cut it wide for a double helping. There was something sensual in the kitchen. It was a warmth that made it part of our family and part of a home. The smell of the spices that went into fixing dinner still lingered. There remained a few things that would have to be put up, but this was something Dickey and his family didn't have. At least not today. It was too bad. For all the disorder that we had gone through today, we had resiliency in our family to salvage what was important and to enjoy the holiday.

Mom and Dad were sitting in the living room, and so were Len and Kate. And then here was me feeling like a fifth wheel, and pining for a girl to be here. Most of the guys I ran around with had steady girls. It was something I desired-that someone to make the holiday complete, a wholesome girl. The feeling of being alone, in an odd position without pairing up was not a bad thing. My family cared for me. There were not many things one could be sure of, but of this there was no doubt. Things turned around, and it was not bad at all.

In an unusual way, my friendship with Dickey Brink had become better. If his stopping at our house and putting trust in me to help was the cause, or something else, I wasn't sure. But we strengthened our friendship.

My suspicions of the stories Len would be telling could be far from what earlier was thought. Len acted like he was okay with our family. As long as Kate was nearby he felt good about sharing Thanksgiving with us.

/////

CHAPTER VI

It was early December, and the day started out gray with the chance of the sun showing through. My feet were still taking me most everywhere, today being no different. Enough money had been saved from yard work done over a few summers, and now the job at the grocery was adding a steady amount. With this there was my intent of buying a car. A number of guys knew a lot about cars. Some of the guys could be jerks about helping out an ordinary guy. Most were okay though. One of the guys in particular kind of kept a distance from many but was said to be good with cars. I talked to him some, and he happened to be friends with Dickey Brink. It seemed reasonable to make contact. The guy's name was Bart Fellows.

Bart Fellows was an unusual kind of person. While many cliques developed at school, he easily could have been a crowd figure but opted to avoid such groups. Recently one of the guys that was well known for his athletic ability in football, basketball, and track, had a chat with Bart in the hallway near a chemistry classroom. This took place after our return to school from the Thanksgiving break. A guy named Eugene Michaels had approached Bart and asked, "Why does a guy like you avoid all of us? You aren't a bad looking sort. A little polish here and there, and you could fit right in. You could be dating some of the top girls around here. Running with some good people."

"I have a girlfriend that I like very much. I don't particularly care for the way you and your group move around as if everyone else should bow down to you," Bart answered.

"Why you smartass son of a bitch! I could bust you up here and now!" Eugene affirmed as he got nearly nose to nose with Bart. Bart stepped back about three steps and lifted his hands in a boxer's pose.

"Here and now!" Bart said confidently. The chemistry teacher, Mr. Archer, and I were the only two that heard the exchange between Eugene and Bart.

"You're not worth the trouble," Eugene responded, then feigned a pushing away to distance himself, put a twist on his face and walked off. Mr. Archer was partially behind the classroom door taking it all in. He grinned a little about these two nearly mixing it up. It was unusual. Bart was impressive. He was easily outmatched but stood his ground. Eugene had a stocky build. Bart had nearly the same height and was agile on his feet. He might have been more than Eugene wanted to deal with. Bart was one of the smartest guys in the school. As earlier mentioned he was friends with Dickey Brink. He was one of the few people that would associate himself with Dickey. It was Dickey who told me about Bart knowing a lot about cars. The word gets around on things such as this. It's often rare when a good student would also know a great deal about cars. For some reason this doesn't often happen. Anyway it was a logical decision in asking his help, being in the market to buy a car. I spoke to him about looking over some cars, and he agreed to help me today..

It wasn't too far to walk over to his house, about a mile or so, the day being kind of gloomy but not all bad. And before long, viola'. We were at his front door. After knocking there was a wait. Usually some movement can be heard. It was quiet. During this wait it came automatically to give an inspection of the upkeep of the front yard and the overall appearance of the home he lived in. It looked nice, and there was a flag on a pole near the driveway. Old Glory was moving with the gentle wind. While thoughts moved with the flag, someone approached and the door opened.

"May I help you?" the words came from a lady of perhaps forty or forty-five, and she looked like she might be Bart's mother. The motion of the flag caused me to lose my train of thought for a few seconds.

"Uh, yes, ma'am, I was hoping to see Bart.."

"Bart's not here. He said he was going to one of his friend's homes, but I'm not sure who it is," she said kindly.

"Maybe I can locate him, and if not could you tell him Wes stopped by?" I requested with little concern, having an idea where he might be.

"Yes, I'll do that. That was Wes?"

"Yes, Wes." The lady and I went back and forth like a rhyming game, and it struck me as kind of silly. It might have affected her the same way. She giggled some with this banter.

Bart often stopped in a pool hall that was about a half mile from his home. Dickey Brink said something about Bart going there often. He was recognized for a keen eye with a cue stick. Bart was just an odd fit. The pool hall was a place he didn't seem to be the type to frequent, nonetheless he was very good at pool. He was a very calculating individual that was good at anything he took interest in. I walked in and drew attention from a couple of guys. The smoke settled over the lights that hung above the tables, and a radio was playing on a country and western station.

Other sounds went on too. A pinball machine was being rattled as the thumping ding sound accumulated points, and a crack from the cue ball and the spread of the other fifteen balls on the table was common. There was Bart with a cue stick in his hand. He was evaluating the position of the balls on the table. It was fun watching as he used precision in his shots and eventually won two dollars from the other player. He played pool with great skill. Others in the room looked on, possibly wanting to challenge him.

"How's it going, Bart?" I said, as he gave the impression that he didn't expect me to be here.

"Hey, Patterson. What's new?"

"I thought I might have a look at a car today. You said you would go along with me if you had the time."

"Well... I'm finished up here. Let's hop in my car and see what they're selling. " We went outside and got seated in a black Ford with gold trim that had been fixed up inside and out. It also had chrome wheels and added chrome pieces with the finishing touch on the tail pipe. It had bucket seats, fuzzy dice hanging from the mirror, and it was jacked up some in the rear. Radio speakers bounced the sounds off the rear window with echoed music from a popular AM station. The bottom of the dashboard had gauges that displayed oil pressure, amperes, and something else that couldn't quite be made out. A car like this would be great. He started the engine, and it rumbled with force.

"Anywhere in particular you want to go?" he asked, glancing over as I shrugged my shoulders, and then he took notice of the mounted gauges. He then revved up the engine and eyed the tachometer that was affixed on the column behind the steering wheel. We were soon leaving the parking space and going toward a part of town I was unfamiliar with.

"Here's some money for gas," I told Bart as we had been going somewhere for about twenty minutes.

"Save it, Wes. You buy a car and you're going to have to get insurance, gas, and if you got a girl you don't want to go Dutch treat constantly, do you?"

"Probably not." My thoughts went to expenses that little thought had been given to. So, buy a car and then can't afford to drive it. How was I ever to take out Arlene, or Rebecca, or any girl? God! Everything attempted has things added on and keeps me from being where a young man wants to be. Bart has an edge. He's smart, and he has this car. He's got a steady girl. Maybe hanging out with him could be worthwhile. It might prove to be a good thing. "Bart. Do you work somewhere? You know. You have this car and you seem to have a grip on things. Just had an interest on how you manage?"

"I work at Montgomery's Ice House in the summer. Then there is some janitorial work during the other seasons."" A minute later there were some words said by Bart that needed to be repeated.

"Wes! Are you listening? How much money can you spend on a car?" he asked emphatically.

"Probably about $500, but this thing with insurance. I don't think the old man will pay my insurance. No! Definitely not! He won't pay my insurance, so I might have to scale down.

"Good thinking, you might want to cap it at $525. Cars can be financed. We can discuss your management of cash later. And insurance for guys our age is a killer."

"Okay, with a nod of approval. Bart might be helping me get things situated as hoped. Since my father doesn't seem to put forth much effort toward this, and Greg is in the military and George will soon be away at college, there was confirmation in the earlier thought that Bart might be a good guy to run around with.

"Do you make any money hustling at pool?" It was an uncomfortable question but he was good at pool and why not ask.

He smiled some as he thought about it, then said, "Well there's a dollar picked up here and there. There are far too many good players around to think that you can hustle the game on them. It would be fun to play pool and make some big bucks though, wouldn't it?"

"Yeah, that would be cool," came my answer in a low voice along with thinking how pool hustlers had it made.

We went by two car dealers that had little to offer other than monthly payments that it might not be possible to make. Then we saw a dealership named Perry's Used Autos. There were maybe thirty cars on the lot. There was a Studebaker that might be bargained for. It was medium brown with fairly good paint. The appearance from a distance was good. Bart said he would like to go over it, and it perhaps could be purchased for a little less than the $459 that was on the windshield. He pulled in a space that was near the lot, and we walked to the car.

"Watch a salesman come out like a hawk toward its prey," Bart said. His prediction was accurate. A man that looked to be in his late thirties or early forties in years with straight dark hair combed back and wearing a checkered sports coat walked up to us and smiled broadly.

"How do you like that car? It's a real value that someone will be happy to drive home. By the way, my name is Ned, Ned Irwin, and I am assistant sales manager here at Perry's."

"I'm Wes," I said, and reached to shake the extended hand from Mr. Irwin. Bart hardly paid any attention to the guy. It seemed that Bart was trying to avoid the salesman and went about checking the car. He mumbled something and then circled the car twice. He dropped down to look underneath the front then rear and had me turning around looking for him. Momentarily, it seemed he had walked off.

"Can we get a look at the engine?" he asked a bit impudently after bouncing back up.

"Let me get the keys. I'll be just a minute.

"Let me do the talking on this, Wes. And don't make any offers. If it checks out, we can go from there."

Ned was returning, whistling some, and looking confident. "Wes, I thought I should say something before we get too far along in this. I have to know how old you are, or your brother... or friend?" Ned asked and raised his eyebrows some as he approached us, then grinned widely.

"He's my friend, Bart."

"Are either of you eighteen years of age?" the man asked. I looked at Bart and he shook his head no, so I looked over to Ned with a sinking feeling grabbing my stomach.

"Neither of us is, sir. But I have a job and have saved up some money."

"Can we take this out for a test drive?" Bart interjected. Ned was taken aback by Bart and took a deeper breath than normal.

"I will have to drive!"

"That's fine," Bart told him. "Let me look over the engine." The hood was raised on the car and Bart made some mental notes on the car. After about two minutes, he pulled the hood down and walked to the rear of the car. "Okay. Start her up."

The car turned over without effort, and Bart ducked down for a second and another second or so he was jumping up and into the car.

"Are you men ready? Ned asked, trying to make us feel older than teenage boys.

"Head on out," Bart commanded. Ned drove around another area that was unfamiliar and came to a straight section of a street and accelerated some.

"Mash it to the floor!" Bart told him. He did so as Bart looked out the back window. Ned only held it for about two seconds and eased up. He looked around and floored it once more. The car responded well, and then a police car pulled out from an alley near a building.

"Ah, shit!" Ned exclaimed.

"What's wrong?" I asked.

"Our salesman Ned is going to have to answer to John Law,"

Bart chuckled the words out. Ned pulled the car over and stopped as the police car with flashing lights pulled behind us. The siren was not used, and we were kind of thankful for that; but an uneasiness came on that caused me to squirm some as Ned opened the door and walked back toward the patrolman.

"What do you think will happen?"

"Don't know," Bart answered mischievously. He turned around and looked at Ned, and gave me the impression that he hoped for something like this to happen. It was nerve wracking when this first happened, but Bart's sense of humor put me at ease. It seemed like a long time before Ned came back to the car. His face showed red as he opened the door.

"I'm going to drive back to the lot if you boys don't mind, He said in a humiliated way. He then had a simpering look for a few seconds. Neither of us said anything but understood. He pulled the car into a parking spot and, although a little irritated, he remained under control. "If you can have your father come by with you, if you still have interest in the car, we can discuss this and maybe settle on the purchase. It's a fine car."

"I'll see what I can do." Before I could say anything else, Bart indicated with a finger to his lips to say no more. Looking back at Ned, I gave a nod of my head.

"If you got some money to hold this car, we can keep it for a while so it isn't sold before you return.."

Bart made a facial expression and shook his head no. "I'll risk the chance and return later. I'll call and see if you still have the car. How's that sound?" I said confidently. There was a feeling like a deal was being made speaking like this.

"Don't say I didn't give you the chance," Ned spoke directly. This made me a little nervous. Seconds ago there was assertiveness in my manner, and now Ned was turning the tables on me. My arm was gripped as Bart had a hold of me and guided me away from Ned.

"Don't deal with that guy right now.. You were doing fine just a while ago. Let's leave him guessing. He doesn't have every car in town." We walked off and went to Bart's car. We soon drove away and it felt like we did something illegal. Just walking off like that was odd, and if a deal is met, it would be better if we were more courteous. Bart acted as if everything would work out. That type of attitude might be a plus to me one day.

There were many thoughts as Bart was driving, and the thoughts were going everywhere. Arlene came to mind at first. Imagining her sitting close to me as I held her shoulder. The smell of her perfume could almost be taken in. It was always light. She always smelled nice. Something like a flower in a garden during late spring. There was actually a feeling as my arm flexed thinking about pulling her closer. Then while continuing down the road in my car, steering with one hand and pulling Arlene closer still her eyes were looking into mine. This almost seemed real. It then faded away, but there was soon a replacement with Rebecca in the same spot. Everything was just the same. I had actually kissed Rebecca before and knew her feel. Rebecca was different but also pleasant. There was the looking into my eyes just as Arlene did. Then Rebecca began to leave this silly thought.. For a few seconds both girls seemed so near and real. None of the guys I knew or ran with would turn down a date with Arlene or Rebecca.

Moving the Tassels

Something that made this worrisome, silly thoughts, were entering the picture. Rebecca's boyfriend. He had a nice car. Much nicer than the car I was wanting to buy. Rebecca looked comfortable in his car. And back to Arlene. She was used to nice things. She sometimes went out with guys in college. They probably had sports cars and big cars like the one Bart drives. Probably later models too. Would she even like this car? This is not so sporty a car. This car was basically transportation. Damn! Are girls so influenced by the car a guy drives? Here goes this crazy mind rambling again. Thinking of a good thing and then turn it about on how it really might be. God help me!

Bart drove up next to the pool hall where we met up earlier. "Got to stop in here for a couple of minutes," he explained.

"That's okay. I think I'll walk home from here. Want to kind of think things over. How to approach matters with my dad."

"You sure you don't want me to drive you home?"

"No. This will be better. I'll get back with you on the car deal." He had a satisfied look after I said this.

Shooting pool almost seemed the thing to do. It wasn't my strength as far as competitions go. It was just a neat pastime. There must have been a reason for Bart going in there. He might be collecting on money that was owed to him. He might be dealing in drugs. That was something that was beginning to surface in our part of town. Bart didn't seem the type to deal in drugs. A thought on this, some of the people that deal in such things would do well not to draw attention to themselves. He was the type that was more like a spy for the Government. Someone that moves about well, almost fearless in things he is involved in. Bart is really one cool customer. He doesn't put on like many others in school. Arlene or Rebecca, either of them, would like Bart as a boyfriend. I'm glad he has a girlfriend. It would be tough competing with him in getting a girl. Bart's girlfriend is pretty most likely. Someone said she goes to a private school. It seems she would just be pretty.

There was a car that came too close to me while I was walking toward home. It was necessary to step in the grass to avoid the car.. This actually wasn't all that close but the goofy bastard that was driving had the entire road at his disposal. I might be driving my own car soon there, jackass, so watch out! Now a play act in speaking to my dad was being rehearsed in my mind. There were a couple of different things to say to him. Saying them aloud to get the feel of how he would react was a good idea. It doesn't matter if it isn't actually heard. Maybe the old man would go along with this. It wasn't costing him anything. Remaining optimistic on buying a car was tough.

Upon walking into our house, Mom was busy straightening some things in the dining room. Dad was working on a lamp that had a chip on it that was noticeable. It was an off red colored lamp that had the shape something like an hour glass except for the two gold-eared handles near the top. We had this lamp for probably ten, maybe even twelve years, and it was one of those items that becomes part of the home. It is noticed most when it is missing. So Dad decided to make the chipped area as inconspicuous as possible.

"I'm home." My use of a few words may cover the nervousness that was being experienced.

"Everything okay, Son?" Mom asked. She doesn't call me son often. Maybe something is wrong..

"Ready to buy a car," I answered. Mom's face showed surprise and most of the color in her face went away.

"What kind of car do you have in mind?" Dad asked but kept his eyes on the lamp, though he remained attentive. Directing my voice to the both of them about the car took a little effort. Maybe it's best to open up with something positive.

"Bart thinks it is a good car for the money. Bart even figured we could haggle on the price and perhaps get it a little cheaper than the asking price."

Dad agreed to go with me, and after placing the lamp back properly he drove me to Perry's car lot to have a look for himself. As we were going that way, there was the idea of mentioning to dad the concern that maybe the car would be sold to someone else. Ned should be called to see if the car was still there. Maybe money should have been given to Ned to hold the car. Bart convinced me not to, but you never know.

"Dad, should we pull up to a phone booth and call Perry's and make sure the car is still there?"

Dad lectured me on the do's and don'ts of business. The uncertainty came again. What if the car has been sold and he did all this driving for nothing. The thought of the car changed to thinking about Christmas. Maybe think on this and take away worries of purchasing a car. Dad pulled up to the car lot. He must have known where this lot was because he didn't ask much in the way of directions. Ah. There was the car. Waiting for my money to exchange so it could go home with us. There was an exhale of relief. The car was still here and things looked pretty good. We parked and stepped out of Dad's car to do business.

Ned spotted me and noticed my father. He had a different approach with my dad than he did with Bart and me. That was fine. He talked respectfully to dad. He wasn't disrespectful too much when we were here earlier, he was just a better salesperson with my father. Dad drove the car. After some disclaimer or something of that sort was signed and the deal sealed, it came time to drive the car home. All that was done was sort of confusing, but the processes led to me buying my first car at a better price than was on the windshield. Dad actually did talk Ned into selling at a good price and with a guarantee on paper for a period that extended into the new year. I wasn't even aware of how long exactly that it was. All that was important was ownership of some wheels. Man alive! I drove home with my own car.

The following Monday this wonderful automobile was steered into the school parking lot, and it gave a good feeling to me. There is a pride in having a first car and ownership would bring on questions for sure. It drew some attention from people in class. Everybody wants to see your car. There are always a bunch of questions to answer, and of course there is always some smart ass that has to be critical of what was bought. With suggestions from Bart, the comments were kindly brushed away. There was no time wasted in setting up some rides to and from school. It would help me pay for gas and insurance. There was a good feeling after setting up these riders. A little extra money is always nice. This was something Bart would approve of.. It wasn't mentioned to him but he was influential. It was time to do some sensible things. Bart was a few steps ahead of the rest of us, and if positioning one's self to a better financial state while in high school was possible, then one should do so. Welcome the small benefits.

Christmas break was upon me before I had the chance to catch my breath. There was the work at the grocery. There came a strong desire more than ever for Arlene to go out with me. Rebecca was still working at the grocery, and we often saw each other. She always spoke, but she was going with that jerk that she had been dating for a couple of months. Every time the thought came to mind of him dating her, a lousy feeling would surface. These thoughts would bring a derogatory sensation or words toward him. It was best to keep these to myself. This was a self-conscious thing. Difficult to understand. I didn't know the guy, and who could blame him for going with Rebecca?

My car was not drawing much attention from Rebecca, but there was a compliment from Yance and Mr. Tromveck. Mr.

Tromveck was almost completely bald and looked like a comedian that often appeared on television. He usually avoided eye contact and predictably wore a white short-sleeved shirt and sometimes a tie at work. He had broad shoulders that hinted to me he had worked hard all his life. This could have been incorrect, but it kind of looked that way. He especially went on about my car, and his first car. He might have been saying things because he and my dad are friends.

When he looked off to the left toward the ceiling while describing his first car, he brought something out worth thinking about. He would go on about dating then marrying the prettiest girl in Deermont. There was an empathy for this man's story. The boss. The man who paid me to work for him. There was something for the first time in his voice that made me realize that he was a good guy. He usually gave the impression that he only concerned himself with store business. Working at the grocery was not difficult. After listening to Mr. Tromveck on the car and his wife, my going to work for the next couple of days was easier. It would be nice to hear more of his story.

There was a department store that Arlene would sometimes shop at. It was about five miles northeast of where she lived, and about the same distance from our home. My mom occasionally shopped there. The store tried to rival the well-known stores in New York and Chicago, and probably did well for its location in carrying and selling products, clothes, and name brand merchandise that larger, better-known store names handled. I went there in my car, with some money saved for Christmas gifts. There was only a need to buy for my family. There was no steady girl; not even close to one. Dating was something rare. Rebecca had been the last girl I was involved with. So much for that.

There were a couple of things to buy for mom. She did without many material things that other ladies living near us were purchasing. A perfume that was advertised on television would have her pause at her household work when the commercial was aired. Okay, why not get this for her? A young lady at the counter walked toward me.

"And what can I help you with today?" the words came from her as she smiled, displaying her perfect, bright white teeth.

"There's a perfume that is advertised and it looks like the bottle sitting there. I pointed it out in the lighted glass display case.

"Okay." She then sprayed the atomizer at her wrist and held it to my nose. From this inhaling my thinking went completely off balance. How could a woman smell so good? Then looking toward her, she turned her lips into a gentle, beautiful smile. "How's that?"

"Proper."

"You are saying that it is good?" she asked.

"Uh, yeah. Yes, ma'am. Sorry, but I don't know what to call you." This uttering came slowly while trying to tell her it was fine and the often self-conscious thinking of how poor my words were. How stupid she probably thought I was. Her pretty smile was comforting.

She hinted about gift wrapping the perfume but the suggestion was declined while reaching for my wallet to pay for this. My sister would wrap the Christmas presents, and that would save money. Kate would probably say something complimentary to me for buying this for mom.

It couldn't be legally purchased by me, so handing over some money to Kate was the thing to do in order to buy my dad a bottle of brandy. He would like this. No doubt about it.. Then the shopping would be complete after buying some earrings for Kate. Bingo! All through!

Moving the Tassels

My sincere wish was to buy a gift for Arlene. This could be done in a tactful way. She would be gracious and she would accept it as a gift from one friend to another. Then she would feel obligated to buy me something. This would have the same friendship kind of exchange.. When mentioning this to Bart there was no word who this gift would be for. Bart was logical. He was the one that said the girl, not being a steady girlfriend could feel uncomfortable. There was mentioned to him that she was probably out of my league. He convinced me to hold off on a Christmas present to her. He was right. It was the best thing to do, but there was a desire to give her a Christmas gift. Then the thought came, maybe next year.

Christmas Day was a few days away and there was a feeling that is difficult to describe, but it is joyful. I had just come home from work and parked my car behind Dad's car. There was a little admiration that both cars looked good. Then a stroll in the front door of our house and hollering, "I'm home."

"Wes, how was work?" Mom asked.

"Not bad. Things went rather well," came my answer with emphasis on the word rather, trying to sound British. There wasn't a purpose for doing this. Just a quirky response.

Mom looked at me, kind of surprised, then mentioned that two phone calls came for me.

"Who were they from?" I asked excitedly. There's always the thought some girl might call in a state of slight desperation, or in need of company.

"One in particular was from Mrs. Cray." A call from her was far from what was wanted. Mrs. Cray either had bad news about Mr. Cray, or... well, that call wasn't wanted. My heart sank a little from getting her call. It couldn't be good.

"The other was from Bart, I believe.'"

"Okay. I'm going to use the phone for a couple of minutes."" There was no answer at Bart's house. I dialed the number again to be sure it wasn't messed up the first time. There was still no answer.. Why would he call?

"Mom, I'm going to run out for a little while. Be back before long."

"Make sure you're home for dinner. We seem to never eat at the table any longer as a family should," Mom went on with her complaint.

"I'll be back!" Then jumping in my car, there was a quick drive to the Cray home. There was only the one automobile at their home that belonged to the Crays. It was a '68 Plymouth, with a dark golden brown color. It looked sporty for this elderly couple. I pulled behind it and made my way up to the door, then knocked lightly.. Nerves sort of took over about what might be found out. Mrs. Cray answered the door "Hello, Wes. Would you care to come in?"

"Thank you," was all I could say. My glance was toward the television that was playing, and there was Mr. Cray sitting in a chair. His eyes looked my way, and they were weary. He looked so very tired. There was weight loss that was obvious, but he smiled and spoke in a voice that seemed to be an effort to speak.

"Hello, young Wes. How have you been?"

"Well, okay. Trying to get ready for Christmas." In came their dog, a Yorkie named Nelly. He was a very friendly dog that shared warm company with Mr. and Mrs. Cray.. It caused reflection on a dog we had. It was a Collie that always welcomed us for a few years named Steamer. He looked like Lassie on TV, and he was a very comforting dog. How he came by the name was really unknown, but he gave that welcome that made one feel good. He one day disappeared, and I never knew what happened to him. Mom spoke of the chance he might have been stolen. All of my family was upset after he was gone, even my dad, although he tried to hide this emotion.

Mrs. Cray moved toward Mr. Cray. Her dress was dated. It looked gray with a medium blue stitching that had wave like patterns that moved horizontally. She had her hair up in a bun, and that is how she usually wore it. Her eyeglasses rested on the lower part of her nose. She just seemed like a grandmother to me. She adjusted a pillow as Mr. Cray leaned back in the chair he was sitting in. His legs were covered with a type of blanket. He moved with Mrs. Cray's adjustment and rested easier.

"So Christmas is keeping you busy?" he paused, and before my answer he spoke to Mrs. Cray. "Carla, haven't we got something?"

"We do," she told him. She left the room and walked to the dining room and picked up something with both hands as it shined through the dim lighting in the room. She came into the TV room with a tray covered with aluminum foil. "I baked these for your family and you," she said with a smile, and handed them to me.

"Hey, that's a nice thing to do. I didn't think to get you all anything."

"Why we're happy if you will accept these. We weren't expecting anything?" Mrs. Cray handed me the foiled platter and the aroma whetted a desire to have some of the cookies immediately. She mentioned the number of different type cookies she made. I wasn't actually listening, but knew to thank her before leaving.

"Your family and you have a Happy Christmas," she said, as I was leaving. In the chair Mr. Cray remained. He moved his head and my acknowledgement was about the same as his. He was exhausted by talking for a minute or so. His face had changed some. A short time back it had a look of some red or even more of a purple in spots. Now it was kind of an ashen look.

Arriving home I walked to our kitchen table and put the cookies down, then peeled back the foil and saw all the different types. Sparkling red, green, and shapes like Santa, angels, and Christmas trees. Some looked like reindeer, elves hats, and about anything that had to do with Christmas. One of these cookies was munched on and soon gone as Mom walked near.

"Where did all these come from?"

"Mrs. Cray gave them to me. To us.""

"So sweet of her. Wes, I don't want you to spoil your appetite by eating too many of those."

"Okay."

Mom went toward the den and she was gone a minute, returning with a note that she put near the refrigerator. It was a reminder she wrote on the paper. Christmas gift for Crays. Mom was a very considerate person. She and Dad exchanged Christmas gifts with the neighbors across the street, and now she felt obligated to buy something for an elderly couple she barely knows. She kind of knew them mostly through me.

That night my car would be seen in most of the frequented places, but these were not busy at all. Most of the guys were out with their girlfriends. I drove over to the Christmas tree stand that was a few blocks from an elementary school. Dickey Brink was selling trees there. He said he was doing this for some Christmas money. So was Mick, the guy that had dated Kathleen, the sister of my friend Jimmy.. I saw Dickey at school, we were hanging out more often these days, and sometimes I would hang out with Mick. He had now dropped out of school and was picking up work wherever he could. The tree lot put Mick and Dickey to work. What a team. This place had lights that beamed down making it look like a concentration camp. It took something from the spirit of the season.

"Hey Mick. How's things goin?" I asked. It seemed kind of awkward because he wasn't known to me in comparison to most of my friends.

"Making money.. This job and the carpet laying have most of my time used up.""

"Are you still dating Jimmy's sister Kathleen?"

"Man she dumped me like a load of gravel. She chased me out her parents house with a beer bottle!" There were probably some things that could have been asked, and Mick might have told me, but it was probably best leaving it at that. Most everyone knew her temper. It took very little to get her fuming. When last seeing them together it figured to be a short affair.

"Hey, there's Dickey! You look like the man with the plan. How is the tree business?" purposefully starting to talk with him and walking over his way to cut off my chat with Mick. It was a convenient way to end what we were talking about.

"This is working out well. The guy that runs this told Mick and me we could negotiate with the customers since it's so close to Christmas. I've sold quite a few tonight. I think Mick has too, he said with a bit of pride. He was going over the different trees and the prices."

"Wes! Dickey!" Our names were called out loudly by Mick. "I need some help over here."" We walked quickly to where Mick was. He had the trunk of a car opened and was studying the size of the trunk and the size of the tree he had just sold to a lady standing near. A very pretty girl was next to her. They looked alike enough that they had to be mother and daughter. The light came at my eyes getting only a glimpse of the lady's appearance, but the angle of light from the tree stand shone on the girl. She was most likely the same age as us; maybe a year younger. She was wearing a coat that covered her hips, and had heavy warm looking gloves and a covering on her head that rounded off and pressed her hair down on her forehead, kind of like a toboggan, and the sides kind of pushed her hair out. She looked like one of the actresses from an old movie. Her cheekbones protruded some and she didn't say a word. She just watched the three of us move about.

"How do you want to load this?" Dickey asked.

"Get some of that heavy twine near the fire barrel. We'll cut off a long piece, then double it, then wrap it as much as needed.'"

"The two of us can get the better part of the tree in the trunk, can't we," I suggested, and looked for an okay from Mick.

"Yeah, I think so. Let's do that while Dickey picks up the twine." Mick lowered his shoulder and I grabbed a thick limb on the tree and we moved it deep into the trunk as Dickey walked over with the cylinder of twine. Mick took another look at the tree and drew about sixty feet of the twine, cut it with a pocket knife, then put the ends together and brought it to half its length. He wrapped the top of the tree and tied the latch of the top of the trunk to something inside that wasn't visible. He was satisfied that it was fastened and looked at the lady and the girl to get approval.

"Thank you, and Merry Christmas," the woman said. The girl looked on and gave a smile. They got in the car and drove off. The three of us commented about the girl.

"How would you like her under the tree?" Mick said with a laugh.

"She'd be quite a present, wouldn't she, Wes?" Dickey looked my way after saying this. I just did my typical musing about another girl that would be nice to show off, walking about with her on my arm. Then there sometimes comes a feeling of hopelessness.

"You must have sold that tree for a good price," Dickey spoke to Mick.

"Two dollars."

"Are you kidding? That tree had to sell for at least fifteen dollars!" Dickey exclaimed.

"The boss said we could bargain. I bargained. It's near Christmas. I thought that girl would give me her phone number. She just didn't talk any at all."

"She's probably got a boyfriend. Girls that look like that are not available. If they are, they're off the market in a hurry," I said, as if I were a guy in the know.

"That's for sure," Mick added.

The guys had a few customers walking through checking the trees, so it seemed a good time to leave. There was also something else on my mind.

A while back a few of us stopped at a restaurant a couple of times after a football game, and we got something to eat. The waitress was kind of nice to me and it might be a place to stop in for a hamburger or something. My car looked pretty good under the lights when parked near the restaurant entrance. It could be called vanity, but there was a swell of pride walking to the door and looking back to admire my car. It wasn't a car that draws all that much attention, but it seems to be reliable. Tonight it looked good. That was what was needed. It was in my thoughts while driving to this frequented place.

The stools at the counter were empty, so I took one furthest from the cash register, then looked to see if the girl that waited on us was working. She might not even work there any longer, but it was worth the effort to see. There was an older woman moving about. She was probably as old as my Mother. She had frizzy light brown hair and was about as average looking as could be imagined. She was going to the tables and booths waiting on the customers that were occupying them.

"Can I get you something?" a voice asked and surprised me as the older waitress had passed by seconds earlier.

"Uh... yes. I, uh... would like to start with a cup of coffee, and maybe a dressed cheeseburger."

"Do you want onions on the cheeseburger?"

"No, leave the onions off." There had been a late movie on television about the Indian fighter Custer recently, and he liked onions. But the onions were too strong on his breath when he exhaled. Good God, do my thoughts go everywhere when talking to a girl? In this case it was the waitress that served my friends and me some time ago. She looked much the same. Dark hair and eyes, and every so often she would smile. Very nice smile. Friendly. And her name... yes, remembering her name. It was Charlotte. She wore a nametag that displayed it.

"Here's your coffee. It will be a few minutes before your cheeseburger is up."

I told her thanks and tried to look more adult. Drinking coffee seemed more adult, and of course it was ordered quick, when she first got my attention this evening. Sipping the coffee took some patience for it was very hot and seemed too strong. It must have been sitting for a while.

"How about a fresh cup of coffee? I'll have some made. Your face twisted some when you were drinking this. It could have been made an hour ago" Charlotte said, putting a comical look on her face.

"Okay. That would be real nice."" She turned and walked toward the kitchen area. What a stupid thing to say on my part. It wasn't cool at all. "That would be nice." Better think of wittier things to say to a girl. Or lady. Or older girl. Whatever she is to me. A guy just isn't with it when making a remark like that. Some guys know just what words they should let roll off their tongues. The words are timed right. They have a keen wit. Not me. There is so often the stumbling about, attempting to say something. Maybe the sayings of witty things come with age.

Moving the Tassels

Let me see. Her name is Charlotte, and girls enjoy hearing their names spoken. Something cool should be said when she brings back the fresh coffee. Three girls walked in and were giggling and making a lot of noise. It caused a loss of focus. Trying to concentrate became harder.

"A dressed cheeseburger and fresh coffee," Charlotte offered as she set both items down on the counter in front of me.

"Thank you. It looks like it will be well worth the wait," I told her. She smiled that nice smile again..

"I'll check back with you in a few minutes.."" She then turned and walked back toward the kitchen once again.

The cheeseburger had that alluring smell. A big bite of it proved its taste equaled the alluring smell. It was very tasty. It kind of hit the spot. Then the thought about what was said when Charlotte brought this came to me. Hmmm. That wasn't a bad thing to say. It wasn't even planned to say this, but it was a good thing to say. Ah! Failure to mention her name. That's not so cool.

The older waitress had stepped to the booth where the three girls that had walked in were sitting. It's nice that Charlotte is waiting the counter. She was waiting the far side of the restaurant, but the counter seemed to be hers alone. The coffee was tested with some hesitation. It was very hot and fresh. The difference was obvious, and it smelled the way coffee should. There is something about coffee that gives off that aroma, that special smell. What the television commercials emphasize. It was very hot and I tried to drink some of it down so Charlotte would have to give me a refill. Glancing to my left the other waitress was about to come by and check the counter. That's what it looked like but she gathered some dirty plates off a table that was behind me. The girls were making some racket again. One of them let out a laugh that was too loud. It was one of those things a person does when wanting to draw attention. One of her friends laughed at her and said something to her that had both of them laughing. She also gave an easy hit in the back with the palm of her hand to the girl with the loud laugh.

"More coffee?" Charlotte asked as she quietly moved right in front of me.

"Yes, of course," was my response. It was so automatic. She had come up while my eyes were averted by the three girls, and the question was almost startling. "I remember you waiting on me before."

"Did I?"

"Yes, it was a while back, but I remember..""

"There are so many people that come in here." She gave a little more concentrated look. "I think I remember you. Remembering everyone that stops in is nearly impossible," she said in a nice way. "I'll check back on your coffee in a few minutes."

"Okay, that'd be good."" She walked off and this affected me by how nice she actually was. What was she like away from here? It was a good feeling for her to say she might have remembered me. Then again a challenge how to ask her about things? What she likes? Where she lives? The kind of car she has? Just talk about stuff to get acquainted. While thinking about this and drinking coffee, there was a little more feeling of ease. Charlotte was coming back with the coffee pot.

"Would you like some more coffee?" she asked in her pleasant voice.

"Uh, sure. It's, uh, good coffee," adding this, just trying to say something and not come off as being so awkward. She filled it close to the edge of the cup and smiled comfortably. She sure had a pleasant way about herself.. Did she act the same way to all her customers? My study of this was brief.. Except for me at the counter, her customers were on the other side of the restaurant. It seemed she was nice to everyone. Supposedly that is how waitresses get good tips. A piece of pie would go with the coffee. When Charlotte came nearer I spoke up, "Could I get a slice of that coconut cream pie?"

"Why, sure you can. Let me see if they have a pie in the back. The piece behind this glass has been sitting in here more than likely all day.."" It wasn't but a few seconds and she came to me with the slice of pie. "It looks very good. Bon appetite!"

With the fork in my hand, the pie disappeared in seconds. The pie was delicious, and after finishing it off there was a desire to ask for another. Instead it would be better and more an adult thing to stop. A guy has to show some sophistication. Overeating is not effective in impressing a girl. It doesn't do anything to impress a woman either.

Out of nowhere Charlotte appeared again with the coffee pot. "You must be spending the entire night here. Are you waiting for somebody?"

"No, not really. Had the night off from work and most of my friends are out tonight. Just passing some time until later..""

"It's nice to have some free time, she said. My shift doesn't end until 2:00 a.m. Then my roommate is coming by to give me a ride."

"You don't have a car?" I asked, trying to act like some real smooth customer in control of the situation now.

"Not yet, maybe before too long. I have to stretch my earnings." She glanced to a booth that a lady who might have been in her mid twenties and some guy that might have been in his forties had taken. "Excuse me," she politely expressed, "I have to check on that couple." She whisked off to wait on them. The thought came again about what to say next. There was an opening with what she said. Now it seemed like this adult type of feeling. My shoulders drew back to improve my posture. It felt like being in a movies, sort of cocky and very sure of myself now.

Looking over to the booth that had just been occupied, the guy was all smiles at his young girlfriend. He was holding her hands in the middle of the table, and she looked pleased to a degree. Charlotte came up to them, placing some glasses filled with water on the table and was ready to take their order. They had resumed a more proper position. They had little time to look at the menu but must have had an idea what they wanted. She took the order, writing down what was requested. She turned and walked off. My thought now was that he is probably what is referred to as a "Sugar Daddy" Some of my friends have talked about younger girls having interests in older men. All kinds of terms and so forth go with it-May and December, old man robbing the cradle, old bird and his young chick. It means about the same thing no matter how it's called. I wonder if I'll ever be that way? Charlotte is no doubt older than me. If we were together, how would people talk about us? She was walking my way again.

"Would there be anything else?" she asked, and again very pleasantly.

"I'll just finish up my coffee." Then out of the blue came the words, "Say, if your roommate can't pick you up when your shift ends, I could probably give you a ride home," and this was said with more confidence. It was surprising to myself that the words were blurted out. She looked at me for a few seconds as if studying my eyes, or some sort of detail that would make her feel okay with my suggestion.

"Oh, I don't know," came a reply from her with a touch of uncertainty. She walked off, continuing her work. A couple of minutes passed. She returned to the counter. "Let me think about that offer. Okay?"

"Yeah" the response came automatically. The clock on the wall read ten minutes of ten. She had plenty of time. The restaurant was not too busy, and even cars that pulled in would usually drive on through. It was someone looking for someone else most of the time. Somehow people looking for one another hook up somewhere and sometime during the night. A lot of times it was stragglers driving around, kind of like me tonight.

Maybe another three minutes had passed and she again walked to the counter. "I have thought about your offer," she said. "Can you be trusted to be here at 2:00 a.m.? Definitely?" she added.

"Why, yes! I mean, you can rely on me."

"Okay. Now I'm really counting on you. I don't even know your name."

"Its Wes. Wes Patterson."

"My name is Charlotte," she offered.

"Yes, I know," I interrupted. "It's on your nametag," My intention was to let her know this was read and not snooping around.

"Okay, Wes. I mean this for sure. I am holding you to this.'"

"Great! I am going to check with my folks, but everything will be fine. I swear!"

Charlotte nodded. "I have to get back to work. Two o'clock, now."

I walked to the cash register and the other waitress took my money for the order. She said something to me, and what it was could have been anything. There was an overwhelming desire to dance out of the door, but it would be better containing myself. When getting in my car I turned the radio up and started singing to a song that was being played. It was by Dionne Warwick, and it made me feel good singing along to it. And before long arriving home, pulling in the driveway, there came an exclamation, "Damn! I forgot to leave a tip." The front door was unlocked and I made my way into our home.

"Well, I didn't think you'd be home so soon," Mom said, as Dad was just being Dad, looking my way and not making much of the fact of me being home on a Saturday night.

"I was just coming home for now and letting you know I have to give someone a ride home from their work shift when it ends at 2:00 a.m."

"2:00 a.m.! My lord! Who works until that late hour?"

"It's some girl I know. She needs a ride home tonight. I told her I'd give her a ride. She's counting on me," this plea would take on strong concern for sure.

"Wes, this is something I don't know about. You get your car and suddenly you're taxiing people around at all hours of the night. What do you think, Dear?" Mom asked Dad, as her hands cupped one another while her fingers moved in a fidgeting way.

I didn't want to have to tell Charlotte I couldn't give her a ride. My thoughts went toward coming up with another way of begging.

"If he has someone expecting him to drive them home from work, and he's made a commitment, then he should hold to what he said. But, in the future I expect for us to be notified before doing something such as this!"

This was a surprise. Dad was backing me up. "Yes, sir," I said in the sincerest way possible.

"Remember, don't make a habit of this. And I want you to drive your friend home, and then you're to come home immediately after. Do you understand?"

"Yes, sir," I said once again.

"How far of a drive is it?"

"Just a few miles from here," I answered and figured she couldn't live too far away. Nothing more was brought up about it.

It felt like the weight of the world was lifted from my shoulders. Mom and Dad were questioning and it could have led up to fighting me completely on this. There was even a fleeting thought about sneaking out of the house later. Now things were set. I sat down and watched television, and kept an eye on the clock as the time moved slowly. At 1:30 it was time to leave the house and go on to the restaurant.

It was about ten of two when arriving at the restaurant. This robust confidence had waned some. The idea loomed of waiting outside and beep the horn when spotting her walking out, or going inside letting her know I was here and waiting. My decision was to go inside and let her know. She deserved to know she had met someone that was keeping their word. It took a bit of courage to do this. Why? Who knows?

"Hi!" I spoke as I saw her cleaning a table off..

"Well! I am so glad I could count on you. I was beginning to worry a little," she let it be known.

"The car is parked over to the side near the entrance," I told her. "I'll just wait out there for you."

She nodded in approval. The walk back to my car had a restored confidence. If someone were watching me they might have thought I had strutted to my car. There was this feeling of being on top of the world.

Charlotte walked out the door of the restaurant just after two a.m., and I beeped the horn on my car very lightly. She looked my way and walked to the car, looking to see if it was me as she was buttoning her coat. She opened the car door and sat down. She was near the passenger door but she was turned toward me. The engine was running so I put the car in gear and then realized she hadn't mentioned which way to go. and I asked, "Where do you live?"

She had me pull out on the highway and head north. There was a scent of perfume not noticed earlier. Not strong but pleasant.

"I want to thank you again, Wes. My roomy is a good kid, but she can run late. She sometimes loses her train of thought. You know how those people are?"

"Yeah,"" I cleared my throat and felt nerves slightly. "Turn right just up here," she directed.

"Are you from around here?" I asked, actually being curious about where she was from.

"I moved here a few months ago. I'm from a small town." She said the name of the town but my habit of hearing something and not picking it up clearly was in its normal state. She continued, "Almost dead center of the state."

"You have a boyfriend?"

"Ex-boyfriend. I thought we were going to get married last summer but he decided he didn't want to. I came here and enrolled in beautician school, working in the restaurant at night. There are shared expenses with my roommate. For now I'm just trying to get by."

"Well, you seem to be doing okay," I said encouragingly.

"Certainly trying. What about you? What do you do?" she asked, in a nice way as I looked for only a second and saw her eyes meet mine. She had beautiful dark eyes.

"I am a senior in high school, and work at a grocery store part time; I hang out with friends sometimes, and… well that's about it." After relating this I glanced her way to see if she would have a reaction to me saying the bit about being in high school. My eyes returned to the road.

"It's a couple of miles out this way," she indicated." "You seem to be doing better than a lot of people. Did you say you live with your parents?"

"Oh, yeah. They rule with an iron fist."" I let on, though knowing that they were actually fairly lenient. "I have an older sister that lives at home too. She's a senior in college. She got all the brains in the family."

"What did they say about you taking me home? I mean your parents. Did they have anything to say?"

"Mom was a bit upset, but Dad kind of understood I think. They're actually more understanding than the parents of some of my friends.""

"It's nice that they are that way. Do you have a girlfriend?" she now asked. That question had to be thought on for a second.

"I did," clearing my throat, and continuing with my answer. "One of the girls I worked with, but it just wasn't working out according to her," I answered, and felt it was an honest answer.

"That gets you out of buying a Christmas present.""

"Well...yeah, it does." We both laughed a little at that comment. The drive continued and Charlotte still held her position leaning against the passenger door of my car, but she was comfortable to talk to. We both knew she was older than me but that was all right. There was nothing actually serious about this. It was how she made me feel when talking to her. She had me pull up to an older house in a neighborhood that was unfamiliar. It had steps on the outside leading up to a second floor apartment of a two-story house. I stopped the car to let her out.

"Listen, I can't let you in, and I'm so sorry, but..." she said kind of apologetically.

"It's not expected. That is, I didn't think you would let me in. And I need to be heading home anyway."

"If...if you aren't busy tomorrow night, say seven o'clock, maybe you could stop by. That is if you wanted to."

"Say, that would be nice. Maybe I might," I answered real slow not wanting to appear too anxious at the invitation. "That'd be pretty good.""

"Okay. Now go home and be happy you have parents that care for you. Thanks for the ride," she leaned over and gave me a kiss on my face, then hopped out of my car and ran toward the house and up the side steps to her upstairs apartment. Then a light came on so this appeared that everything was fine now. The drive toward home had me turned around in the neighborhood, but soon the way out was discovered and it was easy to get back on track. The thoughts were mostly about Charlotte while driving home. Her face kept coming to mind. Focusing on the road proved difficult. Her face returned again and again. There was still some good feeling where she kissed me. My hand patted my face every once in a while as a feel good type thing. This was silly, but like most guys, it was easy to be silly over a girl. And in this instance, woman.

In a short while I was safe at home and moved quietly in the house. While lying in bed there was the thought about Charlotte for a few minutes. A date with her at 7:00. Man alive! This is working out good. So glad to have bought my car. I turned over in my bed a time or two and was soon asleep.

The working hours the following day were from 1:00 p.m. to 4:00 p.m. Most of this consisted of stocking, and it seemed the time moved quickly. Rebecca was working this day too. She was at the checkout, and naturally she looked picture perfect. She was wearing her hair differently from most days she works. It rounded her face and came down under her chin toward her neck. She had parted it in the center and wore a white bow on the right side of her head. She had remained on good terms with me, but that was only as far as speaking to me. She was still seeing the same guy that was despised by me. Today though, the feeling wasn't quite as hateful.

At four o'clock I punched out on the clock then started to walk out the door. Rebecca was at the checkout and not busy and spoke, "I'm off until after Christmas when I finish up at five. Have a Merry Christmas.""

"I will. I uh, hope yours is a Merry Christmas too." The words didn't flow.. They were spoken in a detached manner and came out of my mouth like it was full of barley soup. God, it's terrible speaking awkwardly. I smiled her way and walked out the door. The drive home had my thoughts going everywhere once again. Rebecca didn't have much to say to me. She could have just said bye, or something. Maybe she knows about this date with an older woman tonight, and she wants to spoil it for me. She could too. That way she looks, and her hair looking so good. Every hair was in place. Does she ever go anywhere and not look perfect?

My thoughts went toward Charlotte. She is a woman. She knows more than girls in high school. She is built a little heavier than most of the girls in high school. More around the waist, but still, she's older. She moves differently from high school girls. She doesn't try to make it so obvious about swinging her hips to get attention. She just moves more naturally, and it kind of draws me toward her. If we danced slowly with my hands on her waist, she could do that hip action girls do, or women do, and I could squeeze her tight. My home was very near, and these stirring thoughts were working me into a frenzy, This thinking about Rebecca and Charlotte, and just then while pulling into the driveway there came the thought about Arlene. What was she doing for Christmas? Lordy, these girls, or women, females! They're driving me mad!

The so called date with Charlotte was at seven o'clock, and it was a high priority today. The drive there was now an easier find and the walk up the steps to the door was what seemed a dance. There wasn't a doorbell, so a spirited knock on the wooden door was in order. There were muffled footsteps coming near. Charlotte had opened the door and asked me in. She was dressed in red and green, and had her hair different. She wore it down, and it looked soft and dark, framing her face; making her look a little younger.

The apartment was not very big. All the areas were sort of combined. It was well kept though. On a lamp table was a Christmas tree, not too big, and decorated with what looked like snow and silver garland that festooned around the tree. There were just a few lights that had been placed on the tree. There were several cards that were standing, most likely sent by people that cared for her or her roommate.

"I just made some hot cocoa. Would you care for any?" she asked.

It was much like being in the restaurant. "No thanks."

"Well, let me give you the tour of Charlotte's Villa. I should probably say Fran's Villa. She actually lived here before me and pays a little more of the rent. She has a little more say of what goes on. But we get along.""

"Is she here now?"

"She has left for Memphis. Her mother lives there. Fran wanted to go there for Christmas. She left around noon today."

Charlotte showed me the kitchen stove, and where they cooked and ate was a small area. She then walked me around the rest of the place. She showed a picture of Fran to me. It was black and white and was an outdoor shot of Fran sitting on a concrete structure that encircled what looked like a fish pond. She placed the picture of Fran back in its place. To the right of it were two dummy heads that had wigs on them. Beside them was what looked like a textbook with something printed about a hair stylist. A door to the bathroom was barely mentioned, and a Murphy bed was Fran's sleeping arrangement. It would probably be embarrassing and before my asking, Charlotte patted the top of the sofa. The sofa had folded blankets and throw pillows neatly placed.

"And here is my sleeping space. It is small but comfortable. Maybe another few more months and I'll have something better." Her humble expression and living order was kind of pitiful in some way. She never let it get her down.

There was no reason for this but kind of out of the blue it was brought it up by me, "Charlotte, I'm sorry I didn't bring you anything. Candy or flowers or something. I think I should have."

"Why, you didn't have to do any such thing. You gave me a ride home last night. That was a nice thing to do." Her voice had just a trace of a twang; kind of country, or Southern, something like that, but not an affectation. It was just something noticeable.

She walked toward a hi-fi and put a record on with Christmas carols being sung. "Do you like Christmas music?"

"Of course. It...well, it's pretty good.'" Boy that response came out dumb. We continued to listen, and Charlotte sang lightly along with the words being sung by some choral group. I had sat on a chair and listened and looked around the apartment. Different pictures and trinkets were placed in a tasteful way. She then said she was going home Christmas Eve for a few days. She missed her family.

"Come sit beside me," she said as she had taken a place on the sofa. There was some nervousness on my part while walking to where she was then sitting. "Are you afraid of something?"

"No, I just... well, I am not used to being with a girl in an apartment alone."

"I'm not a femme fatale."

"I know," I answered, but had no idea what she said she was, or wasn't. We continued to listen to the album of Christmas music and she took my hands and looked directly in my eyes. The smell of perfume she delicately wore came to me and so did a shiver.

In a matter of seconds we had kissed. Very passionately, and the kiss was for a longer time than any other girl that had kissed me before. Our desires were beginning to be very strong, and I drew her up from the sofa and hinted at the Murphy bed, but she would not use her roommates bed. "Here," she quietly demanded. She stood up and changed the record albums on the hi-fi to some easy sounding orchestra, and turned on the bathroom light, then turned off the light that glowed for most of the apartment. She opened up the sofa and spread the blankets out. Then crawled beneath them and welcomed me to join her. This was something. So much quicker than could have been anticipated. It was very exciting and I practically tripped while moving under the covers with her.

"Are you still nervous?" she asked.

"No. Very...happy to be with you.". After saying this there was a pause for a second and we soon embraced again in a kiss and started removing our clothing. The body heat was intense and I thought we would burn up before we positioned ourselves in complete bodily contact. This had excited my breathing, causing tremors in my shoulders. Her neck was smooth, so very smooth. It was drawing me to her more, as her hair covered both our faces momentarily. The smell of her skin with the perfume was fresh, clean, and caused me to rub my nose and lips over her neck and shoulders. Her breath deepened as I did this. We exhausted ourselves on the sofa in this frenzy for a number of hours. I felt like an actor in a love scene in the movies. It was almost midnight when our lovemaking had ended. We held each other for a while after.

"I don't want to ask you to leave, but to keep things on good terms with the landlord and your mother and father, maybe it's best we say goodnight. You should probably leave..""

Moving the Tassels

My thoughts were addled, as my answer was "Okay." There were some embarrassed motions and moments of putting my clothes on and restricting my glances toward Charlotte. She covered up and walked quickly to the bathroom. A bit of straightening my appearance a little more in the dark then a thought about all the jokes and stories guys tell about sexual union with a woman. There was now a smell of perfume she wore that transferred to my body. Most of it washed off after washing in the bathroom after she finished. It was a small bathroom, having an appearance of girly stuff, and with imitation flowers and pictures that had the same idea. My thoughts kept moving to this extraordinary sexual experience. Wow, oh wow.

"How are you going home?" I asked after regaining my composure some.

"I'm taking the bus."

"Do you have a ride to the bus station?"

"I'm working a morning shift and my boss is dropping me off. It's all arranged."

"I see."

"I'm glad you came by tonight, Wes. It was nice not to be alone today...all day.""

"Thanks for having me here, I replied and watched her pull her hair back and place a clip on it in ponytail fashion. Her hair was so pretty it mattered little of the changes. Every way it was presented was becoming.

In a short time I was at the apartment door, and Charlotte kissed me quickly on the lips and backed away. "Thank you again for coming by," her words softly came, just prolonged and understanding. She was a pretty lady, but there was this sensing that she was very lonely. A loneliness people feel when they have no family around. It wasn't said to her at this time, but it may be mentioned to her sometime. This is the place where I was born and have a number of friends, and many times there comes a very lonely feeling. Sometimes it brings me to the point where sitting down and crying could be of some sort of relief.. As for Charlotte, I liked her and hope she'll be okay.

The walk down the steps was far different from the earlier walk up the steps. There was that car of mine holding a position on the street. Kind of like a trusting dog. Maybe more like a cowboy's horse. Waiting to be put back to use providing the necessary transportation. The drive home was kind of automatic. There was little regard of what roads were being taken. There were many thoughts of my first sexual experience with Edna. It was much different. And this night with Charlotte. It was so pleasing with her.

Upon arriving home there was a porchlight on. With cat burglar silence the door was opened without a squeak. Then kind of a tiptoe to my bedroom and under the covers. The thought of Charlotte came to me quite a bit. She was so warm. A hint of her perfume seemed to be in my room. Looking around for her shadow in the dark was a brief and ridiculous action, but it was done and with a deep exhale, my eyes closed for their rest.

At 6:30 in the morning my mother woke me up. "You had better have some breakfast before you go to work."

Work! Good God, I forgot I had to work a full day today. There was a pair of khaki pants to wear, just like my coworker Yance, and a clean dark blue shirt. Then a push of my hair to the side with my hand. On to the breakfast table where sausage, eggs and biscuits were sitting on the kitchen table; Mom had everything ready. It was finished off in minutes and Mom may have enjoyed watching me eating this so fast.

"You could eat slower and maybe enjoy it, Wes."

"It's great, Mom. Thanks."

"How about some more biscuits?"

"Maybe two more, with some jelly," I answered, and the thought of Charlotte speaking of parents that cared for me was pondered on. Breakfast was over, and soon there would be eight hours of work. We were busier than I expected. Yance told me we would be. People were buying ham and turkey like it was going to be a final meal. With so much to do, the hour reached four without my realizing it. Yance let me know it was time to punch out for the day.

"It might be a good idea to shave before you come to work," he said bluntly. Taking my fingers to my face and stroking the whiskers, it became obvious. It was not a heavy beard like some guys could grow. It was there though.

Christmas Eve was here and a morning shift was to be worked. This was a busy time just as yesterday. No matter. A four-hour shift could be done without thinking about it. Customers were building a small line near the back where the meat department was. I was taking it all in. There was much to do, but it was fun seeing people come in the store for orders that had been placed or the last minute groceries. It was Christmasy. We had Christmas music playing and those spicy aromas were drifting around; this stuff was popular at this time of year. There was a thought of Rebecca moving up an aisle, but it was not to be. She would not be here today; not until the 26th.

The shift ended, and for that matter the store was closing at noon so all was going good. The drive home felt empty. There wasn't a girl to be with. My family would celebrate, but no girlfriend nearby. I would just have to put on an act.

We had our home decorated modestly. There was our tree that showed through the front room window. It had some presents already spread under the bottom branches. Mom and Dad put a foil cover on the front door. It was a medium blue with white letters that vertically spelled out NOEL. It was the finishing touch. Dad always added something around Christmas as a last decoration piece. Who knows why? It could have been Mom that urged him to do this.

At about six o'clock, we had our Christmas Eve dinner. We talked about the things that were in reference to family. Mom didn't want to discuss social issues. There was some special on television that entertained us for a while. Tomorrow my aunt and uncle were coming by for part of the day. The Tylers that lived across the street might stop by for a drink of wine. They often exchanged gifts with Mom and Dad. They were good neighbors and good friends of my parents.

Len called Kate at 9:30 and she had the phone tied up for a while. She seemed happier than I ever saw her. That was good for Kate. There was a loneliness of Christmas that had to be fought off. There was not a girl here for me, and the one most recently in contact with me would cause a problem if she were brought here. She was sensible. She probably wouldn't come here anyway.

TV had some shows on most of the night that were all right but the yawning led to a need for sleep around eleven o'clock. Besides, there wasn't anything to wait up for so it seemed the thing to do.

At eight a.m. Mom and Dad were having their coffee and were partially ready to go to church. Kate was getting dressed too. And it was time for me rise out of bed and get ready. There was quite a bit of time and a second thought was why hurry to get dressed to go to church with Mom and Dad and my sister? It was kind of hokey. Before church we opened up our presents. New clothes from the folks, and Kate gave me a cologne and aftershave that were receiving a lot of air time on the television commercials.

Well, church went okay, although it was long and drawn out, and the day was going to be a bore for sure. My Uncle John and his wife Enid were coming by around noon and would stay through the evening meal. Uncle John was one of Mother's other brothers that thought he had a handle on everything in the world. He acted superior to those around him and could only be tolerated for a short while. He would be bragging about how his kids are doing. My gifted cousins that never did anything wrong. Straight A students. The eyes of my relatives would most likely move toward me after this mentioning of grades. Yep, that was me. The unproductive student. The one that didn't try. It would not be said aloud but they would be thinking this. They were always asking how I was doing in school, what subjects was I taking... anything that could be asked that would make me feel like a snail. Then they might lay part of the blame on my parents. If this happens something could be said that could spoil the whole day. My parents try to get me to do better. They can't be held responsible for my lack of academic drive. A question came to me. If those kids are so perfect, how come they aren't coming along with Uncle John and Aunt Enid? It was no matter.. Who would want to be around them anyway?

It was about noon and Mom was putting the final touches on our home looking as she wanted it to for guests. A rumbling sound from outside was noticed. I walked to the front window to look outside. It was Bart Fellows and getting out of the passenger side was Dickey Brink. Now what were these two up to? Is Dickey having more holiday problems? Maybe his home life is in shambles again and Bart figured he'd bring him by. Outside it was windy and the sun would break through a little. My jacket would likely be enough for walking out and seeing what was going on.

"Wes. I have something I think you need to know about," his words came sincerely with a slight stutter.

"Sure. What's so important?"

"It's Arlene. Did you hear about her?"

"Arlene! What about Arlene?" An unsteady tremor came over me for a second or two.

"She went to church last night with some..." Dickey stuttered more and began to fight back tears before finishing what he was trying to say.

"What? What?" I cried out.

"Arlene. She was killed in a car wreck last night."

"Killed! That can't be," I said, almost stunned into what might have been a bad dream.

"She was; she and some guy were in an accident and both were killed! The car crash killed them both! I wouldn't tell you this if it weren't true.'"

"That's what happened," Bart said, backing up Dickey's statement with a little more calm.

"They ran off a cliff where Coleridge Pike is at. It's on the news, Wes."

"I can't... well, I... Arlene! My God! My God!"

"I know man. It don't seem to be real. Arlene was like... well, like someone?" Bart added incompletely then looked skyward and to his right.

The shock was making me cold. My attention to what Bart and Dickey were saying was lost in the visions I was placing in my head. These were of Arlene in her most beautiful appearance. It was as if she were right before me. Perfect composure. Laughing off anything that might come across as negative. The nice clothes she always wore. Her hair fixed always in place and she was always nice to me. More than any other girl she was the one that always spoke. She would sometimes tease me about something. She did her best to make her parents proud. She did everything right. Her face appeared again, and there were clouds behind her. A blue sky that made me shiver and shake, and then Dickey said something else to Bart.

"Wes, I have to go. We both are leaving."

"Sorry to break this to you, Wes," Bart added dejectedly. "Dickey has told me how much she meant to you. Both of us decided we would tell you in person.. So sorry man!"

"Yeah, just unbelievable," I mumbled and still looked away, thinking she might reappear and be real. All this stuff was not real. Bart and Dickey were talking low as they got in the car. Bart started the motor, and the rumble from its power and the pipes he had on the machine were soon moving down the road.

With a look toward the car the sense of unreality came again. Were they really here? The car was leaving my sight. It seemed like Arlene was with them and was leaving me forever. There came an urge to cry out, but it would just cause some kind of scene. While standing outside for those few minutes there came the thought of going by her house. I walked into our living room and called out to my mother.

"I have to take off for a short time."? A nervous shiver was felt.

It could not be controlled, and held this way for a few minutes.

"Where are you going? Aunt Enid and Uncle John will be here soon!"

"I know, Mom. Please. There is something that needs to be done. It won't be too long."

Mom had made her way in the living room and was looking at me. She attempted looking into my eyes. They would reveal too much. She did sense something was wrong.

"Be careful, Son. Okay?"

"Sure, Mom. I'll be okay, and back before supper for sure." My car sat in the driveway and was now like a dear friend. Ready to help out in a trusting way. At first there was the wanting to drive to Coleridge Pike. It dawned on me that, that would be no good. The car was probably a mess and the site roped off. What good would it do to see the wreck anyway? There was something though. It was the remaining hope that Arlene might have walked away and would be standing there looking at what happened. Dickey wouldn't lie to me about this though. He said it was on the news. Maybe driving over to Arlene's house is the thing to do. I could help her family out. No, I couldn't.

Maybe it would help to call someone? Arlene has many, many friends. They would know. Somebody she was good friends with would have the confirming story. They could let me know if something really happened. The thought of calling Regina Westerfield was probably the best thing to do. She is a good friend of Arlene's.

It couldn't be explained but I drove my car back toward the high school. There was a pay telephone on the corner not far from the school. The directory was opened and searched through as my eyes were getting teary, but I found a Westerfield name. It was only a guess that it was Regina's home number. Tears began rolling down my face and were blurring the number even more. I wiped them away and sniffed my nose to clear my nostrils. There was a need to find some composure and be like Bart. A need to handle myself as Bart would.

With the phone number put to memory, I dialed the phone. A man answered and called Regina to the phone. She began to speak and her voice trembled when saying hello. She told me about the car wreck much as Dickey and Bart had. Whatever else was said after that was not registering. Back to my car, my refuge for now, and slowly driving and continuing to wipe away tears, with the thoughts of what life would have been with Arlene. In a couple of years she might have been convinced to consider me to be a good guy. A guy she might consider marrying. Lord, she had all the qualities. "Everything!" I heard myself cry out. My tears came without control, affecting my eyesight as the car was pulled to the side of the road.

Moving the Tassels

There is a park near the high school I was near, and my decision was to turn the engine off for a while. The school looked so quiet with Christmas vacation. Many of the students were out of town for the holidays, and some had part time jobs in stores to earn extra money. Stepping outside of the car, there was this something that was so bleak. An enormous sense of loss. Nothing would ever be the same with Arlene gone. Damn, tears rolled down my face continuously. It mattered not if someone saw me like this. My nose was running and tears continued. My watch read a few minutes before 4:00 p.m. It was best to go home. If Uncle John made the wrong remark to me, he could receive a punch in the nose. He had it coming anyway. Mom and Dad would have a fit though. This would be too disappointing to them. I would still like to punch him. Maybe just punch somebody, anybody!

My car was started and put in gear, and I circled the block a couple of times before going home. God, why did you let Arlene die?

She was a good girl. A good human being. The typical questioning of faith. That was something in itself. It's hard to know one's own faith. Many go to church and are taught things from the Bible but don't actually know the faith. And who does one really know to ask? My sister Kate, maybe. Bart or even Greg if he were here. George is smart too. He acts religious. He would probably get all scientific about it. So unusual and not a good mix..., science and religion. Here was that feeling of being alone. Maybe the feeling Charlotte gets. Charlotte would think highly of Arlene. Good God! Alone and mixed up. Especially mixed up over Arlene no longer alive. The religious beliefs didn't make sense. People die all the time. Sure, but someone like her. Oh, God!

The next few days were somewhat of a blur. The year was coming to an end and Christmas was one that supposedly would never be forgotten. Arlene had been buried, and I couldn't bring myself to go to the funeral home or burial. Concentrating at work was an effort that was often difficult. Rebecca had returned to work, and she spoke to me about Arlene. She vaguely knew her. She probably knew of her more than knowing her as a friend or acquaintance. She was somewhat comforting though. She spoke of her as if she might have known her well. She told me she always thought I held a special place in my heart for her. She said I should keep good memories of her. This remark had me walk away without comment when it was said.

On New Year's Eve there was a party at my friend Jimmy's parents' home. There were about ten of us there, and every so often some of us would sneak out of the house and have a swig of whiskey. My head felt like it was swimming before midnight, and when the New Year had arrived, I kissed Sally, the young girl from California. There was an attempt to kiss her passionately but she was not doing so the same. To my dismay some of the other guys kissed her. Minutes later it seemed it was no big deal.

I went back outside and turned a bottle up, drinking more than could actually be dealt with and was nearly the cause of throwing up. Then it was back to inside and carrying on for a few minutes before passing out on the sofa. Jimmy's parents must have known we had been drinking, but they both were more than a little drunk, and everyone was okay so they just allowed us to enjoy seeing the New Year in.

Waking in the morning, the feeling was horrible. Jimmy's mother had some breakfast fixed and asked everyone that had stayed over to have something to eat. It was about the last thing that was wanted, but it was a good idea to get something on my stomach before going home an hour or so later. My Dad knew what had happened. He questioned me about a couple of things. He even considered having me rotate the tires on his car but took second thoughts about it and lectured me about the foolishness of drinking too much. It would have been better to have taken a beating than listen to him talk about this, but he did understand I might have had a bad ending to the year. He probably said something to Mom too. They knew when to come down as strict parents and when to temper it with understanding.

The year was now in the past. The last week of 1968 had been really tough.

//////

CHAPTER VII

School had resumed... a new year in progress. It sometimes felt as if everyone was staring at me. There shouldn't be a reason to feel this way but it might be natural when things have not gone very well. It seemed as though Arlene was haunting my thoughts. There was a likeness of her in my mind. Sometimes words would come out, talking to myself as though talking to her. Sometimes other people would find me doing this. Often they would laugh it off, or put some distance between themselves and me.

A class period had rolled around at school, and it was the boring English IV. This was attended impassively as most classes. The grades were so-so in English. It's what often happens when doing just enough to get by. Our teacher was an all right guy. His name was Ulysses Short. The last name was very misleading. He was six feet four inches tall and had been a college basketball player. His talent at the game was not enough to go beyond college, but he was an assistant coach for our basketball team, and he got along well with most of the students, especially the athletes. This particular day he brought something to the attention of the class.

"The month of January has opened a new year to us. It has closed the door behind us on a year that will be studied in the history books. This month, this year, the remainder of the decade will bring about many changes to this class and the entire class of seniors that will graduate," he related as he paced across the floor, first to one side of the room, then to the other. His voice was strong. It projected out as that of a stage actor. "Janus was a god from mythology that was known to keep a vigilance on doors. He is often shown to be two-faced. Putting the past behind us and looking to the future. Or closing one door and opening another. This month is named in honor of him. We should return the honor in making the future exciting. At the very least worthwhile."

Looking around the classroom, some of the students were drawing in the words Mr. Short just delivered. Many others were yawning and displaying the boredom that classes often have. This was different. I liked what he told us. There was no plan to excel in school the remainder of the year, but this piece of information from mythology helped for the moment. What Mr. Short had just told us about Janus could be useful in some way; it seemed interesting. The mention of one of the old gods made the English class a little less dull.

Later, the sixth period bell rang, bringing class time to an end. I met up with Dickey Brink and he looked depressed. My English class surprisingly had me feeling a little better for the first time in nearly two weeks, and Dickey looked like he had lost all his money in a poker game.

"Why the long face, Dickey?"

"Ah, Mom and Dad are at it again. If they could only act like they care for each other even if they don't"

"Yeah, I'm sure that's tough to deal with. I don't know what to tell you!"

"Nothing is really expected. I just thought I would say something about it to somebody. I might have to smack the old man in the head again. You know I'm pretty good at that," he said and smiled slightly.

"You have a mean swat Dickey. Maybe you can put that talent to use and try out for the baseball team this year. If somebody asks me about your handling a ball bat, I'll testify that you have a swing like no other. If you're coming after me with a skillet, I'm making tracks," I joked, trying to make light of his situation.

"Hey, thanks for listening. I'll get back with you later."

That's got to be hard to deal with. My parents aren't perfect. My dad sometimes acts as if he would rather not be bothered by me, and Mom can treat me like an infant at times. It's often frustrating how they can act, but they do care about my sister and me, and I have never seen them in a fight. The have had disagreements, arguments and such, but it doesn't last long, and they don't throw things or take swings at each other. Our home is probably peaceful in comparison to many others.

The Saturday that followed took such a long time to arrive. The first week of school had really dragged on. Saturday night was time off from work and here was the desire again to be with a girl. No date and no prospects. Most of my friends were out with their steadies and here I was, as was so often the case, by myself and without a girlfriend. One of the real shockers that Bart mentioned was Dickey Brink now had a girlfriend. The most unlikely of my friends to date a girl on a regular basis: Dickey Brink. He had been seeing some girl off and on, and now was going with this girl! What's the world coming to? Just a few days ago he didn't even mention this.

With girls on the mind, the notion to go to Charlotte's apartment came to me. Going to her apartment was probably not a smart choice of things to do, but doing things impromptu was not completely new to me. The restaurant she works at was much closer, but there was this feeling she would be home. Driving near the apartment there was a light spotted that must have been from the kitchen area. It didn't look as if her roommate's car was around, so possibly Charlotte would be there alone. I parked my car and came to the steps leading to the apartment. The steps were taken two at a time, moving quickly to the landing and knocking on the door. The night air was crisp and caused me to shiver some. The thought about going inside and getting warm was comforting. It would be nice to warm up with Charlotte.

There was no answer so a knock again, only this time a little harder. The window had curtains that were gapped where peeking through was possible and no one looked to be home. It was little trouble to wait a couple of minutes, but the apartment was empty. Looking again and still the same. Nosing around was not such a good idea. Someone could mistake me for a "peeping Tom" and that could bring on all kinds of trouble.

There was a morbid feeling while walking down the steps and these were checked for balance with my hand on the metal handrail. It felt so cold. A shiver came over me again. Then the thought of being all alone fell on me while walking back to my car. This was really distressing. It stinks! These weekends like this tore at me. Weekends are supposed to be fun. Arlene has died; there are no girls that are showing an interest toward me, and Charlotte isn't home. Well, she's probably at work just like she usually is on weekends.

Damn, what was I thinking? Just drive up to the restaurant and see if she's there. That's simple.

Arriving at the restaurant, most of the parking spots were taken and it was quite obvious they were busier than usual. There was a parking place that had just opened up and my car eased in between the lines. Charlotte was visible through the windows of the restaurant. The dark hair partially pinned up, and the way she moved confirmed this. Maybe, just maybe she can spend some time with me. The hours she worked could have some bearing on this. There was a need on my part to be near someone. For now, if she could talk to me for five minutes after she gets off work it would be a little comforting. It was no surprise of her being at work. Waitresses work on weekends. Damn, I knew that. Anyway, seeing her made me feel better right away.

Inside there was only one stool available at the end of the counter. There was some guy that could have been 30 or 35 sitting by the available stool. He was solidly built and needed a shave. Sitting next to him was not my first choice but he made a gesture in a friendly way. I did the same, then looked for my favorite waitress, expecting her to stop by. It took a couple of minutes. She moved from one booth to another and then came to the counter.

"Hi, Wes. How are you tonight?" she asked in her usual nice way. "Doing okay. How are you?"

"Very busy. Can I get you something?" she asked as she seemed hurried with many customers to wait on.

"Coffee, and maybe a fish sandwich."

"I'll get your order in right away."

Something was not quite the same. She was being nice, and not avoiding me, but something was different. Her smile. It was not like before. This was a little bothersome. While sitting there fretting over something with uncertainty she placed a cup of coffee before me. "I have the rest of your order to you as soon as I can," her sweet voice said.

"Okay, thank you."

"Say, do you know the pretty lady?" the stranger next to me asked.

"I've known her for a while. She's kind of a friend."

"Well," he paused and gave me a look that was sort of disrespectful. "She must like 'em young,"

There was this urge to say something but the right comeback was not available. This guy was not too threatening. He acted like an all right type when first sitting down, but that was a smartass remark. It's best just to let this comment go. Five guys came through the restaurant doors at that moment. They were near my age and looked like they were wanting to start some trouble. A fight with a group was the last thing to be involved in tonight. The guy sitting next to me was less of a concern than these five that had just walked in. He lit a cigarette and blew the smoke up toward the ceiling. He looked their way again, studying their behavior. Trouble could start with them as with any bunch when more than a split second glance in their direction was considered a threat.

There was no one recognized. One of them did call out to another waitress. The stranger next to me looked at them with the same measure of disgust that he had showed me after my speaking to Charlotte.

"Hey, Miss Waitress," one of the guys called out slowly and in a smartass tone, "is there a phone around here I can use?"

"There's a phone booth just across the road," she informed him and she pointed toward it. Without saying anything back to her he mumbled something to his friends and two of them raised their voices to draw some attention as they all walked out. While watching them leave Charlotte walked up with the rest of my order.

"Here you are. Anything else?"

"Uh, just wanted to stop by...see how you're doing."

"Busy," she paused a second or two. "Wes, I probably need to tell you something. I have a break in a half hour. Will you be here?"

"Yeah, For sure,"

"I'll talk to you then," and she walked back toward the kitchen after saying this. She just moved so natural. A nice walk without intentionally wiggling her hips. Her hips just moved correctly, and were slightly hypnotic.

"Hey, the lady does have a thing for you, huh?" the guy next to me said, with just the slightest amount of respect that was picked up on.

"Like I said, we're friends,'"

"That's good,'" he acknowledged and moved his head up and down with his thoughts kind of holding in place.

My mind was coming up with what could be problems. It was moving here and there about what she had to say. Maybe she's pregnant! Oh, God, I hope not. Nah, that couldn't be. Maybe she's finishing her beautician school. Maybe she's going back home. Damn, why did she say something about having to tell me something. The sandwich was in hand and being eaten but hardly enjoyed. There was a concern. It was about what Charlotte was going to tell me. My sandwich had been finished automatically with no enjoyment at all.

She came back around and put more coffee in the cup. She smiled and kind of turned on her heel then checked on others that were seated. There was this passing of time, waiting and looking over the other people that were near and eating what had been ordered or waiting in one way or other. Most everyone was with someone else. This was miserable. It didn't make sense. Why was I so alone? Why wasn't there a girl? There was a want, maybe a need to have a girl to be with. Be around. Laugh with. A strong need to find a steady girlfriend. Then was the thought of Arlene and nearly breaking down and crying hovered. With a change of thoughts there came a control to my composure. Guys aren't supposed to cry, especially in a place like this, sitting here! Hell! Crying was out of the question, especially since this oaf was sitting beside me.

"Wes. I heard my name spoken."

"Yeah!"

"I have a few minutes. Can we step outside?"

"Sure.'" Stopping by the cash register and paying my bill was a must. One time last year I walked out of a place by mistake and the restaurant manager caught me by the arm and made a big scene about it. One time of that is plenty. We hurried outside, not wanting to lose the time of Charlotte's break. It was apparent she had something to say, and an uneasiness was running through me.

"My trip back home had me getting back with my boyfriend," Charlotte related. "We talked things over and decided to renew our relationship. I'm sorry to tell you this but knew that I should. You've been very sweet, and I thought you should know."

That's the kiss off. It must be something like that. There was a few seconds of relief. It wasn't her saying she was in a family way. There were no comments or anything at first, and just a scuff of my shoe against the pavement. Looking up to meet those dark eyes would be very hard. Then an uncontrollable movement of some sort would wrinkle my face. With a deep inhale and then exhaling my words came, "Well, if that's how it is to be then maybe I should move on. Bye, Charlotte." As I was about to walk away, my hand was grabbed by hers and I turned back to face her.

"Thanks for being a friend when a friend was needed, Wes," she spoke in that voice I had learned to listen for when she was near.

"That's all right. I might stop in and check on you," came my response. It was a line a movie actor might voice after a disappointment, yet handling it well. It even felt good saying this, but only for a little while.

"Stop by here. You're one of my favorite customers."

There was the turn and walk off that was so very hard to do. The desire to turn around and go back was all over me but fought off, and the walk across the blacktop to my car was difficult too.

When in my car this hopelessness weighed on me and there I sat for a couple of minutes before starting the car up. What was there to do? Nowhere to go. Nobody to see. Once again that being alone, and a feeling of wanting to cry. This world was unfair. Unfair to me. Then the words that were said some time back about feeling sorry for one's self touched on my thoughts.

After a couple of minutes, it was time to drive off and head toward the site where Arlene was killed. Before getting there I turned the car around and drove closer to my home, but made a quick stop by the pool hall. It was open and had a few cars parked outside of it. A couple of older guys were sitting around on stools and smoking their cigarettes. They blew smoke toward the lights and added to the haze that the pool hall continued to always hold. The manager asked if I needed something and I paid to shoot at a rack of 15. It was not anything pretty. The balls usually dropped in the pocket by slop. A term used for the unskilled in pool.

"Shoot a game for four bits?" one of the older guys asked.

"Nah. I'm not very good and probably leaving here after I finish this.""

"That might be all night," the other man said in an almost inaudible voice. This was heard though. I almost reacted to it but suddenly got tickled about what he said. He was close to being right. This took longer than most players but eventually all the balls were in the pockets and the cue stick was placed back in a holder and I walked out. Back in the car and starting it up, my mood stayed low and the drive down the road was a place to nowhere in particular. After some time there was the realization of driving toward the other side of town. The last time out this way was when a couple of us guys went in this direction after a football game. Nothing of real interest and nobody known. Just a waste of time. Damn, is the rest of my life just dawdling the hours away?

Moving the Tassels

My friend Jimmy often has people stopping by his house at all hours of the night. Especially on weekends. My decision was to stop by his house and see if any one was around. It didn't take too long before arriving there and noticing Mick's car was parked in his driveway. Well, it had to be Mick's interest in Kathleen. Maybe he was trying to get back together with her. She's a pretty girl. No need to blame him on that account, but that temper is just too much. The door to the house needs painting and maybe a touch of other maintenance. The doorbell had never worked. In an automatic move my knuckles were knocking on the door and before anytime seemed to elapse, Jimmy's mom opened it.

"Come on in, Wes. Where have you been lately?" she asked, showing her always friendly manner and opening the door wide for me to walk in.

"Just driving around here and there. I didn't have to work tonight and was hoping to locate some of the others."

"Hey there! Wes.".

"Mick. How's it going? I saw your car outside. What have you been up to?"

"About the same as you. Trying to find something to do. Watching television." Jimmy's younger brother was watching television and Mick was looking in on the same program.

"Anybody else around?" I asked, wanting to do something besides watch TV.

"Everyone's out enjoying their weekend,""

"Suppose so."

"You want to drive around some?"

"Why not," I answered. "There's not much of any place to go, but we'll go there anyway."

"You boys are welcome here if you want to come back." We both thanked her for her kind invitation. Leaving a car at Jimmy's house was more the rule than the exception.

"Let's take my car," he said, as we were walking toward them. Mick's car was fairly new and he probably figured if we were to meet up with anyone it would be best to be in a newer car that had good paint and a bit more appeal. No reason to contest his choice. We drove by a bowling alley. It sometimes had stragglers such as us stopping by. There were only a few people in there. Toward the far end were two couples using a lane. They were laughing, cutting up and seemed to be having quite a good time. We walked almost to where they were.

Laughs were continuing and one of the girls picked up her bowling ball, took an awkward stance, then stepped toward the pins. She brought the ball back high behind her, and the ball went flying in the opposite direction from where it was supposed to go. A loud boom on the back part of the lane was sounded. It rolled off the raised part of the lane and made another thumping sound. It struck me as really funny.

"You can't do that!" the other girl cried out and began laughing aloud. The two guys they were with started laughing too. The girl that dropped the ball had brought her hands up to cover her mouth and nose, almost prayer like and joined her friends in a cheerful laugh.

"She's a real charmer, isn't she?" Mick commented.

"It's kind of silly, but they're having fun,'" I responded. They were having fun. Exactly what I would like to be doing.

"Hey, Mick, I meant to ask you. Are you trying to get back with Kathleen?" He gave a look that was showing mixed emotions.

"I don't know if I want to or not. When we were dating she would get set off over nothing. I didn't know if I was doing things right or wrong. Tonight, I just thought to stop by and see if she was home. Maybe we would ride around. Maybe get a hamburger or something like that. She was out with some of her friends.

There wasn't a place I could think of to go, so the television at her parents' house was holding my attention."

"It's tough when you don't know what sets a girl off. You think you're doing things right then all of a sudden you might catch a smack on the face," I spoke as if an authority on ambivalence.

"Kathleen sure is a different kind of chick. I just didn't know with her. But she has a way about her too," he said with a thoughtful laugh. The lady that was in the bowling alley bar waiting on customers walked out toward the lanes. She picked up some paper plates that had been discarded, and a couple of beer bottles. She threw the plates in a garbage can and set the bottles on a flat part of a Dutch door that separated the bar from the bowling lanes. She looked our way and made eye contact with Mick. He gave the impression that he was making a play for her. "How are you fellows doin'?" she asked in kind of a Southern flirtatious way as she continued to look at Mick.

"Never better, Ma'am. And you?"

"Doin' okay for myself," she answered Mick. She then threw her shoulders back some to let her figure be noticed. She pulled her stomach in slightly to bring more notice to the rest of her figure.

"Now, she has a nice structure doesn't she, Wes?"

"She's probably thirty Mick. She's probably struggling to hold her belly in for so long of a time,"

"Probably. And probably knows how to make a guy happy. You know, if I had her alone, I would play some soft, slow music and drink some cherry vodka, and keep her under the covers, pulsating until morning."

"You sure have a different way of saying what's on your mind. I don't know about cherry vodka, and the music... I like rock and roll."

"Wes, old man. I'm going to tell you something. Soft, easy music is the thing to play for being in bed with a girl. The rock and roll will have you romping so fast you wouldn't know how to enjoy it. Easy music. Even classical music is the way to go." Mick expressed, and nodded his head with the confidence of an expert.

Mick had been out with a bunch of girls, most of them not known to me. He might have thought himself a ladies' man. Kathleen was the only girl he dated that I did know. So who can say? He might be a so-called ladies man. He might be right about the music too.

We finished watching the two couples bowling. The laughs had continued as the one girl showed a technique that was hardly professional. She then took a bite of a candy bar she had partially covered with the wrapper.

Mick watched her and spoke so he would not be heard by others, "Candy may be sweet, but sex won't rot your teeth."

"Never heard that before," I rejoined.

The ball often found the gutter for the girl, but she didn't seem to care. They were out having a good time. I would have gladly traded places with the guy she was with. Mick's insistence, had both of us going into the bar in the bowling alley. It was very dark inside and had stools and a mirrored wall that was partially blocked from different liquor bottles that lined across. The bartender was the only person in there besides us two.

"Draw yourself back and hold good posture," Mick whispered. We sat down toward the far end of the bar, and Mick ordered us glasses of draft beer. We were eyed suspiciously by the bartender, but he did not ask for ID. The beer had a peculiar taste, and I finished it, acting kind of adult but also somewhat uneasy.

We left the bar and the beer didn't appear to affect either of us. The temptation to drink some more was considered but we decided otherwise. What a lousy Saturday night.

Monday, after the school day was over and those that rode with me had been dropped off, the drive home went faster than usual, and the idea of going to work had an unusual appeal. At home there was a change of clothes for work, and then a snooping in the refrigerator for some sort of snack. Most of my homework was completed in study hall and just a few minutes were needed to go over some things we covered in one of the classes. We had tests at the end of the month, and my grades had started improving. Janus might be having some influence. The doors may be closing on me before getting the chance to make my mark in the world... maybe on the world, whatever that might be.

It was off to work and punching out at eight o'clock. Then leaving the store and turning on the radio in the car as a song was aired that was an oldie. It might have been from the 1950's. This was so recognizable to me as the words were sung with such honesty. The words were never known to me nor the name of the song. It was the melody. It brought on some sort of sadness. I pulled my car in the driveway and went inside our home. Mom was sitting in the kitchen and looked sad.

"Hey, Mom. Why are you looking so blue?"

"Mr. Cray, the elderly gentleman you know, passed away, Wes. He died this afternoon. We found out about a half hour ago."

"Good God! He just..." my sentence wasn't finished. It was no surprise but it was still something you never want to hear. The people that were like my grandparents. They were just decent people. Upon hearing this there came a feeling of something that words could not express. My plan for any additional study would be on hold. I ate some dinner and went into the living room and watched something on television. It didn't matter what it was. The thought of that nice old man and now his widowed wife. How would she get along? They had been together for so long. Then came the thought of Arlene. She was killed in an accident and now a disease had taken the life of Mr. Cray.

When people die it confuses me. Grandparents die all the time. It is not so unexpected. Even great aunts and uncles. All of them are at that age. When a younger person dies it is so much different. Some young people lead one to think that they might live forever.

I went to bed about ten o'clock that night and perhaps in the last phase of my sleep had dreamt of working in Mr. Cray's yard. Arlene came by to give me an orange soda.

It was morning and I sat up in my bed. Darkness was still about and something kind of lingered. It was very strange. The dream I woke from was so real. Well, it was to me. Arlene was there, and she was typical Arlene. She looked just as she always did. Her hair in place and wearing tan pants and a checkered red and white blouse that had sleeves that came right to her elbows. She said something that could have been the word piety but maybe not. It was hard to read her lips and she said it so low.

"Do you understand?" she did make that clear. My words didn't come out soon enough to ask her to repeat what she said. But she smiled, and that was it, and it was nice. She was perfect.

I put my head back on my pillow, pushing my face into it as the ends came up by my ears. Then I turned over on my back and tried to retrieve the dream of Arlene. It was useless to try and go back to sleep. The shafts of light angling in my room crossed the face of the wind-up alarm clock. The hammer that struck the bells would be activating in about ten minutes. I pushed in on the stem part that shut off the alarm and sat on my bed for another minute.

"Damn! It's almost like a taste of orange soda in my mouth."

CHAPTER VIII

The first month of 1969 had come to a close, and February had arrived on the calendar. Arlene had been dead for about five weeks now, and thoughts of her came to my mind constantly. One might think this was obsession. Perhaps so. When meeting someone like her... well she was just one of those types of girls. What else can be said?

Life does go on. When a man hires you to work at his business, then you are expected to be there. This sometimes helped take my mind off of Arlene. Now to the thought of Rebecca; this too could also take my mind off Arlene for a while, and it was something that did have me thinking. Rebecca was going to be working for a newspaper a few nights a week. Her interest in journalism was allowing the opportunity for her to actually report there. She was nice to look at. So businesslike though. Keeping up with a young woman like her would require enormous effort. Maybe that boyfriend of hers can keep pace. That son of a bitch was still around, and it looked as if he was going to stay around. Who could blame him?

This idle thinking went on for a long while. The jobs around the store would vary. Staying busy helped in a number of ways. Thoughts would resurface while pushing a broom and cleaning one of the aisles. Dickey Brink had stopped in the store. It was just before work was done for the day. It was almost 4:00 p.m.

"What are your plans tonight?"

"Not sure. Probably go home and get something to eat. Then clean up and go out for a while. How about you?"

"Valery was wanting to see a movie. I thought you might get a date and double with us."

"I'll have to see," I told him. Telling him I couldn't find a date was not the thing to do. It was still hard to believe he was going with Valery Carlisle. She was a good-looking girl. She had a great figure too. Dickey didn't seem to be right for her. And here was me, Mr. Stag. What was it that no girl wanted to go out with me? At bat and striking out, and he, pinch hitter Brink is hitting home runs! I put the broom in a cubicle behind a checkout station, took off the apron and punched out on the clock located behind the cash register. Dickey followed along like a pet dog. Sometimes life is so hard to figure He was so uncool, so weird. He was just something different. He was a friend though, and was now a good friend. Even Bart, who was cool, thought he was an all-right type. What really got me was Valery. She finds something in him. Before my saying something about getting a date, he mentioned this:

"Valery might have a friend that would go along if you want me to ask her, or actually have Valery ask her."

"Give me a call at my house around six. I should be cleaned up by then. I'll see."

"Yeah. That'll be good. I'll call you," he said, while walking out the glass door and me following. He then turned and waved. He got in his dad's car and drove off. It was an Oldsmobile that was typical of a parent's car. A nice car, but not sporty enough. His old man was letting him drive it though. Thinking on this, my car wasn't sporty either. It was transportation. Using my dad's car was not something he was in favor of. He didn't even like my mother driving the car. If it means relying on getting from one place to another, and having to work out the wherewithal of getting there, then a reliable car that doesn't look so good beats a sports car that doesn't run. Some of my thoughts run high on good common sense.

After getting home, eating, and showering the phone rang. "I'll get it!" I called out.

"Hello.""

"Is this Wes?"

"It sure is. Is this Dickey?"

"This is Dickey Brink, the one and only. Have you given any thought to going to the movies with us?"

"That would probably be okay. Hey, what's with the goofy way of saying who you are?"

"Oh... nothing, just in a good mood tonight. Say, Valery's friend is actually her cousin who is in town. She'd like to go out with you. That is if you'd like to. If you haven't got another date. She's just here for the weekend."

"Yeah, Dickey, I said I'd go. What's she looks like?"

"She has blonde hair, brown eyes, and about as tall as Val. She's pretty in the face.""

"Okay, great. Where do we meet at?"

"We'll pick you up in my old man's car. Seven o'clock,"" I answered, and he had a way of saying it that was giving me an indication that he was coming around to being hip.

"Ok. I'll be looking for you."

Mom was picking up some dirty dishes and putting them in the kitchen sink. She was often moving through the house straightening up after Dad or me.. My sister Kate was also good at picking up things. She took after Mom in this respect. Dad would work and come home, watch television and expect to be waited on. No doubt he worked hard but he did little around here. He did things around the house only when necessary.. Normally it was Mom that kept order, and here she was again.

"Mom, I'm going out tonight. Dickey has some girl he wants me to take out."

"Who is she, Wes?" she asked with a mother's curiosity, as she put the last of the dishes in the sink.

"Dickey's girlfriend's cousin. I'm only doing it as a favor for him?" This was not exactly true. There was a desperation to just be around a girl. It wasn't the thing to say to my mother, nor to Dickey for self-esteem. It was nice being a big timer in some people's eyes.

"You don't know anything else about the girl?"

"Only that she's from out of town. She's blonde-haired and I'm taller than her."

"Well, you and your friends be safe. By the way, where are all of you kids going?"

"They are wanting to see a movie, and we'll probably stop and get something to eat after. I shouldn't be out too late." Then looking at Mom after giving her the lowdown there was something in me that felt this was misleading, but it wasn't. This bit of giving information to either of my parents about where or who I was seeing was kind of square. Nobody else does it. Sure, there should be concern, but I was nearly eighteen and would be getting my draft card soon. I wasn't the teenager that was speaking with a cracking voice like a kid beginning to go through puberty. Although it came to me suddenly that mom and dad might not have approved of my being with Charlotte. Her age and our experiencing each other was something Charlotte seemed to understand. She was on a closer level of understanding than most anyone. She also handled things better than my parents.

Sometimes my mind moves in directions that could never have been imagined. From a friend's girlfriend's cousin, to hero worship, to an older girl that works in a restaurant. It's no wonder my mom asks my whereabouts. She probably knows the confusion facing a high school kid. If I would sit down and talk to her, she'd probably tell me to find direction in my life. My dad would hint at the same thing. Maybe there should be dialogue. We should talk more. If I started really opening up, they would probably suggest psychological help. Maybe. Maybe not. It's been tough talking to some of the guys. Bart, Greg, Mick, and others. The only person that could sometimes be of help was Mr. Cray. He was understanding. His wife was too. But then he would occasionally get philosophical and get away from the subject.

One day last summer we were talking after the work assigned to me, cutting and trimming their lawn, was complete. Sweat was pouring off me and after wiping my brow Mrs. Cray brought me some iced tea.

"The sun sometimes beats down on me. It would have been nice to have been born rich," I kidded with them as they enjoyed a breeze circling their home. A deep inhale added some poise and there was an appreciation of the same gust of air from this blue sky that had a grip on the heat.

"Most people that haven't learned to do things for themselves are often uncomfortable. Money is needed, but it should be earned. If things come to one too easily, then nothing is learned. There is always the question of how to deal with the unexpected. If too much is given and little is worked at, it can be quite a problem." Mr. Cray explained as he made his point with a little laugh.

"If they have the money, they can pay someone to do what they have to have done," my input came out as if I were knowledgeable in such matters.

"If there is no one available at the time, the money might not be so helpful. Self-reliance may be a much more valuable asset. It's comforting to learn to do things. Even handling a power mower."

This was a nice thing he said. It had nothing to do with girls, but it gave some confidence. The work felt good, and cutting the grass and the trim work was not so bad. It was enjoyable to listen to him because his down-to-earth mannerism made me feel better. That thought about preachers and Sunday mornings when some of them are so long-winded came to mind. I mentioned it to Bart, one day after coming out of the pool hall. "It sounds like he was possibly referring to existentialism," Bart noted.

"Yeah, maybe so," was my response, having no idea what he was talking about. A guy can pick up on things happening on the streets. The thinking is: You know everything necessary to get by. That was how I felt for a long time. What a dumbass I am. Mr. Cray knew so much, and Bart knew a lot too. Where does that leave me?

These thoughts were broken up by a honk of a horn. Dickey and his girlfriend and my date were outside waiting for me. I said goodbye to mom and dad, telling them I'd be out for a while. Mom and dad had been fairly liberal on my staying out. They told me 1:00 a.m. should be the time to be home, but if it was to be later than that, make sure to telephone them. Usually 1:00 a.m. was late enough.

Dickey was sitting in the driver's seat of his dad's car like some authoritative figure. He acted like an airline pilot. It was tempting enough to make a remark, but really no need to. Let him show off.

Moving the Tassels

"Hop on in, Wes. This is Sylvia, Valery's cousin. Of course you know Valery. Sylvia, this is Wes?" The introductions were given as such by Dickey.

"Hi, Sylvia," I said with a bit of shyness.

"So nice to meet you, Wes" she spoke and then giggled. Why she giggled was strange. It sure is uncomfortable to have someone giggle when first being introduced. She was kind of pretty, in fact very pretty. Her outfit looked a touch unusual. She was dressed like a cheerleader. Almost anyway. She was wearing a red sleeveless ensemble that reminded me of what cheerleaders might wear. There was a temptation to ask if she was going to a game to lead cheers after the movie, but I kept quiet instead. Her giggling expressed itself once again.

"We're going to see Romeo and Juliet. It's supposed to be a fantastic movie," Valery informed us with excitement in her voice.

"At my school, the entire senior class was taken to the theater to see this. It was all the rage," Sylvia exclaimed.

"Are you a senior?" curiosity had me ask.

"Not quite," she giggled again.

"What year are you?" I prodded.

"Sophomore. I could be a junior but my parents thought it best I started school at age six rather than five. My birthday is on December eighteenth. The week before Christmas! I'm a Sagittarius," she informed me. Her giggling continued to erupt every so often. This was something that was unsettling. Giggling like a girl six or seven years younger than she was. Why?

It was kind of embarrassing being out with a sophomore, but it wasn't a bad thing. A lot of guy's date sophomores. There are even some girls that are seniors that date sophomore boys. With seniors and sophomores aside, it was best to let Dickey be in control of driving us to the movies, and letting him be a big shot for his girlfriend. After all, he has had some bad times. And he was thoughtful enough to have me go out with Sylvia. Glancing over at her, it was apparent to me that she was a little prettier than my first look at her, and her looks improved as we drove along. At this point she could be a freshman for all I care.

We arrived at the theater and purchased our tickets. The line for seeing this movie was long, but everything and everyone moved fairly well. Sylvia would giggle about nothing in particular, and it started to annoy me. It was forgivable. She was cute enough to be forgiven for about anything.

A curious thought entered my thinking. Do attractive, pretty girls realize that they can pull nearly any stunt and get away with it? They more than likely know this. If it happens to be a beautiful, stunning woman... well, a woman such as this has her choice of whom she will let serve her. About a year ago our family attended a wedding and the bride looked very pretty, but she was upstaged by one lady that was her aunt. This lady couldn't help but look beautiful, and everyone looked admiringly at her. She was no doubt used to it. She probably knew she held power over most men. Many women such as her can be the sole female around powerful men and these women can be comfortable. They understand their power. Like the queen on a chessboard. The king can move in all directions but the queen can also, and extend beyond that of the king. She often checkmates the king.

The movie seemed long to me. I knew Shakespeare had penned this and it was considered a great piece of literature, but something different was expected. Dickey's girlfriend Valery had teared up over the movie. Not so unusual. And there was this young girl, my date, who giggled about the movie.

As the theatre let out, the four of us made it to the car and drove to a seafood restaurant. We went inside and were quickly seated. With numerous items to eat, every one of us ordered a fish sandwich, coleslaw and French fries. The restaurant was tastefully decorated with things that dealt with the sea or what might be shoreline articles. Fishing nets were attached in corners, and a huge clock that would chime in according to nautical protocol was mounted on a wall. Large fish that had been caught and handled by taxidermists were placed with care and judgment on what looked to be every wall of the restaurant.

We ate and had some laughs. We teased Valery a little for crying, but Dickey might have cried a little too. It might have been something he wouldn't want to be kidded about. Why do that? The night was going fairly well.

After eating I was driven home. There was another giggle from Sylvia, but I tried not to let it bother me any longer. She must do this all the time. It was about 12:30 when we reached my home and it was time to say goodnight to all. I looked at Sylvia and attempted to kiss her good night. She turned her head away and offered only her hand. "I don't kiss on the first date," the words quietly came from her and subsequently a slight giggle.

Okay, I said and took a calming breath. Then looked to see Valery and Dickey's reaction. They were kind of wooing and cooing and looking at each other's eyes. I grabbed Sylvia's hand and covered it with my other hand. "Goodnight again, everyone"

It was bothersome thinking about this while walking toward our front door and my hand squeezed tightly into a fist, then a pounding on the wood rail that bordered our front porch. There was the sound of the Oldsmobile accelerating away and the group that was just here was now down the road. Then it didn't seem as bad. Now going inside to give the lowdown on my date with Valery's cousin was most likely to come. These question-and-answer sessions were detestable. Why did they have to always ask? What did they think I was up to?

Going through, the living room was surprisingly quiet. No television, nothing but a medium watt bulb in a parlor lamp was on. I stopped suddenly to listen for anything being said, and there was not a word. So I went to the bathroom and washed my face, used the toilet and only wished it would flush without making much noise. While walking toward my bedroom, I heard Mom.

"Are you okay, Wes?"

"Fine, Mom," I answered in a low voice. "I'm going to bed now."

"Good night?" "Good night, Mom."

In my room I changed to my pajamas and then pulled the covers up to my chin. While lying there, the night was reviewed. Sylvia was a cute little gal. Why wouldn't she kiss me goodnight? She doesn't kiss on the first dates. That's a bunch of bull. That's what girls might have said in the movies in the 1940's or 1950's. Things are different today, girl! It should be explained to her. Damn! On the other hand, you can't force yourself upon a girl. It sure was awkward. She could have kissed me. Girls kiss guys on the first date all of the time. The Victorian age is long gone. A guy spends money on a girl, and he expects a goodnight kiss. It sort of gives a guy the idea of asking her out again.

The thoughts echoed again. With a turn on my side, the disappointing night gave way to a deep sleep. I awoke startled. It was a dream about Dickey and Valery being in a car wreck, along with Sylvia. I was not sure if this actually happened. I was in my bed, sitting up for a minute and having to decide what to do? Maybe call Dickey's house and see if he arrived home safely? Was Sylvia okay? Would it have made a difference if Sylvia had kissed me good night? Maybe goodbye! God, it is disturbing to have a dream like this. The best thing to do is call later this morning. Maybe just drive by Dickey's house to see if his Father's car was there.

Dickey and Valery, along with Sylvia, had gotten home safely. Dreams, or nightmares can sure cause an uneasiness to the person having the dream. It's a weird thing. Why do dreams like this happen?

For a while, the feeling was gloomy, taking it to heart that the last girl I had been out with would not even let me kiss her good night. It might have been about the giggling. Maybe Sylvia thought there was something funny-looking about me. Maybe there was. The notion never occurred of being that way, but there might be that part of narcissism owing to my appearance of being okay-at least average or even slightly beyond. Maybe it was me fooling myself. My looks could be a lot worse than what the mirror reveals. Dickey seemed to look funny to me. He always wore clothes that never fit quite right. He waddled along most of the time rather than having a nice smooth walk. He was not athletic at all, yet he had an uncanny balance. With these things that were apparent, it was likely that Valery was aware of this. She still liked him. A lot. She was pretty too. It's hard to understand. Maybe Sylvia was giggling at Dickey. No, she wasn't offering her hand to him. It was me, and a handshake instead of a kiss. It could be my breath. It is usually masked with some kind of peppermint or gum. I had not been told this, but maybe I'm funny looking. This is difficult to figure.

This moping around carried on for a few days when I met up with Bart at the pool hall. He was making a few dollars as he chalked his cue and studied the angles while adjusting the horn-rimmed glasses he would sometimes wear, making calculations on the table that usually proved to have him winning games. He sat down on a stool to let others play. All four tables were now occupied and a radio playing put out enough sound that we could talk and not be heard easily. "You look like a dog that has been dropped off and abandoned, Wes."

"That's about how I feel.."

"You should get out and enjoy yourself. You have a car. Ask a girl out and have some fun. Go somewhere and do something. Your car is doing okay, isn't it?"

"The car is fine. Just getting a girl to go out anymore seems to be a challenge. All the girls are taken it seems."

"Now your way off base there, my friend. There are a lot of girls that are waiting to be asked out."

"None that'll go out with me. It's got me feeling feckless. I'm not sure who to ask out."

"Have you got enough money to ask a girl out to the upcoming Valentine's dance?" Bart asked and showed a serious look as if it would be very expensive.

"Probably. I've been working steadily, and getting money for driving some of the guys back and forth, you know, the school thing."

"Great! My girl knows Regina Westerfield, and she doesn't have a date to go there. I was going to contact you about this, but didn't get around to it. You know Regina, don't you?"

"Sure, but I can't believe she doesn't have a date. She's gorgeous," I excitedly answered.

"Listen. Her boyfriend broke up with her. He is in the Air Force and is going out of the country.. He told her he didn't want to tie her down."

"Bart, I think I'll call her. Yeah! For sure, I'll see if she'll go."

"You look like a new man already. Give her a call. Get yourself ready to go out on the town, man. You'll be back to your old self."

"Thanks, Bart. Maybe that will be just the thing."

When she last spoke to me it was just after Arlene was killed in the car wreck. She was upset and so was I. There was no intent on going out with her then. One has to wonder.

Regina accepted my asking her to the dance. Arrangements were made, and the evening of the Valentine's dance we were sharing a table with Bart and his girl. Dickey and Valery, and Jimmy and Sally, the young girl whose family relocated from California.

The hall where the dance was held was decorated in white with red hearts in a number of places. There were white and pink balloons clustered together in the very center about twenty feet above the dance floor.. The music the band played was rather calm if comparing them to some of the bands that were performing around town nowadays. They were good, but played a lot of ballads and older songs, occasionally letting loose with a real rocker.

Regina was dressed so nice. She looked as if she were informed of the decorations because her outfit was also white with embroidery just off her shoulders and twists of the material festooning toward her neck. She moved like a dream. It was as though she had on ice skates and was gliding across a rink. Regina danced in a way that could almost hypnotize someone. When we slow danced she moved gracefully and the feel of her waist was trim and firm. It was hard to believe I was out with her. Here this night, with friends and everything. She was with me at this dance.

We sat at the table with the others, and everyone was laughing and talking about school, and graduating, and the things that each was planning in the upcoming months. One of the things Bart said was so funny that it caused Dickey to spray some of his punch out of his nose. Everyone laughed at that. And Valery squeezed him like a favorite pillow after this. It was just a great time.

When driving Regina home after the dance, I felt apprehensive. There was an attempt to make conversation, but it wasn't going well. Then my talk went to cars and then work. This wasn't what was intended at all. I pulled into the driveway of her home, and she moved toward me. She kissed me good night. My hand trembled some, only slightly from shock or whatever. We got out of the car and walked to her door. She gave me a quick kiss again, and I asked if we might go out another time.

"That would be nice," she said. "Tonight was so enjoyable."

"I'll call soon. Thanks."

"Good night," she said, smiling as she opened the door to her home.

This was a great night. I wanted to do handsprings to my car. There had never been this kind of feeling before. Never like this! With a jump up and click of the heels of my shoes, the car door was quickly opened as if by magic. This was wonderful. How great can life be? Starting my car, and listening to the engine was a great sound and it would be hard to convince me that my car wasn't running better too. This night was great.

"Damn! She kissed me!" I cried out in my car as I was driving down the road. "She kissed me! I kissed her back, but that girl… that woman, and I do mean woman…kissed me! It's so hard to believe!"

The drive home was giving me a little time to think. Why would any guy break up with this girl? He must be crazy. Is there something wrong with her? The driving continued. Now there was something so mixed up about the night and Regina, and how pretty she looked.

A girl that's a sophomore and doesn't live here wouldn't let me kiss her goodnight. Not even a quick little kiss on the lips. Then Regina. A girl that looks like Venus moved toward me and kissed me! Wow!

I started talking to myself aloud in my car. It was beginning to look like no girl would go out with me. Was my appearance troubling? Were my actions too immature or dull? Was I too cheap? It was difficult to be sure where the problem was. Self-consciousness was coming into play. Girls certainly talk about guys. Who they have gone out with. They probably say if the guy was a real loser to be out with. God knows what else they discuss. If the guy kisses like a slob or pig. Whatever! It was just disheartening not to be able to go out and enjoy being with some girl. Especially a pretty girl. It's nice to show off a girl you're with and let the other guys make comments over the girl you're with. Saying things such as how they would like to trade places, and all the rest of the remarks. I've made those remarks, too. A lot of talking to myself had been going on. If someone saw me doing this, they'd think I was off my rocker. What the hell! Did it matter?

As for Regina, she was something, my, oh my!

The drive home had taken longer than was expected. Driving a couple of miles out of the way by missing turns can do that. The speech from me to me was distracting too.

Regina and I had a date the following week. It was kind of a cheap date. We went with Jimmy and Sally. This was a party that Sally's brother Alan invited us to. He had met up with some people that had the same interests as him. One of them was a guy whose parents were out of town. He had the house to himself, along with his older brother. I didn't know them or even catch their names but the house was really big and in a nice neighborhood that was new to me also. When we went in there were seven, maybe eight people already there. None of them looked familiar. A few of them looked our way, nodded, or said hi. Most were interested in their chance to take a hit off the joint. They were burning incense in a brass holder and passing around joints in circle fashion.

"This is not what I was expecting," Regina commented.

"Let's just see who's who and where they're from," Jimmy suggested.

"There's Alan over there," Sally said and pointed as Alan was about to walk up the steps that led to the second floor of the house. "Alan! Over here," she called out. He turned, stepped down one step, then made his way over and grinned like a monkey..

"What's happening with the proletariat?" "Who lives here, Alan?" Sally asked.

"These are some real cool people I met. They're with it. You know. Things are so ragged out where we live."

One of the girls was passing a bottle of wine around. Everyone partaking would turn it up and take a big swig. I was curious and walked around some. Regina followed closely. She was definitely out of place with this group. Her clothes didn't fit in with what most of the other girls were wearing. When we walked by, no matter who we passed, she was given a scoffing look as eyes trailed our movements. Sally was in a more relaxed-looking skirt and top. Nice, but not too nice. She was not receiving the warmest of greetings either. Jimmy talked to a couple of people and seemed to be accepted more than the rest of us.

Alan said something again, and it sounded like some of the partygoers were either doing or about to do some LSD. This was getting very uncomfortable. Where it came from was anyone's guess.

I didn't know as much as Alan did about it. Alan talked like he knew everything about it; how easy it could be made in a lab, and often boasting about taking LSD all the time when he lived in California. At times he would mumble the words lysergic acid diethylamide. It must have made him feel important. After this he usually mentioned how backward it was here.

It was probably time to leave. My interest had me wanting to stay, but it was unnerving too. The idea of a house being raided would be a nightmare. We stayed about a half hour longer and opted for somewhere to eat.

"Is your brother always into these type parties?" Jimmy asked Sally.

"He was reckless when we lived in California. He keeps saying he's going back!"

"Has he ever gotten in trouble for using drugs?" I wanted to know.

"That's why we left Los Angeles."

"Hell, drugs can be anywhere. It doesn't have to be Los Angeles or New York. They're right here," Jimmy acknowledged as he shrugged his shoulders. All the while Regina remained quiet and looked away.

The remainder of the evening was not very good. Regina asked to be taken home and our relationship didn't continue as was hoped for. I tried calling her, and pleading my case, whatever it might be, but nothing was working. There had been a couple of dates with a simply beautiful girl, that I happened to like, and there was the thought she had liked me. Now she had the idea of me being involved with drugs. She wanted nothing more to do with me. The situation was back as it was before. The guy without a girl. It was not good either.. And as usual many times there were thoughts about Arlene. She and Regina were good friends. Regina was every bit as pretty as Arlene. If it had been Arlene that went out with me and we went to this party with a bunch messing around with drugs, Arlene would have wanted to leave too, but she would have listened and knew there was not involvement by me. There was the difference between the two girls.

On Friday night, the last night of the month, Jimmy stopped in the store while I was at work. He walked toward me and asked, "How late are you working?"

"I get off at nine."

"Something happened. I'll tell you about it when you get off work. I'll be outside."

"Yeah, okay, Jimmy." It was about twenty of nine, and the way he acted was not good.

Nine o'clock came, and it was time to check out for the night. Outside the store Jimmy was leaning against my car. "What's going on?"

"Mick," he said. "Mick was in an accident and was killed."

"Killed!" I shrieked. I hated the sound of my on voice but hearing of a friend being killed caused me to lose control.

"It was this afternoon. He was traveling with the freight on a flatbed truck. The truck stopped all of a sudden and then everything shifted forward. It crushed Mick to death!" Jimmy exclaimed as his words picked up speed while telling this. He leaned back against the car and brushed away a tear away.

"Damn! It's hard to believe Mick," I said. "Damn!" I repeated in a softer voice.

There came the thought of us drinking beer in the bowling alley. Mick, the guy that dated Jimmy's sister and had a way with girls was dead. It was mentioned that Mick had died at the scene. His ribs punctured his lungs, and word was another bone tore into an artery going to his heart. All of this was hard to hear. Mick took chances no doubt, and he worked at different jobs trying to make money. Several of us muttered some things about this. When associating with someone, it's hard to put them at fault over something when it is easier another that is someone you don't know. Why would Mick be on a flatbed truck in February?

February had come to an end. At this point of my life it may have been the worse month ever for me. There had been memories of things and most things resulted in not being good this February. Less than two months ago the car wreck around Christmas time was so hard to take. It's very hard dealing with friends dying at such a young age.

Moving the Tassels

Last month Mr. Short mentioned the Roman god Janus, and the opening and closing of doors. Janus closed doors on three special people. The month didn't matter. It was a confusing thing and I so often stay confused. I wish Mr. Cray was here to talk to. It would definitely help. Yeah, it sure would help.

///////

CHAPTER IX

This is Sunday, March 2. Kind of a gloomy day. The weekend has been rotten. My birthday is tomorrow, Monday the third. Birthday number eighteen. Time to be recognized as a man. Time to sign up for the draft. Maybe it is time to knuckle down and make the last weeks in high school respectable in the way of my grades. Failing is possible. Sitting out from graduation is not a pleasant thought. Some of the classes are going okay, but that doesn't guarantee that all my teachers are going to give passing grades. Everyone has to pass English. That's for sure. It will take five classes to earn enough credits to get my diploma. Man it's crazy when goofing around all this time, and the last months it comes time to be serious. Graduating after completing a class in summer school is not an appealing thing. Bart Fellows doesn't worry about such things. He prepares. He's smart enough to know better. He has college in mind. Most everyone in my school is confident that they will graduate. I wish I were.

Mick's funeral is the day after my birthday. Mick should have gone back to school. He wouldn't have been working on that truck Friday, and he would still be alive. We will have birthday cake tomorrow night and let on as if everything is rosy, then I'll go to the funeral home for Mick. God, it's crazy! The next day he will be put in the ground. A smashed body going into a casket and buried forever. Or is it forever? The preachers always say we live on. Our souls live on, and the thought of a soul is kind of weird. But something seems to be another part of us other than the bones and what covers them. Damn, if Mick hadn't been on that truck these thoughts would not be rolling around in my brain.

A couple of days had passed and Bart was hanging out at the pool hall again. I stopped in and we started talking about Mick and dying and things. In a pool hall of all places. He was tightening his personal cue stick that unscrewed in the center.. The question posed was if he believed in God and a soul and the hereafter. A hint of a laugh preceded his response..

"My Dad has a cousin that is a college professor and much of the same thing was discussed among some of my relatives at a family reunion.. Something he talked about was an analogy to this."

"What's an analogy?" Kind of embarrassing to ask this but if you don't know, you don't know.

"It's a similarity of some type. Often to bring across a point or idea. That's what I think it is. Get a dictionary; look the word up," he stressed as his patience was tested.

"All right. I thought it was something like that."

"'Anyway my Dad's cousin was talking. He never got around to the soul as most of those listening had wanted exactly, but described the earth, and solar system and the universe; he kind of compared it to a balloon that was being filled with air. He even said it was as if the breath of God inflated it. Then he said that he thought everything, all beliefs, whether science or faiths and everything, every soul and morsel of food was a necessary piece of this. Even every molecule, but as the balloon continued to expand the significance became slightly less, although it was still part of the overall item. It was something like that in how he talked about it."

"That's wild. Who'd come up with something like that?"

"My Dad thought he was too smart for his own good and said he was always teetering on the edge of insanity, but I liked to listen to him. It made more sense to me than a lot of what I have heard before."

We changed our subject and talked about a car show that was going to be in town and planned to go to it. He took off after this. Here am I standing around thinking about what had been discussed. Mind blowing.

Some guy about twenty walked over and asked me to shoot a game of nine ball just for the game itself, the loser would pay for the game. Why not? He had the rack in his hand. "Hey, can you do this?" He held the triangular rack with his wrists on the inside. He turned them inward and circled the rack around..

"It looks easy enough," I answered and positioned the rack just as he had and flipped the rack around and it busted my lip. For a second or so I thought I chipped a front tooth. Then spat out blood onto my forearm and wiped some of the remaining blood away.

"Damn! I never saw anyone bust his mouth up like you did. You okay?"

"Yeah. But forget about shooting the game."

"Take it easy there."

I walked out of the poolroom and spat again on the sidewalk. The split on the upper lip stung a little but my pride hurt more than a busted up lip. Boy was that ever a show of how to twirl a pool rack. Plain stupid.

While heading home the thought about a balloon swelling and what part of this human beings were kept coming to mind. It was almost scary. Bart was fine with it though and if he accepted such an idea it should be considered. The confusion just went a little beyond its normal state. One last spit toward the ground to get the taste of blood out of my mouth.

There was the thinking again about Mick. He could give a look to a girl and put her under a spell. At least with most of the girls it seemed. He couldn't do this with Kathleen, but just about any other girl. George seemingly had the same power in his eyes. Mesmerizing! That was it. Both those guys could do that. Mick had the ability and so did George. They did something most guys wished they could do. This was something Bart should comment on. Maybe we'll talk about it next time. Bart and I might toast a beer to Mick.

In school our English class had an assignment by Mr. Short and it required reading "The Tragedy of Julius Caesar." This was an historic person we studied about, Julius Caesar the leader of the Roman army, and he was kind of interesting. The movie "Cleopatra" was in theaters not long ago and Caesar was a big part of this. If the movie is historically correct it would be surprising, but it had him playing a person with enormous power. Caesar being a powerful leader in history was mentioned in the same way of Hannibal or Alexander the Great. One of the guys in class commented on something like this in our English class and was given an unusual answer, from Mr. Short.

"The records of history told us much of the decisions and strategies Caesar made while leading Rome's army. Shakespeare will give us a somewhat fictional account of the man himself and how those that served under him felt. How prophecies and omens are sometimes considered and may also come into play. The characters in the play are to be studied, maybe as we would study our present day politicians!

After hearing this there was more confusion than ever. I had had enough of Shakespeare from the movie. All the characters spoke so haughtily it was hard to understand the plot. Shakespeare confused me. What did he really mean? Most high school students don't know what he meant. This was discouraging when a teacher went on about such things, but there was also something admirable when someone that put forth the effort to speak to a senior class about politics, Shakespeare, and Caesar, and knowing the difference of the subjects being studied. It made me want to know, but it was so hard bringing myself to study. My sister Kate could study all the time. She would probably know exactly what Mr. Short was saying.

It was Thursday, just after my birthday and in hand was the play in book form. So, the thing to do is take it home and try to get through it. The way he writes makes it hard to understand. My fingers were gripping my skull as the palms of my hands were pushing into my eye sockets. "Good God!" I whispered. The book had footnotes throughout, but it still tested my patience. Here at home, sitting at our dinner table reading lines and comprehending nothing. My sister Kate had just come in from school.

"Hi, little brother. What are you reading?"

"Julius Caesar." I paused for a few discouraging seconds. A frown of disgust was felt on my face. "Did you ever read this?"

"Yes indeed." She looked at me and conveyed that she understood my struggling. "" Are you reading it by yourself? Isn't this being read in class?"

"We are to cover some parts of it but not all of it. I have to write a paper on this and turn it in. After that we will discuss it."

"I remember Caesar's wife warning him. She had dreams. "Dreams! I have dreams, Kate! We all have dreams.."

"This was to warn him. What was it?" She asked as if summoning some invisible guide.

"You're asking me?

"I can't remember the lines, but it was good. If you get to that part, the plotting and murder of Caesar, it is written well.. It's things you've probably heard before. It really is a good play. I think if you would see it acted out, you would enjoy it."

"Okay, thanks, Kate. I'll get through," I responded, and felt, as was often the case, like I was missing something that I'm supposed to pick up on. I finished this eventually and it was somewhat exhausting. It was almost haunting thinking about "the ides of March" that was mentioned early in the play. This term is frequently used, and it drew my attention after reading it. It kind of kept me going, pushing myself to read this and concentrate. Most likely the grade on my paper will reflect how much was gotten out of this. Mr. Short told us our papers are due on March 17th. He is letting us feel the full effect of the play. At least that's how it seems.

Wednesday the 19th, my grade was returned for the paper I turned in. I received a B+. That's a good grade for me. This was a grade to show my parents and Kate. Later, thinking on this, it felt how a kid in the third grade would be showing a report card to parents in hope of receiving a prize of some type. It was silly, but nonetheless I was proud of getting a B+ on this. This was Shakespeare, and his writings are tough to figure out. Getting a grade above a C is good for me. With a Shakespearean play it can come to mind that a D is what is expected and usually received. So why not boast a little? Another line to remember from the play Julius Caesar is "the good is oft interred with their bones." That was Shakespeare at his best. Anyway it's a line that struck me. And somehow this applies to my friend Mick in some way, and it easily added the saintly in regards to Arlene..

That following Saturday there was to be a full eight hours work at the grocery store, with much bagging and helping some of the customers put their groceries in their car. It was around noon when Valery, Dickey's girlfriend, came in the store. I waved at her and she waved back. She was wearing blue jeans and a light blue sweater. It still seemed so odd that she was his girlfriend. Of all people. She was very shapely and a pretty girl. She had a nice way about her. Her appearance would turn a guy's head. Being out with Dickey just didn't make sense, but she gave the impression that she thought so much of him. Of course it was no secret he was crazy about her. Before long she was checking the items out. All were food items her mother no doubt wanted.

"Do you want me to help you out with those, Valery?"

"Oh, would you? That would be nice."" We went out the door and to a station wagon. She opened the back door where the groceries could be placed on the seat and floorboard.

"There you go," I said and felt a grin on my face. "Thanks Wes, are you working late tonight?"

"I get off at 4:30."?

"Dickey and I are going to the movies tonight. Are you doing anything after work?"

"Nothing special. I don't have a date if that's what you mean."

"If you want to join us, I'm sure Dickey wouldn't mind."

"No, thanks. I'd just be in the way." Then I had to ask without getting too personal. "You and Dickey sure seem to have something good going. Everything still going fine for the two of you?"

She glanced away slightly and a happy look came to her as she pushed her hair behind her ear. "Wes, he makes me feel like I'm the most important person on earth. I couldn't be happier?"

"Hey, that's great. Listen I'd better get back in the store. You two enjoy the movie tonight."

She smiled and waved and was soon steering that big car down the road as I watched for a few seconds and remembered there was work to be done.

For a couple of seconds this thought lingered: My life is changing this year. All of us will be going on to different things and what we experience now will be a long gone memory like Valery in that big car going down the road. The world we have all known is taking on a different expression.

The afternoon hours were soon past and the workday was over for me. While driving home there came the thought of what to do tonight? There was no plan to stay out very long. It's back to work in the morning, so going out for a little while seemed a good idea.

After cleaning up I drove over to Jimmy's house and saw his sister Kathleen. Her looks were always noticeable. The part American Indian with the high cheekbones was apparent, and the basic looks she possessed were something most any guy would check out. We talked for a quite a while. The subject of Mick was brought up and it appeared she was still saddened over him. She had broken off their relationship some time ago, but the thought of him dying had bothered her more than most anyone expected.. Jimmy joined in and talked some also. He had a date with Sally tonight. He was getting ready to leave. I decided to stay and watch television with Kathleen and her parents. A program that was regularly scheduled was on and it was worth the time to watch. Mom and dad often watched it at home. Kathleen's mother fixed some popcorn and gave me a soft drink. My stay was about two hours after the program was over. We talked over a few different things and the night turned out better than might have been expected. Jim and Kathleen's parents were always very nice. After thanking them, I mentioned having to work in the morning.

Arriving home, there would probably be the account of where the night took me and what places I had been. This was often the case. Mom and Dad were watching television as usual and didn't ask much. Now they acted differently. It had me trying to figure this one out. Who knows why? No need to bother asking them either so I let them know it was off to hit the hay. The hours started early. Work would be another full day and the bed seemed very inviting.

The covers brought a comfort and a yawn. Sleep was not far off. The bed felt good and there was very little noise to disturb me. It seldom mattered anyway. What had been on my mind was continuous. Valery and Dickey. Here they were going out nearly every weekend. It had been fun being out with them. They so often looked into each other's eyes as lovers do. He told me he thought Valery was super. Why not? She had the figure and the looks. She was a nice girl, and she liked him very much. She may have loved him. And what about this? This guy had a bunch of troubles just a few of months ago, but now he seemed to have the world by the tail. He knew the secret. He put it to work with Valery. She was his world, and he let her know it.

Kathleen came to my thoughts for a few seconds. Here was a girl still upset over a guy she had dated and decided it was not a good mix. Then the word mix could take on a different meaning. She was part Indian and part Irish. It's probably not uncommon, but the mix with her produced a temper always prepared to boil. She might get rattled and throw a tomahawk or a shillelagh. One has to wonder about her.

Two completely different girls. Girlfriends, or at one time girlfriends of guys I know and knew. Altogether different and yet they have probably been brought up much the same. Girls are so hard to figure. Maybe Dickey Brink had solved some of this. My eyes closed for a few seconds. Thoughts of Edna came to mind. Our time last summer. Thoughts of her left just as quickly.

"How simple can it be?" I asked myself as sleep was postponed momentarily. Here talking to myself in bed. No one around. "Well, Dickey Brink, you're way ahead of the rest of us poor slobs. You found your girl and maybe you know how to keep her, the thought came to me again. This echoed through my sleepy thoughts once more. Of all people, Dickey Brink.

///////

CHAPTER X

April Fool's Day was on a Tuesday. At school everyone had their guard up expecting a prank or some kind of joke to come about. Some happened and some didn't happen. It made me feel foolish in behaving this way. At one time supposedly everyone has been the butt of a joke. Everyone had fallen for April Fool jokes, usually if these are played early on. This time-nothing. For some reason I was thinking at home on this and heard the phone ring. Mom had answered.

"Oh, yes, Ill get him," she spoke. "Wes...telephone?"

"Okay, mom," I picked up the receiver. "Hello,"

"Hey Wes, how's it going?" the familiar voice asked. "Is this Jimmy?"

"Of course. Were you expecting anyone else? "No, not really. What's new?" I asked.

"You know that jerk of a brother of Sally's? Alan? Well he left town this morning and is headed back to California. Do you believe that?"

"Just took off, huh?"

"Yeah. You know how he thought everything and everyone is so screwed up around here. Well, he had enough it seems and headed west."

"Aren't his parents, uh, Sally's parents going to try and do something?"

"There's not much they can do. He's eighteen. He can do about anything like that and legally they can't do much. Sally's mom is all upset, and Sally is kind of beside herself."

"Wow! Just take off like that," I kind of said to myself. "Say, is this an April Fool gag?"

"I wouldn't joke about this. I'm worried about Sally though."

"Yeah. Well I guess she'll be all right. There's nothing she can really do anyway. Man, he would be graduating soon.. You'd think he would wait until after school was out."

"You're right. Kind of stupid thing to do, but it must have been that he had enough of the dull life, to his way of thinking. I just thought I'd let you know. I'll be talking at you later," he said.

"Yeah. Take it easy." I hung up the receiver on the phone and questioned why Jimmy would call me about that? I didn't really like Alan. If he wants to go back to California, that's his business. Maybe there were a few people in California that liked him. His attitude just bothered most people, and he bothered me too. He wasn't anything like his sister. She was very likeable. Maybe Jimmy was concerned about her and worried she might go chasing after her brother to get him to return here. That didn't seem likely but sometimes people do things that surprise everyone. Maybe Jimmy didn't want that kind of surprise. It would be quite a joke if Alan was pulling an April Fool joke on a bunch of us. A guy like Alan was just the type to do this.

Things were moving along at work dealing with regular grocery dealings on Thursday night when Yance had answered a phone call in the office area. My curiosity had me moving closer to the store office trying to listen in part. It didn't work out so I saw some empty shelves in eavesdropping distance and readjusted items on them. The conversation remained fairly private. So with the shelves in order a broom nearby could be put to use by sweeping and casually moving closer to the office. Yance spoke very low. He then hung up the phone and walked to Phyllis, a cashier. She was the first black employee of this store. A nice lady. He said something and she was then nodding her head. A customer had just walked up to check out so I walked to the back of the conveyor belt to bag the groceries. Yance walked up from behind and pulled me aside.

"Wes, Mr. Tromvek had a heart attack tonight and it may have us working some extra hours. Do you think I can count on you to help?"

"Sure," I replied. "Is Mr. Tromvek going to live?"

"His wife said it was not a severe heart attack, but he would definitely be taking time off."

"I'll help when and where I can." My thoughts ran kind of goofy after this. Thinking about Yance running the store and coming out with a new dress code. He will have everyone wearing clothes that look kind of military, including the ladies. Yance had a lot of that in him. That was probably a good thing if a store was to function properly. There's nothing wrong in abiding by his rules, but if he suggests a dress code other than what we normally wear, he might have to be called out on that. This was a silly thought. At this time Yance was going to try and supervise the store the best he could. There was doubt in any radical changes taking place. The store was profitable and keeping it running as it had been was probably the best thing to do. Yance was an all right guy, and if we just do as we had been doing it would be fine. Mr. Tromvek was the owner and manager. His condition didn't seem to be all that serious. He would probably be back to work before too long. It wasn't the ideal thing to think about at this time but a couple of extra hours each week would be helpful, and actually good. Who couldn't use a few extra bucks? Mr. Tromvek would probably be thankful that all of us were keeping the grocery going as usual.

Spring break was here and it felt as though something was being missed out on. Tentatively there were plans to go with a couple of friends to Florida during the break. Now this had to be cancelled because of work. Wayne Borden was driving to Florida and he hounded me some because I backed out. It didn't do much good to explain. Anyway, Wayne was not the type person to be around for the better part of a week. He would be taking off when we got there and rejoining us later; letting us know how many girls he had been screwing. He might be a favorite of the ladies, but he could be irritating a lot of the time. Missing out on this was not so much a bad deal after weighing the pros and cons. It was a little disappointing with the idea of a bunch of pretty girls on the beach.

Mom handed me a letter after arriving home from work. It was from my friend Greg. He wrote that he was going to be stationed for thirteen months in Vietnam. He had qualified in some field the Army found he would be good at and he would be carrying out a particular job there with an increase in rank. It was not near the border, so he felt much at ease in where and what the duties would be. He gave an APO address and encouraged me to write to him. A year ago Greg and I were goofing around like we didn't have a care in the world. God, what a change! Well, it was difficult to know what to write, and informing him about the weather was the last thing he would want to know or care about. With Kate's help a letter was completed, and after rereading it before mailing, there was much in it. The letter had some impressive content. It was a sensible good friend letter..

Greg might find I have matured the last few months. The truth was Kate knew how to put pen to paper. It was a fortunate thing having an older, intelligent sister that was willing to help..

There were a few things about writing that were asked of me while she assisted. She said something about loosening up and letting a creativeness flow.. This might be okay for an English assignment, but to write to a friend in the Army… it just didn't come across the same. In the letter it was related to Greg of some of the things and people he knew.. Mick and Arlene, both dead now, were just two of the unfortunate things that happened. Rereading one last time found me wiping my eyes when reading Arlene's name. Nearly four months had passed and it was still so difficult. It was worth a line to tell him George had transferred to another school. Maybe this letter just needed some fillers.

Working at the store had been a busy time and there was work every day for eight hours during break. Actually I volunteered to do this. A forty-hour week was something different. Combining school and homework and working at the store part time added up to more than forty hours, but all the hours at work away from my friends at school was a different feel. During the week there were working shifts with Phyllis and we talked some. She was in her mid thirties, wore her hair very short, but was an attractive woman. She was married, with three kids. She and her husband were fairly new to the area and were working hard to get their kids through school with intentions of all three children going to college. She wanted them to have advantages that were not so available when she was of the same age. They were even stair step ages of 14, 12, and 10. I didn't know them, and it would have mattered little if I did. Their age difference was too much.

It was interesting that her concerns were on her mind all the time. She mentioned it just about every time we talked. These thoughts never crossed my mind before. It was different than just studying or being aware of civil rights-the marches and struggles people go through but if it is not part of your problem you might never give it a lot of thought. Before it didn't seem so important. Those kinds of problems were never dealt with, nor did they have to be. It surely was important to Phyllis. She clearly wanted a better life for her kids, plain and simple.

Sunday had arrived and it was an opportunity to take the day off. Yance told me to do so. He thanked me for putting in the hours and was decent about bringing this up. Those thoughts about his uniforms had faded. It was just a silly thought imagining he would impose a dress code. He continued to wear these same clothes but never mentioned it to anyone that worked at the store. The work week had come to an end and spring break was winding down. The trip to Florida would now be a memory, and it probably would have been a good memory; but with Wayne it could have turned into something that was not so good. He would be giving all the details anyway on Monday. There was no problem in waiting for this account.

Graduation was approaching and the idea of not graduating continued to bother me. Were these so-so grades enough to convince my teachers to give me a passing mark? Questions kept popping into my head. Maybe the thing to do is go to each teacher of each class and ask her or him if my grades were good enough? Could extra credit be worked out? Turn in papers or extra assignments. Panic was sort of overtaking me. There was an Economics class that I was comfortable with in January. It was one of those classes that was kind of easy. But my last test grade was a D. Mom and dad were not happy with it either. Mom wanted me to take math classes that were much harder. The sociology class was about the same. It wasn't a difficult class, but some of the test scores had been low. There were two other classes I felt okay with. Then there was English. Mr. Short was not one to let a student cruise. He had my attention and enthusiasm at times, but if he decided there wasn't enough effort being put toward English IV, or the core of it was not grasped as he expected it to be, he might just flunk me. That Julius Caesar paper was damn good, but maybe not enough.

My stomach was bothering me, when Bart was spotted walking ahead of me down the hallway.

"Hey, Bart, what's new?" I called out and took some quick steps to catch up.

"Wes, old man we're winding down our time in these corridors of learning. We'll probably look back on this time in our life and laugh at our naivete'."

"Maybe so. You know, I'm getting a little worried about graduating. The grades and course work have been... well, it could have been a lot better. I don't know if I'll pass all my classes. I need all of them too. There is an uncertainty on this, and I'm not sure what to do about it."?

"Surely you've good enough grades to pass. You're not a moron. You turn in your homework?"

"Most of the time. Sometimes no. But most of the time. Does it matter that much?"

"The teachers expect that work to be done. It's not assigned to pass the time of day."

"Yeah," the word came out dejectedly.

"Have you talked to your teachers? Seriously talked about this?" he asked in a most sincere way.

"Not yet."!

"You need to take this up with each of them. What classes are you worried about?"

"Economics, Sociology, and especially English? "What teachers?

"Dotterman, Smith, and Short."

"Dotterman and Smith are fairly smooth. They would only flunk you if you were doing horrible and just weren't trying. Mr. Short... he doesn't fool around. You're right about that. You might need to ask him. See if you can meet with him after school. See where you stand? Bart looked at me and shook his head. "Wes, all this time I thought you had your schoolwork down."

"I should have. I just went through the motions where I could. You'd think I'd know better.. Damn! I'm sounding like my Dad..""

"I have to make my class. Get cracking, Wes," he said and gave me a half salute as he began to walk a little faster..

My next class was a study hall, and our librarian oversaw this one. "Why would you need to do this?" She asked as she looked over the frames of her glasses, considering my request.

"This English class has me worried, ma'am. I need to know if my grades are good enough."" Then I did some acting on my part and put a sad and desperate look on my face. There were the few seconds of looking down and then back up. Her name was Wilma Hatfield. She was a spinster type, or kind of a schoolmarm, but she could fix herself up and probably have a number of men interested in her if she wanted.

"Mr. Patterson," there was a pause. She looked at me again, and the sad doglike appearance again came to my face. She began writing a note. She folded it sharply. "Here! And be back in ten minutes.""

"Yes, ma'am. Oh, yes ma'am," I joyfully said and took the note and made long strides down the hall. After all of the pleading, she gave me a hall pass to see Mr. Short. The pitiful looks and begging worked. Maybe acting should be considered.

High schools must all be designed and built by the same people. The painted concrete blocks and doors with student lockers placed between the doors. All of them look the same. There have been visits to a number of schools and every school looks much the same. The outside is a different matter. I reached Mr. Short's classroom. He had the door open and was lecturing to his class. He saw me in the doorway and continued speaking as he turned his head to face me. I lifted a hand up and a partial wave had him walking toward me.

"Patterson... what is it?" the voice came across with authority.

"Sir, could I speak to you this afternoon when school is over for the day?"

"Certainly. I'll be here for about thirty minutes"."

"Thank you, sir, thanks." I said and nodded like a beggar that was given food. The look on Mr. Short's face showed some contempt. He didn't like my acting this way; that was for sure.

Classes were finished and the kids moved through the hallways, weaving in and out. Some ran, and the sound of lockers opening and closing echoed off the walls. Some selected books that would be needed for home study. I even took my English text although it wasn't necessary for the evening. One of the guys that usually road home in my car had a locker nearby and upon seeing him I told him it would be a few minutes later than normal before we left the school parking lot. Many were still moving about, calling out about something, and making their way from the building. It was a kind of dreaded walked to Mr. Short's room. There he was with his eyes scanning some papers on his desk.

"'Ahem", clearing my throat, and getting his attention.

"Yes, Patterson. Come on in. You were wanting to talk of something?"

"Yes, thank you, sir.'"

"What was it you were needing to speak to me about?"

"Mr. Short, I was trying to find out if my grades in English were good enough to get a passing grade, sir?" The words came from me with a bit of stuttering, and an obvious nervousness that was surely noticed. That unwavering look was on his face.

It almost seemed that he was going to tell me that enough work had not been done and it would be necessary to repeat this class in summer school to get a diploma. The few seconds he took to answer seemed like an eternity. There was an internal fight to control my jitters.

"Do you feel as if you deserve to get a passing grade?"

"I uh,... well, yes. I uh, think I did good work on the assignment last month, and you remarked on my paper that it was much improved work," my words strengthened a little as I mentioned his compliment.

"Oh, yes! You did turn in your assignment, showing that you can achieve something if you desire to. Even the essay questions that were answered in class showed that you put your mind to it. More than usual."

"Thank you."

"Wes, you can make a better life for yourself if you put some effort behind your work. Any work. I don't know your plans after graduation, but I will tell you that you can plan on many things after high school being tough.'" He looked down at his papers after saying this and there was this thought of him digging through papers to pull out an assignment I had messed up on. His gaze came back toward me. "I seldom fail students that try. Continue your work. Maybe some extra effort. I see no reason why I wouldn't give you a passing grade for this class."

"Mr. Short, I appreciate that," I told him and looked him in the eye and shook his hand, just as my dad would have wanted me to do. Then I zipped out of the school feeling as though two or three long leaping steps would bring me to my car that was parked at least two hundred feet away. The weight was gone. It had been unloaded from my shoulders. Damn! Life was good! Life was great!

If there were only a steady girlfriend. That would make everything super. Well, better. It is so difficult to find a girl that likes me, that I would like in return. The same old thought, most of the girls I desired to go out with are already in relationships. That narrows the choices quite a bit. Another thing on this topic was the upcoming prom. It was not far off. Who is there to ask? A thought beyond this is who would go with me? My first choice would be Regina. She has the whole package. Looks, charm, intelligence, but Bart told me she has a new boyfriend. Even if she didn't, she would probably refuse to go to the prom. She still thinks there is involvement with drugs and such on my part.

Rebecca would be a great prom date. She is seldom seen any longer. She's still going with that guy that used to pick her up at the store. He really irked me. He didn't do anything directly to me. It just seemed that Rebecca and I were doing okay at the store. We kind of had a good thing going. Of course we needed to be discreet and see each other outside of work. She didn't think our being coworkers and carrying on a relationship was a good thing to do. Then the guy she is going with entered the picture. He was everywhere. It was easy to grow to hate him. I shouldn't have. He was actually a likeable sort, but it seemed he stole my girl. It was just too hard to come to terms that she lost interest in me, and found interest in another.

Valery's cousin Sylvia is one to consider. She lives so far away though. If there were something we had in common or a genuine liking of each other, then distance wouldn't be such a big deal. Then again it is a matter when thinking of her as being a sophomore and living far away. Being a sophomore though is not a problem. Is it the giggles? That was something to think on. It made me feel self-conscious whenever she started that. If she would happen to be my date maybe on our second date she would do a risky thing and let me hold her hand.

Jim's sister Kathleen is a possibility. Her temper though, and what she could do may spoil the evening. She is liable to get upset with the slightest thing and go off as she has been known to do so many times before.

The party! Yes, the party we went to last year at Teresa's house. She was a nice girl. Nice looking too. Why hadn't I thought of her before? Maybe it would do to find out if she is involved with anyone.. That should be the next step. She may be the girl to ask. Immediate action is needed. The prom isn't far off, and time is running out. A person getting ready to graduate doesn't want to miss their prom.

Thoughts went toward Charlotte. God Almighty! Why do these thoughts come into my mind? Well they do. It's doubtful that Charlotte would go to a high school prom. It would be foolish in asking her even if she were available. There would be too many jeers. Too much embarrassment by bringing someone older like that. She said she was getting back with the guy she was intending to marry, or something like that. If she did go to the prom with me, she would kiss me goodnight. Maybe even more.

After my thoughts about Charlotte, there came the unceasing thought of Arlene. What an angel. If ever a guy could have a prom date and be completely happy with the girl that went with him, it would be Arlene. Such a tragedy. This nearly had my crying at the thought of her. The focus should be on Teresa..

It took a little work to find out her status but it so happened Teresa was not seeing anyone on a regular basis. We talked on the phone and she agreed to go to the prom with me. It was a relief to have a date. This was nearly as good as getting word from Mr. Short on my grades in English. My life was taking some shape, maybe a little, as the concerns for graduating and going to the prom were now resolved. I felt more at ease.

The subjects that concerned me were getting more attention. It happened that Mr. Smith recently drew me aside after class and said, "You have done much better these last few weeks. If this had gone on the entire year, you certainly would merit a very high mark.

The effort and work put forth will be considered for perhaps a grade better than what may have been barely passing.

"Yes," was all that could be uttered. My head nodded in approval and Mr. Smith, the book wormish looking fellow nodded also with the slightest show of recognition.

Work at the grocery was still busy. Mr. Tromvek was supposed to be back at work Monday, May 5th. We had a bit of time to get the store in its best shape. The sale of goods were moving as normal. Every employee had put in some extra time. We also put in extra effort. Saturdays were usually when I worked over, and in talking with Yance there was the option to put in extra time on Sundays too. Now, with constant work on Sundays and a newfound interest in homework, there was little time for anything else.

The schedule showed I had the last weekend in April off work. That was prom weekend. It was here in the blink of an eye. The special night was here. With the time off, much of what occupied me was a tux rental and a corsage of flowers for Teresa, then bingo, ready to go. This car of mine had become so important since its purchase. It had been so reliable. Now the time was to clean it up as best I could, then have Bart give it a good check so trouble might be averted. Finish it off with a tank full of ethyl and we're ready to roll.

I drove to Teresa's home and walked to the front door, rang the bell and waited. The wait seemed ·very long. Damn! She wouldn't stand me up on my senior prom, would she?

"Hello, you must be Wesley?" a man's voice asked. "Oh yes, sir, I'm he, uh, Wesley, Wes Patterson."

"Come on in. The daughter will be with you in just a minute. By the way, I'm Teresa's father. A rustling kind of sound from another room was noticeable. Teresa's mother entered the room.

"Wes! Well, it's so good to see you again. Teresa will be in here in a minute. You've met my husband?"

"He met me, dear. You just interrupted us."

"It was nothing intended. I've known Wes since back in the fall. He was here before."

"Hi, Wes," Teresa said and walked into the front room where everyone was talking and not quite completing what each wanted to say.

"Teresa, you're dressed very nice. I brought you these." and handed the corsage to her. Her mother made over them as well as Teresa, and she helped in pinning them onto the dress.

"Thank you, they're so pretty." She then turned around with her arms away from her sides and her hands out as if she were prepared to catch herself should she lose her balance. The dress was floor length. She was attractive with her dark brown, almost black, hair done up with the bow in her hair that matched the white dress she was wearing. Her Mother made us stand together posing a few different times for pictures. The flash was beginning to affect my eyes. They cleared quickly, and we decided we had better be on our way. In a matter of minutes we were off to my high school prom.

In my car Teresa asked, "Are we going by your house to have pictures taken too?"

"My mother wanted us to, but I told her if possible we would have prints made from some of the others that were taken."

"I think she would like to see us dressed up as we are. Proms don't happen every night.'"

"She would, but we're running late as it is. Mom understands." Glancing over at Teresa there was a show of disappointment on her face. She changed her expression as we approached the building hosting the night's festivities. We were to meet Dickey and Valery and Frank Shears and his date.. Frank was another classmate that needed a place at a table. He was an all right sort.

The dancing was almost all slow songs. Sometimes a song would have some liveliness to it. Nevertheless, it was all enjoyable. Teresa danced pretty well. It was quite exerting to avoid stepping on her dress. It spread out slightly where it reached the ground. It's amazing that girls can move around in those. As for me, there was this feeling of being like Humphrey Bogart. The tux was sized correctly, but it is something that takes some getting used to. There was a lot of cutting up, and pictures with different people. It was one event that would have been enjoyed even if it had continued longer than it was supposed to be.

We went to a very elegant restaurant and included Dickey and Valery. Frank had reservations at another place. Each of us ordered steak and salads, and a choice of potatoes was also on the menu. Dickey nearly made it without a blunder up until his last bit of the steak. It fell off his fork and dropped across his shirt and into the napkin in his lap.

"Dickey, look at you! I'm going to have to clean you up wherever we go," Valery said, and laughed seeming to take an enjoyment in helping him out. He rolled his eyes and quickly brushed where the meat had bumped against him. With him these incidents were always an ongoing thing.

Dinner had been completed and it was decided to call it a night in order to be up and about for the next day. I drove Teresa home and walked her to her front door. She kissed me goodnight in the glow of a front porch light without hesitation. The thought of her father walking outside came to me, but it didn't occur. He just seemed the type that might be a very overprotective parent.

After returning home there was the usual visit to the bathroom to clean up and moving about only in my underwear. The rented tux was placed on a hanger and draped across a dining room chair. Then a quiet walk to my room. Mom and dad must have been asleep and measures were taken not to wake them. There would only be about four hours sleep before having to get up and get ready for a big day at a park. Upon arising and going to the kitchen, my eyes found mom and dad.. They had just sat down to the regular morning routine that was reserved for weekends.

"Where are you and your friends going?" Mom asked, and for about the third or fourth time I told her. She continued to try and get information out of me. This seems to always go on. There was bread to be toasted and with butter and jelly this would serve as my breakfast. There would be much more to eat with the picnic lunch. The toaster was being put to use while the sound of the morning newspaper rustled through my Dad's hands. A thick amount of butter and jelly were added to the toast and was gobbled down like a starving dog. In a matter of minutes I was out of the house.

Teresa was at her front door upon my arrival at her house. She had a pecan pie she said she made with help from her mother. We still had to pick up Valery and Dickey. At Valery's home we found ready a picnic basket of fried chicken, biscuits and baked beans. We loaded everything up, and the four of us were on the road. We turned up the radio in the car and sang along with whatever was playing. This could have been in part to stay awake.

In an hour's time we arrived at the park and spotted several others from school that selected the same location. We romped around, joining others sometimes and moved around, very carefree, as people our age were apt to do. With the expended energy our appetites were soon in need of food. We located a picnic table nearby, and the girls set it up with a cloth and paper plates. Some of the gusts of wind from late April breezes toyed with the plates and sometimes the table covering. This was anchored down and some cold pieces of chicken were a welcomed meal. The biscuits and beans were no longer warm either but it had a satisfying taste. Dickey once again spilled on his shirt. It was not such a matter with the casual clothes. It was becoming an expected procedure once again for Valery to come to his rescue to wipe off the mess he made.

"You're lucky to have Valery along to clean you up.."

"She really takes care of me, Wes."

Teresa was sitting comfortably at this table placed in the outdoors. Everything was so alive, green, and sometimes caused a sneeze. A suppressed "achoo" came from her. It caused little change in her demeanor. She seemed to be enjoying our time here. She watched as others moved about that were at least the length of a football field away. A slightly envious look from me spotted Valery and Dickey. Valery grabbed his hand. He covered her hand with his other and she smiled showing a happiness on her face that might never come my way with any girl. She and Dickey were in love. It was very special. They would look into each other's eyes and their faces would radiate. This caused me mixed feelings. There was jealousy for what he had. He was deserving though. His home life had been kind of lousy.

The picnic and fun time continued on. We ran around near a stream that traversed wooded areas and brought us through some of the most scenic parts of the woods. We played in the water just as kids of five or six years younger might do. Sometimes we laughed over a bit of nothing, and made a little bit of nothing a very nice outing.

It was still daylight but the time to leave was upon us. Our drive seemed to go by quickly and I was soon walking Teresa to her door. She was a very nice girl. Attractive, fun to be with on this prom occasion, and again she kissed me good night. All was fine for these last two days, but Teresa and I were only in a friendship relationship. Something, not exactly sure what, just didn't mesh in our being out together. During the drive home this preyed on my mind. Most guys would proudly be out with her. When she agreed to go to my prom, it brought relief more than happiness. The last two days had been fun but were not quite as wanted, and it appeared she was experiencing the same thing.

The last Sunday of April found me working. After the shift it was directly home for me. There was dinner with the family and a realization that this simple occasion was pleasing. Mom had fixed pork chops and dressing, peas and carrots and baked a cherry pie for dessert. The main course was delicious and here, me, a growing boy opted for two pieces of cherry pie. It was only appropriate to tell Mom how enjoyable the dinner was. Her face lit up with delight from this acknowledgement. It was probably the first time I had ever spoken about how good dinner was over the last couple of years.

After dinner Kate started to clean the table. There was some reluctance in helping, but it was time to help. This rare occasion called for it. Kate then helped Mom with the dishes. Dad went in the kitchen and started repairing a lamp that had a frayed cord. On the telephone stand were my schoolbooks and these were collected, then taken to the dining room table for study. Kate finished helping Mom and joined me at the table.

"Are you getting some of the assignments completed before the last day of school?" she jokingly asked.

"There are tests yet to take. A number of people are getting test exemptions, but it could easily be guessed who is not one of them."

"Did you get exemptions?"

"From a couple of classes, but not all of them. Some teachers don't give them either.."

"How do you manage your time with school and a social life and all? It's hard to see how anyone going to school can have any kind of social life and make decent grades. And people that work. Phew! It's amazing how it's done."

"Little brother... you learn to manage your time. One of the most important things you will do, or have to do." It was all right for her to call me little brother. Not often since my height surpassed hers did she say this. It was okay though. What she was saying was in good humor.

"Go on. Go manage your time somewhere else."

"Len is coming over, and I intend to manage my time. our time."

I threw my hands up and waved them around, then went over some of the things that should probably be memorized. Concentration is so difficult. It's to their credit the kids that study and get lost in the subject. Kate seems to be one of those people. She's just about to finish up her senior year of college. Then she'll be married and what happens to her life after that? All the school, studying, and what will she do with it?

This came across as a kind of musing. Then with the more personal question: after high school, what then? A page was turned in my text, and for a few seconds my train of thought was miles away.

Sleep came that night, earlier than usual. There is now an alarm clock radio in my room and after turning it on there were thoughts about many things. A song from The Beatles was playing. The words to the song were familiar, and I sang along with it. It was released last fall and hit the charts with amazing sales. It gave cause to think about that time in school and my lackadaisical interest in the subjects that we were studying. Just starting work at the grocery. The football games. The song continued and so did my singing. It made me feel good. The song was over and another was being played. It was Aretha Franklin singing. My! She could certainly hit a range of notes. If trying to do a singalong there would only be coverage of the mid-range notes. It didn't matter. These eyes were tired and wanting to close. A drifting off. The radio would continue to play as a sound sleep entered my world.

My most remembered dream that night was being at the prom with Greg's girlfriend before he left for the Army.. This was Edna. Why was I dreaming she was with me at the prom? Nevertheless we were enjoying ourselves. Dancing often, and sitting at the same table with some friends. The faces could not be made out though. The next thought was taking her home. The scene went from the table at the prom to being in my car with her. She began to kiss me pressing her body against mine. There was a scary thought that we would wreck my car, but she was still kissing me and it was enjoyable. There was heard a voice that came from nowhere and awakened me. A startling feeling. It was challenging to get back to sleep, so I was just lying on the bed in the early morning hours. Did it happen again? Softly a voice in the dream said once again, "April Fool!

April had turned out better than it had started off to be. It was a good month. The grass in our front yard was a rich green and very thick. The perennial flowers my mother planted some years back in the beds that bordered our house were coming out, spreading over the soil. The unpredictable weather was still with us; sometimes a morning sunshine was followed with a very wet and windy afternoon. Dad wore a smile more often than he normally did. My sister Kate was preparing for her finals, graduation, and in June her wedding to Len. I received word that Mr. Tromvek at the grocery was doing very well. The idea of not graduating was kind of put behind me. What had been fretted over a couple of weeks ago was no longer such a worry. My car had even showed some sort of feel that it was running better than ever since the colder days of winter were no longer an issue. What else could be asked for?

///////

CHAPTER XI

Everyone in my graduating class was getting antsy. I was no exception. With our diplomas about to be received and each of us considering what to do brought this out, and it seemed an exciting time for school. My enthusiasm had not been such for anything pertaining to school since starting the first grade. Another thing that kind of loomed was what each of us would be doing after graduating. There was still a summer to enjoy, but after that it most likely would become serious. With all that was going on the best thing to do was take as much of it in as possible and enjoy being part of it. Some of this advice came from Bart. He was passing along what his father had said to him.

My classes at school were beginning to get more interesting. What irony. Of all times to get eager about my studies. Graduating near the top ten percent would not be something to expect. Graduating in the upper half was probably a pipe dream too, but school was more enjoyable to attend this last semester. It was as though something was actually showing from my efforts. My study spot on the dining room table had become a regular thing to associate effort, and a calming effect would fall over my being...

the idea of accomplishing something worthwhile. While sitting there one night, my sister Kate walked past.

"Kate, I have actually enjoyed the last couple of months of school. It has come to the point where studying is not so tedious like it used to be. It's kind of strange."

"Oh! Maybe, Wes, you are showing some sign of maturity. All along I could have told you that putting your nose in a book and learning something is not a bad thing. You don't want to be in a hopeless situation all your life. The homework helps for sure."

"I'm not going to extremes with this. I just found a few things that we we're covering in some of the classes that appealed to me," I commented and let Kate know with a shift of my eyes that there was no need for a lecture.

"Carry on Wes," she said and walked toward her room. "Carry on, carry on," I mumbled.

The first Tuesday of May I didn't have to be at work until 6:30 p.m. so after dropping off my riders there was time to meet up with Dickey Brink at the nearby drugstore. We sat at the lunch counter and had a soft drink. It was kind of strange. The last time I stopped here with someone was when Dickey and I were registering for school. Now, here we are again as we are about to finish up our high school days.

"So what are your plans after graduating?" I asked with my usual confidence when talking to him and tipping my glass, letting some ice bounce on my lip and getting the last bit of soda. His face showed excitement.

"I was going to tell you about this, and now that you've asked, I got to tell you I joined the Navy! I leave in August and when I get established Valery and I are going to get married! She'll be with me as long as I'm Stateside. If I go out of the country, she's going to try and be there too!"? His excitement in telling me this was a little overwhelming to the both of us. It caused me to nearly choke on a piece of ice from the drink but there was quick recovery.

"That's out of sight!" I cried aloud, and some of the people in the drugstore looked over at us. I didn't want to draw this attention but with this news it could barely be kept under control. "Valery and you! When did the two of you decide on this?"

"Last week. We were out and just talking. I had thought about the Navy for some time. Dad was in the Army and said he had friends that talked of the Navy always having a clean, dry bed. In the Army it's not always the case. Anyway I was convinced and have talked to a recruiter, and in talking to Valery we went on with plans and next thing I know we're going to get married.'"

"Wow! That's really something. And she's okay with the Navy and all?"

"She loves the idea. It's going to be great," he added, and turned his eyes upward as though envisioning a Van Gogh's "Seascape" type setting. He could have in mind a view of the English Channel. Whatever, his thoughts were far from the drugstore for sure.

"It's a pretty amazing thing. I can hardly believe it. Valery and you sailing off somewhere."

"Valery won't exactly be sailing off with me," he hinted and laughed. My comment and its meaning were completely without thought. There wasn't anything meant by it. Dickey knew my remark was to be taken with good intent. He continued, "I was going to call you and tell you about this. I've been spending so much time with Valery that I just didn't get around to it. Here, telling you... this is better."

"Hey, have you told Bart?"

"Not yet. I will though. I wish he would have been here. He'd like to hear about this, and with the three of us cutting up and all, it would be kind of neat.'"

"You sure surprised me. No doubt Bart will be interested in finding this out. But I think it's great. I hope everything goes good for you two."

"Thanks, Wes. I think it will. Valery is everything to me. I'm going to try with all effort to make her happy," he said and showed a sincerity and a joyous look on his face that told his story.

We joked around for a few more minutes. After that it seemed I better get home, and continue this newfound mild addiction of studying before going to work. While driving home the thoughts could not be shaken of Valery and Dickey getting married. It was great for them, but there was this but there was this touch of envy that he had something I didn't. The pairing of people is something possibly never to be understood. There are all the old adages of "for every girl is a guy" and "there is one and only one certain somebody for each of us." It was the lyrics in many songs. Who knows if these are just feel good words or if there is some truth in them. What was known to me was something is missing with me and it was troublesome. Thinking again on this, there was reason to be glad Dickey had Valery as his steady, or now his betrothed. He was involved with a good girl.

On arriving home there was a letter on the table from Greg. He was still doing his service for Uncle Sam. He wrote that he was sorry to get the news of Mick and Arlene. He added he would be going to another location in the next couple of weeks. His aptitude in the Army was recognized by one of the officers and something to do with intelligence was to be part of his new duties. The reports from TV and magazines were always portraying the fighting over there was carried out in jungles. There were always scenes of vines and weapons firing at God knows what. Then our soldiers being hauled away on stretchers with bandages usually placed on their heads. It just came to mind that the fighting was always in a place like a Tarzan movie or some swampy looking place. Being in an office was a weird setting that didn't register quite the same..

As with many other things, this was a confusing engagement. Vietnam was not only a foreign country, it was almost like a place on another planet. The news would mention how the people were so different. Their thinking was not like ours. But what about people from the Midwest being different from those that lived on the coasts. Those in the South had different views from those in the North.. So everyone is different. One could only hope Greg would do okay during his time in the Army. There were some other things to do, and then I would write him a letter later on.

My sister Kate was at home working on something for her husband to be. Mom and dad were out doing their grocery shopping at the supermart.. Kate had her life so much in order compared to me. Her advice wasn't sought nearly enough, but with upcoming changes quickly approaching for the both of us she would probably give no objection to imparting her knowledge.

"Kate, I have a lingering question of what to do after graduating. college has been something to think about, and mom and dad want me to attend. Mom definitely does, but more than likely I would flunk out or would have. To discipline myself like you do into studying so much is difficult to reckon with. The studying that has been done recently is probably nothing in comparison to college. The Army or Navy is something too. If the draft gets me it's two years, and joining up it's three in the Army and maybe four in the Navy. I don't know about three or four years of my life going by like that. So what do you think?"

"Well, you have obviously given this some thought. College does require more study, more work. But four years will come and go and you'll be 22. The time can be spent in college and you can get a deferment and go in ROTC. The Navy or Air Force can be time served and training and some school can be done while there, I think. A recruiter is one who can tell you about this. You know, you can even ask dad about some of this. He could be helpful. You have some options, Wes."

"Dad is not the person I want to talk to about this. I'm sure he would like me to go to college. He loves the Army too. He would probably have me sign up and be off in a jiffy. He might even have me go in the Navy. I just don't know.""

"How about this? You can always talk to Len. He would tell you straight up.".

"No, I don't think so. He is just like Dad when it comes to this. He thinks the Army is the only way to go. I've heard him and seen how he reacts. He and Dad are just alike on this. I need to get an unbiased opinion."

"Oh! Here's something you got to hear. Dickey Brink joined the Navy!"

"Dickey, that roly poly friend of yours?"

"Well yeah," I laughed. "Get this: He's getting married too!"

"Wow! I'm stunned," Kate responded but didn't display quite the emotion that might be expected. She lifted her left hand up and placed all but her pinky finger near the corner of her mouth "Well, he's the one to talk to. Maybe he can give you advice on getting married," she joked as her eyes rolled up and a bit of laughter followed.

"Marriage isn't the thing for me. Not right now. Good God, I'm not even dating anyone at this time."

"Well, your friend is way ahead of you on a couple of things. Gosh, it's hard to imagine someone marrying him."

"Hey, the girl that he going to marry is really pretty. She thinks a lot of him. I've been out with them. They're right there together..""

"I've got some things to take care of. But don't forget that Len will talk to you, I'm sure. He's very understanding."

"Yeah, and I understand exactly what he would be encouraging me to do," my response came out so automatically that it surprised me. It made me feel kind of witty.

"Okay" She paused a second or two. "Give some serious thought to what I said about Len."

I nodded my head as Kate walked toward her room. The idea of her not being here much longer kind of played on my mind. Thinking about going into the Army or some other branch of the service had me wondering about mom and dad. We would be gone and their life would certainly change. Maybe they want us out. It could be they're tired of us. Kate was twenty-two and me eighteen. That's a long time to be dealing with kids. Kate was always a good kid, but I caused troubles and worries over the years. Damn! The school term is not even completed and I'm pushing myself out the door.

The next day it was back to work for an afternoon shift, and Phyllis was at the first checkout line. My job was bagging groceries for her. Phyllis's husband came in the store with their youngest daughter. She was going to introduce me to her husband and their daughter when a customer needed help putting groceries in the car. It took longer than expected and when I finished Phyllis's husband and their daughter were walking out the door. He was about the same height as me but had a lot of pounds on his frame. He looked very solid. He spoke briefly and the girl smiled bashfully and went along with her father as she used him as a sort of shield from strangers. We've had riots and demonstrations and assassinations and just a mess of things that little girl will learn about, and different things she will experience. And she gives me a smile. I know so little of what she might have to live through. Maybe it will be a better world for her than what has been seen lately. Phyllis stood at her station with nobody checking out when I returned.

"I wanted to introduce you to my husband and daughter. I'm sorry you didn't get to meet them," she said apologetically.

"They met me at the door and said hi. The lady I was helping had to rearrange things to get her groceries in her car so it took a little longer than expected."

"I would have liked you to actually meet them though. Maybe at another time."

"Yeah, maybe so," I told her and tried to let her know I would like that.

People all over the world one would guess, just want a chance to live a life with some dignity. Surely Phyllis would agree with this. She wants to raise her children to be educated and is hoping for their happiness. Why is it always such a problem? It's just another one of those things that confuse me.

The day of graduation was here. In my room were some things that were special to me for this high school venture. A certain tie was in my closet that would be worn. Looking for it caused me to find a few things put back on the top shelf. My baseball glove with a grass stained baseball in the webbing. Dad used to throw with me some years ago. Mom even tried. It was funny to watch and she laughed along with it. But that was mom, always sacrificing for us, and especially for me. Mother's Day a couple of weeks ago had barely been noticed because she was more concerned for my graduation, and Kate's upcoming wedding to Len. Two more things, what might be thought of as older toys, were found. The metal coil that could resemble a pipe, or it could be stretched out like a concertina, or even be made to walk down steps. Then the gyro that fascinated me with its balance on a string, or a pivot pedestal. With a sigh these objects were just some things from some yesterdays. These were placed back on the shelf, and then the tie was found. It felt very becoming as the Windsor knot was twisted into my tie.

Before long mom and dad were driving me to the auditorium. There was a desire to go with some of my friends but my parents had the last word on this. Kate had to meet with Len so she would be absent. It wasn't such a big deal. I didn't go to her graduation. Mom and dad wanted to give a graduation party. I declined. It seemed there was no need in carrying on over this. Just getting out of high school was satisfying enough. Perhaps not having a steady girlfriend was subconsciously and partially my reason to not want a party.

Before we got in my parents' car, dad walked up to me and handed me an envelope.

"Son, you can open this now if you want." I took the envelope and tore the corner to the other corner as neatly as possible. It was a time to act civilized. There was a graduation card, and it was a long card such as money cards are. With some excitement the words stood out on the front. Also on the front of it was a verse and a drawing of a diploma coiled up. Inside was something else written and mom's and dad's signatures saying love and good luck. There was also a $100 dollar savings bond. How about that? That made me feel good.

"I'll hold onto that bond until we get back. You don't want to lose that," Dad offered.

"Yeah, that's for sure. Thanks dad," I said and shook his hand then kind of gave him a hug. "Mom, thanks," I also said to her and hugged her and she kissed me on the side of my face as she wiped some tears off her cheekbones. "Thank you both very much," I added, and said it with sincerity.

"Sorry Kate isn't here. She has a gift she wants you to have and she will probably hand it to you when she is back."

"I understand. All of this is very nice. Thanks again.

The senior class had gathered and was given a reminder of protocol. The diplomas had been given out and numerous students had been recognized for various achievements and awards. My name was not mentioned in this group, and there was no reason to be. My friend Bart did receive an academic scholarship to a small college in the northern part of the state.

There was a long speech given by a local congressman, and he talked mainly of community service. Many fought off yawns as he talked. The speech had come to an end and the principal made one more walk to the lectern and congratulated the class and asked those in attendance to applaud the class of 1969. I scanned the seats and possibly everyone in the building. It didn't take long to find my parents there and that was good, but there was this hope of someone special being there... someone, but there really wasn't. This was a reality check that is difficult, but had come to be expected. Cheers went out, and the mortarboard hats were tossed in the air, with hands clapping as we moved from our positions toward family and friends. The twelve year period had been rewarded and the crowd slowly disassembled. Handshakes with laughter and well wishing went on for a while. Then it was over. I went home with mom and dad and sat in the backseat of the car by myself. For a person that had just graduated, it felt a little goofy sitting there by myself. Mom and dad continued to give me praise for something that seemed almost unworthy of the attention.

We arrived home and had a delicious dinner. A special preparation of meatloaf with potatoes, carrots, butter-seasoned green beans and dinner rolls. After the regular dinner mom came in the dining area with a cake that had "Happy Graduation, Wes" written on the frosting. It was all really a nice family thing. This was so strange, so out of place. When an opportunity presented itself, I asked if it was all right to go out for a while. This was about a half hour after eating. My clothes were too formal so changing into a pair of light brown dress slacks and green pullover shirt felt more relaxing. The shirt was one that was particularly a favorite, probably because of the collar that had dark brown stitching on the outside. With the change of clothes it was time to go and just get away.

"Mom, dad, there are a few graduation parties I am supposed to attend and I thought I would go to them if you don't object?"

"Sure. Just be careful and don't be out all hours of the night," Mom advised.

"I understand. All of this is very nice. Thanks again."

"D on' t go boozing it up and trying to drive home either," my dad said. He almost never did this. He would let mom do the warning or give alerts. He knew more of what goes on than we ever gave him credit for.

I took the tassel that was just given and got into my car. With a loop here and there it was soon attached to the rearview mirror and adjusted. Then I carefully backed around dad's car and out of the driveway. This silly little object that is pushed from one side to the other of a mortarboard head cover was swaying back and forth with an almost mesmerizing effect. All the time spent in classrooms to receive a protected piece of paper and this twist of braids. These were to accompany me in my future. There were no parties that actually interested me at the moment. Maybe later.

The drugstore that Dickey met me at recently was closed. It was so dark looking at this time. It makes me think the chance of stepping inside the place may never occur again. Driving over there seemed a need or go by the restaurant Charlotte had worked at. It has been a while since stopping by this place. After arriving there was some hesitancy, but I decided to go in. The stools at the counter were empty. There was nothing to choosing the one closest to the entrance. "What'll it be, fellow?" a waitress asked. She looked to be in her mid-thirties with a reddish-orange hair in afro fashion. It almost looked to be on fire.

"A root beer for now." My curiosity impelled me to ask her. "Is the dark-haired waitress named Charlotte still working here?"

"No one by that name works here."

"Thought I'd ask?" The soft drink was placed in front of me and finished rather quickly. Maybe Charlotte got a job somewhere else. I finished my drink, paid for it and was soon driving off toward the apartment Charlotte lived at. It took a little while to get there and when doing so there was the curiosity and some nosiness that had me looking around to see if anything was familiar. There was a station wagon with rust spots and metal eaten away below the car door. It was parked near the apartment. Nothing else nearby drew attention. It took some time to build up nerve, but a decision came to walk up the steps and knock on the door. The metal handrail was grabbed in support while moving upward. The rail felt as cold as it might on a winter's day. My knuckles rapped on the door just hard enough to get attention. Some stirring around was heard and within a minute the door began to open.

"Hi. Can I help you?" the voice of a young man, probably a little older than me, asked.

"Yes, I was trying to locate a person,..." I paused and saw a young girl, definitely not Charlotte, walk behind the guy at the door..

"Who is it?" she whispered in his ear as she stood behind him and peeked over his shoulder.

"I'm looking for a lady named Charlotte," I said with a bit more authority.

"There's nobody by that name that lives here," he answered.

"I think there was before we moved here," the girl said softly.

"Okay. I thought she might have moved. Sorry to bother you."

The door closed without any other exchanges and I went back to my car, shut the door and the tassel moved slightly, again catching my eye when the car was started. There was a slow drive away from the apartment, as thinking on past events, swarmed and where to go now? It didn't make sense heading over near my school but... now it was now my former school. It was as cold and lifeless looking as the drugstore. Everything seemed cold today. It wasn't cold though, it just gave the feeling of being cold. To never walk those halls again. There is school tomorrow, but my locker has been cleaned out, and the books have been sold. No reason to go there. There were arrangements made for the kids that rode to and from school. It was surprising how their carfare money added up. Maybe extra hours at the store could now make up for the carfare money that was an asset.

With the car turned off there was an impulse to just sit in it for a few minutes. No more school. The people known will be moving on. Where will they be in a couple of years? The immediate friends there brought ideas about, such as Dickey and Valery, and of course Bart going away to college. He might be around now and then. A lot of others preparing to go to college, and many others are getting jobs. Some people are set up with good jobs. A few talked of getting married and a few spoke of the military. For now my job is okay, but it's not a career job. Who would want to be in that store all of their life? The thought of Yance caused a bit of a laugh. Yance could manage that store. It could happen for him, and he would do all right. So many people know what they want to do. They have looked ahead and made plans. They know what they want to have in a couple of years, or maybe ten years.

The girls I knew came to mind. Regina, Rebecca, Edna, and others. These girls have moved on already. They have begun to change their future. That was how life should develop. Rebecca's boyfriend wasn't such a bad guy now. The hate I had for him was not as it was before. No real need to hate the guy.

There was a graduation party at Bart's house. It was mentioned I should probably stop by.. Starting up the car and putting it in gear, I easily drove off from another memory. When pulling up to where he lived there were so many parked cars in the drive and yard. There were few places available to park, and the thought going to this party without anyone else was not comfortable. Another place to drive away from, at least for today. Stopping by there would involve mostly his family members, and it wouldn't feel right.

Some other parties were going on also, but none appealed much so I decided not to go. The sun was going down some, and another compelling thing pulled me toward a road that was known, and this was almost inevitable. It was Coleridge Pike.

While driving there a strange feeling presented itself. These steady hands on the wheel began to shake. There was a need to increase the grip on the steering wheel and in moments there was the view of where Arlene was killed. My car was steered over to the side of the road. The anxious tremor abated. A deep breath was taken. She was completely in my thoughts, and I wanted her with me. More than any girl I had ever known. Some of my friends knew this. We talked about it. After the car wreck it was mentioned to Bart more than once. He tried to bring me to accept what had happened. He wanted me to be reasonable. He told me there was no need to be in love with a ghost.

"Listen, Wes, she's gone. You have to admit this to yourself.. Even when she was alive she could not have been what you wanted of her.. She was a dream girl. She couldn't have lived up to what you expected of her. Human beings cannot be what we wish they would

be. She would have done things probably unacceptable to you. We are all human and have faults."

It troubled me when he said this. I didn't want to hear it, and I was pissed off at him for a couple of days. He was right though, and in time it was realized.

Suddenly, I noticed an odor, though only for a few seconds, but it was the smell that is around when raw hamburger has been unrefrigerated for too long... the spoiling smell, like the death of something.. Just as quickly, a slight breeze brought a trace of the smell of flowers. Flowers like those in a garden that have come into bloom on a spring day. Something at this moment was different. Arlene's presence was around. It was completely felt. She was moving toward me, or was she? The girl that was thought of so often was nearing me in a blue dress. Blue like the darkening sky of this very minute. Always moving in a direction she had purposed. She knew what she wanted and was happy as she pursued it. Was this part of her spiritual intent? There was a whisper and the words I would swear I heard. Swear to it if my life depended on it. Her presence was stronger now. And she spoke, "Wes, be at peace... there are so many steps ahead.".

My eyes were moist. Rubbing them would make them red, but it mattered not at all. The real concern was whether this was a dream. It couldn't be. It was just like she was saying this. Her voice with that kindness that always came through. This was real, just real.

I sat there thinking about this for a few minutes longer. There remained a love for her. But there was a reality. An awareness now of this reverie or whatever thing this was that could continue to be. There was more a feeling of being at ease. The peace she spoke of, oh yes, it was just like Arlene. The spirit presence began to move away. But it had calmed me.

At home my sister and her fiancé Len were probably back from their outing by now. Kate will want to give me some graduation gift. Mom had fixed that cake, and I should have eaten some of it before leaving. Dad might be sitting in the living room right now eating cake and watching a television program. Maybe I'll have a piece of it when arriving home. Yeah, it's my cake, and that's the thing to do.

"So for now, goodbye, Arlene."

(The end)

www.ingramcontent.com/pod-product-compliance
Lightning Source LLC
LaVergne TN
LVHW011934070526
838202LV00054B/4629